THE DARKNESS RISING

THE MAINGARD CHRONICLES, BOOK 1

CARL F NORTHWOOD

To Sara
Many Thanks
Happy Reading
Carl

PUBLISHED BY CARL F NORTHWOOD AT INGRAMSPARK

For Nicci,
without your support
this would have been
impossible.

AUTHOR'S NOTE

Darkness Rising was written over a period of seven or eight years (on and off). It morphed from one entity to another, especially during the formative years, changing from a single to a multi-faceted POV, and from a YA into a strictly Adult piece of fiction.

At the back of the book is a pronunciation guide for some of the main characters and locations, but frankly you can pronounce them as you see fit. I am not precious over minor details like that. And, as you are the reader, this story is as much yours as it is mine.

Many thanks must go to my wonderful partner, Nicci for all your support, and for being Reader No.1. Thanks also to Mandi for all your help and guidance, and to the rest of our small writing group for the support, but more importantly, for putting up with me waffling about Fantasy. And lastly, a thank you to Pippa for the art, and Nicci (once again - multi talented!) for the cover design.

CFN - May 2021

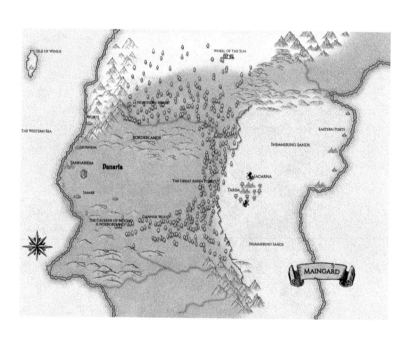

PREFACE

They came on the eve of Sanda Sweven, the Feast Day of the Dead. It was a day when the ghost of those who had passed came to revisit their families. A time to celebrate the living as well as the dead, a day for the living to commune with their ancestors and to receive their blessings and auguries.

It would have been a day of merrymaking, a feast of festivity celebrated from the Isles in the Western Sea, across Danaria and the Shimmering Sands, to the Far Eastern Ports on the far coast. An occasion observed by the majority of the civilised human world.

Instead of a day where the dead visited the living, it would become a day where the living were dispatched to their ancestors, butchered like stock and cattle in the shambles. The Gods of the civilised world would turn their backs and ignore the pleas and prayers of their people as once proud cities and kingdoms would fall under the immense and irrepressible host bent on total destruction.

They came on Sanda Sweven. The Jewels of the East fell first, the twin cities of Jacarna and Tarim. Cities that had stood for a thousand years, separated by the vast oasis that fed their citizens with grains and fruit. Proud cities and a proud people.

PROLOGUE

Gudnar shivered uncontrollably, his arms clenched about himself in a desperate attempt to bring some warmth to his old, aching bones. He had spent the last ten winters on the streets of Jacarna, eking out survival by begging, stealing or scavenging what he could, but this winter was going to be the worst. He hadn't always been on the streets and he found himself thinking of a past a lifetime ago.

As a master tailor he had seemingly had it all or as much as any honest artisan in the 'Jewel of the East' could have. He had made garments for all the nobility in Jacarna, including the Earls of House Kar and House Rogan.

His wife had been as proud as he had when Earl Jan Rogan had commissioned Gudnar to create his outfit for the wedding of the Earl's daughter to King Renta. For months afterwards, people had commented on how splendid the bride's father had looked in his finery. His small shop just outside the Palace had been a busy place, busy that is until a freak accident had damaged his hand and his livelihood. As his work suffered, the patronage of his shop dried up and debts accrued. His wife deserted him, finding solace in the bed of another and then the ruthless sharks of the Moneylender's Guild had circled, taking his home and shop. Since then he had joined the thousands who slept rough and begged for scraps in Jacarna, the so called 'Jewel of the East'.

Already the temperatures had dropped, plummeting several degrees in the last few days and frost had appeared the day after the Feast of Sanda Sno to give an indication of how long this winter may become – and that had been weeks ago.

"Unheard of," he muttered to himself as he turned onto the Street of Souls. "Unheard of," he repeated.

The Street of Souls was the location of many of the temples and religious orders in Jacarna. This was one of the last streets on his circuitous route through the maze of the Lower and Middle Quarters of the city before he reached his little bolt-hole. More often than not, the Street of Souls could be the most rewarding scavenging grounds for him. Several of the priests and acolytes from the many temples and churches along the mile-long avenue would often take pity on a poor wretch if they saw him pass by when attending to their duties.

The first temple that he passed as he entered the Street of Souls was the Temple of Bolam, deity of farmers and husbandmen and one of the major religions in the agricultural heartlands of the East. The temple stood back from the main road and had a central path leading to the main doors. A bronze statue of Bolam stood to one side. The farming god was depicted as always holding a giant scythe over one shoulder and a sheaf of corn clutched in his other arm. About his feet, worshippers had left offerings of gratitude and orisons in the hope that Bolam would take a break from his own crops to bring aid to them.

Opposite was the less illustrious Jarm's House, the Church of the Lonely God, Taker of the Godless. The building's architecture was pleasant enough, but an unwelcoming air lingered about the entrance way. Unlike Bolam's temple which had grounds to the front, the Church of Jarm faced directly onto the cobbled road. Those who took the grey cloth of Jarm were among the least materialistic of Maingard's people. The myths tell of how Jarm was shunned by his brothers and sisters and lived in exile, some say self-imposed, whilst others say Bolam, Noona and Kani forced him away upset at his unwashed and unkempt appearance. The Church of the Lonely God had no congregation per se, except for its retired clergy. Jarm, instead offered salvation to exiles and the unwanted alike. Anyone who wasn't from a congregation of another temple or church ended up here when they passed on, delivered into the care of the Lonely God. Whether they be strangers to the area, unfortunate victims to any of the criminals that thrived in the Eastern Cities or just vagrants like Gudnar many found themselves embraced by the Grey Priests of Jarm.

He passed several more churches until he reached a large temple made of white marble. Tall minarets stood at each corner, each topped with red tiling. This was the place of worship for Tobes, Lady of Luck and Chance. Sometimes the Priests of Tobes left surplus food in the porch late at night for the drifters of the city. In recognition to their patron, this was entirely at the whim of the High Priest. The tall wooden doors to the Temple stood slightly ajar and he nervously peered in. The inner porch was empty, empty of life and empty of food. Gudnar sighed, 'Another hungry night,' he thought to himself.

He left the temple and moved back onto the Street of Souls. The night had started to become foggy and gave the darkness an appropriate eeriness. Tomorrow was Sanda Sweven, the Feast day of the Dead, reputedly when the ghosts of those who were passed away revisited the mortal plane to commune with families and descendants. He looked up and down the wide street and concluded that he was the only soul out in the city that night. As the tall spires and domes of the temples loomed out of the mist, his mind conjured up a disturbing thought –

maybe he was the only *living* soul out that night but maybe there were other souls abroad. Now when he looked down the wide boulevard ahead, the Street of Souls seemed less deserted. The candles and beacons that would normally illuminate the way for the pious and nervous to prayers and absolution now lit the way for the souls of the dead to dance again. Figures seemed to swirl in the mist and shadows, merging together then breaking apart in a macabre dance of death.

It may have been his mind, almost delirious with the cold and hunger, or just years of solitude and despair on the dangerous and dirty streets of Jacarna, but to Gudnar the spirits were really there – and they wanted him. He squealed with fear, his old legs shaking more now, but not just from the icy wind and he ran – ran as fast as he could down the long temple highway.

Red-faced and wheezing, his heart threatening to burst, he made it to the end of the street where it opened out into the huge, open public Square of the Redeemed, so called as it was the natural meeting place for the recent visitors of the various temples. As with the Street of Souls the square was deserted. Columns and statues of stone stood silent in the mist across the quadrangle. He rested with his hand on the low boundary wall of the last temple, The Temple of Noona and there he waited until he caught his breath, his body bowed and his lungs pumping like mad from the physical exertion.

He found himself laughing at the madness of it all – of course the spirits didn't want him, it wasn't his time to die. After all, they were just playing, the one night of the year when they could visit the mortal plane again and be free. Now he was only a few hundred yards from his favourite bolt hole, a small shed at the back of the Burnt Oak Inn. It was small and cluttered, but that kept it a little warmer than the outside and better still, it seemed to be unused and unowned. He started, struck by a thought.

'I hope that weasel Snomm hasn't claimed it! I'll kill him', his hand went to his pouch and he half unsheathed his blade. It was dull and rusty, but it still made him more dangerous than some of the unfortunates that found themselves living rough in Jarcana. He thought better of drawing the whole blade in case the City Guard were nearby.

A sudden BOOM cracked the silent, icy air and the echo resonated throughout the square. Several cats squealed from nearby alleys and then a cacophony of barking from dogs and hounds went up. It wasn't the huge sound or the reaction from nearby animals that made Gudnar jump and nearly die on the spot. Nor was it the moment when several more bangs sounded, this time though, they seemed more distant and slightly duller. It wasn't even the whimpers that the dogs' howls became. Nor the strange green light that reflected from the mist all around him.

It was the sight that met his eyes when he turned, his knife now unsheathed fully and held out in front of him. His hand shook, the rusty blade wavering, as he realised that the knife was of inadequate protection to the danger. Ten metres above the Street of Souls flew a huge dragon, luminescent green patches glowing on its black and brown scales and green lightning crackling from its dark form, arcing across to the temples on either side.

Gudnar stood petrified and in his fear induced paralysis noticed that it wasn't a true dragon, but a ship designed with the appearance of a flying lizard. There were no wings and the head that he had mistaken for the head of a dragon was just a figurehead. Unlike the drakkars of the north where the figurehead rode high on the bow, this dragon head was thrust forward as if the giant worm was in flight. It was also immense, much larger than any seagoing ship Gudnar had ever seen or heard of. Yet this ship was built to fly through the sky and not the waters of Maingard.

Gudnar could see no sign of life on the deck but the towering walls of the hull made it difficult to see the whole deck. He jumped as the green lightning discharged once more, a powerful arc to a stone gateway to the gardens surrounding the Temple of Noona, which shattered and exploded as the bolt hit it. Smoke billowed from the nostrils of the dragonhead and the carved, ornate maw seemed to leer at him. A growl like sound came from the ship and a dark red liquid poured from the mouth onto the dusty street below, so much that it started to pool. And the ship started to sink slowly to the ground below, its immense size flattening the boundary wall of the Temple of Noona.

Gudnar dropped the knife and turned to run across the square. 'Oric's Grave!' He swore. If he had looked up when he was running, he would have seen another of the green glows above the market in King's Way and another over the North Gate, and three more over the City Palace complex. In fact, he would have seen many, many more.

As he ran, he heard the screams from far and near. It wasn't far now, there was the Burnt Oak Inn just ahead. He could see the lights flickering through the windows which meant that the landlord, Bal Torak, was still up, clearing away and cleaning the mess and debris of the day's drinking. He wasn't sure if he had time to warn him. It wasn't as if the old landlord was a friend, Bal Torak only tolerated Gudnar living behind the inn, the old tramp becoming a free nightwatchman.

Gudnar hesitated. In the end, it wasn't the hesitation that cost him his life, just bad luck. Not just bad luck that he lived on the streets, but bad luck that he existed at that time and place at all. The bolt of energy struck the Burnt Oak Inn, obliterating the old building in an instant, Bal Torak, the Inn and the shed at the end of the yard gone in a blink, vapourised into a myriad of pieces. Gudnar felt a punch to his stomach and looked down. A splinter from the front entrance of the inn protruded from his stomach. The piece of door was thicker than his arm, then he noticed the pain, coming from his belly and his back. He tentatively reached a shaking hand behind his back and groaned as he felt the end of the splinter sticking from his lower back. The old tramp's legs wobbled. He collapsed, first to his knees and then, as his vision went black, onto his face.

1

Over two hundred leagues away to the west, a dark garbed figure crouched on a rooftop overlooking the docks of Tannaheim. From her vantage point she could clearly see the First and Second Wharfs which were full of merchantmen from all over the known world. A few dockers and sailors alike wove their way along the dockside, the sea legs of the sailors making them appear as drunks on terra firma. Small lanterns flickered and swayed at the stern of each squat ship. In the distance, the larger flames of the Twins of Tannaheim broke the darkness. The beacons lit atop two tall stone towers situated on the sea wall itself, warned ships of the rocky approaches to the huge harbour of the capital city of the kingdom of Danaria.

In addition to the docks, she also had a perfect view of several large warehouses, in particular, one owned by a certain Yab M'vil. The watcher knew of M'vil as a trader not only in valuables and luxuries but also in misery and death. The vast income generated by his trade in commodities such as fine wines, silks and spices, was dwarfed by the trafficking of thousands of slaves from the far reaches of the world. These unfortunates, smuggled in by his own trade ships, found their short and painful futures in the hands of the brothels and gangs operated by the unsavoury guilds of Tannaheim.

As was common in Tannaheim, most of the warehouses had living quarters for their owners and this one was no different. M'vil used the rooms here as offices but kept house in a large villa outside the city walls. She watched as a corpulent figure dressed in a robe of garish blue silk made his way out onto the warehouse balcony. The bald man took a seat at the small dining table that was set up close to the ornately carved wooden balustrade, placing the small crop he carried onto the tabletop. He raised his hand and beckoned to someone in the room beyond.

An older man, white of hair and beard, stepped into sight and bowed slightly. His slightly swarthy skin indicated him to be the same nationality as the trader – a native of the Far Eastern Ports, far beyond the Great Asken Forest and the Shimmering Sands. He was dressed in a silken smock of a clerk, dyed to a dark grey to hide the smudges of ink common to their work. The fat trader addressed him directly and he turned, clapped his hands in the direction of the interior room and then withdrew. The watcher was too far away to hear the words spoken but as the clerk turned and withdrew from the room, she guessed that the merchant had called for his carriage. The last two nights she had watched him, and his routine had always been the same. He worked late into the evening and then ate a light supper on the balcony at the back of the warehouse. This overlooked a small courtyard and was obviously the client end of the warehouse, where customers called to make business. The far end of the warehouse opened out into the docks and included a large wagon yard.

The clerk's clap brought forward another servant, a young female clad only in gossamer slave-silks – a few thin strands of material that did little to obscure her nakedness. Her red hair and almost pure white skin betrayed her origin as an Istarian, an island west of Tannaheim. Her long hair was bound into an elaborate knot on the top of her head. She carried a small jug which she nervously poured wine from into the M'vil's goblet. As she did so, the trader reached out and stroked her leg causing her to flinch and spill some of the rich, dark liquid onto the table.

Yab M'vil glared at her and spoke again, standing as he did so. The young servant backed away, holding her hands out as if to ward off the trader. She started to wail and cry as the trader reached for his crop. Despite the distance, the watcher heard the next word clearly.

"Kneel!" the word was spat out in a strangely effeminate pitch. The young servant finally lowered herself to the floor, her face clearly showing her terror. The trader moved behind her as she continued to wail.

Despite the terrible ordeal for the young slave the watcher forced herself to continue watching. The scene seemed to play out in slow motion as Yab M'vil lifted his crop. He seemed to take as much pleasure in delaying the unnecessary punishment and therefore prolonging the girl's agony as delivering it. Then he struck like a viper, the hand flashing down and the blow knocking the breath out of his victim, momentarily silencing her. By the third blow, she had started screaming, and by the fifth she had fallen forwards onto the floor laying prostate, still and mercifully silent.

With that note, she watched the merchant disappear into his office chambers and reappear moments later in the court-yard where he stepped into the carriage. The watcher dropped her hood slightly, displaying a shock of black hair running like a horse's mane down the centre of her head. The hair cascaded to one side covering intricate tattoos inked into the skin of her scalp. Her clear skin was only marred by an old scar that ran down her face from her hairline to her left cheek, its path only broken by her brow and eye. Her dark eyes followed the carriage as it pulled out of the courtyard. "But first I want to find out what this secret your men found in the woods is."

As the carriage disappeared out of view, she stayed crouched, her posture like one of the many carved gargoyles on the surrounding roofs. The young woman was called Bex and hearkened from the small coastal town of Samak, and she absentmindedly rubbed the scar that run down the side of her face, a jagged reminder from her past. The physical wound, as ugly and as noticeable as it was, had healed far better than the mental injuries inflicted following her youth existing on the streets of her hometown and then, in her teens, in the nefarious criminal guilds of the Western Kingdoms.

Instances like the treatment of the servant girl brought the ugly memories to the surface of her mind. The indignity, the shame and the pain suffered in the simple task of surviving. Yet survived, she had. Free from the chains of the Guilds, she was no longer Bex the beggar, Bex the pickpocket, or Bex the whore.

She smiled grimly and thought, still Bex the thief amongst other more legal trades. But at least what she took was now hers and hers alone. More importantly, she could choose her marks, such as the corpulent Yab M'Vil. Especially like him, she thought, those that traded in the misery and pain of those too weak to stand up for themselves. This drive to escape her own past often led her to helping others in circumstances like hers. Hence, she found herself overlooking the warehouse and offices of her latest victim.

Indeed, the last three nights had let her know and understand her next victim's routine. Yab never left his offices for his villa until at least the Bell of the Cat, well into the night. This, she surmised, would give her plenty of time to break into his villa. Time enough to find out what this damn secret was! All she had been able to glean from her many contacts was that it had been found in the forests near his villa several nights ago.

What 'it' was, no one said, but Yab had been overheard to say that it was going to make him a lot of Crowns. What was known about 'it', was that Yab had stored it at his villa and had spent most of the night hours awake, sitting and staring at it.

Bex's plan was simple. Establish Yab's routine. Break into his home, find this secret and steal it, hopefully send the fat, old pervert into an apoplectic rage. She lifted her hood, covering her face once more, whispering to herself as she did so, "Soon, I will pay you a visit, old man."

Slowly she moved across the rooftops before sliding down to the streets and making her way back to her lodgings. Just maybe though, if she hadn't been as focused on her prey below or the events of her past, she might have noticed that the watcher was being watched herself. Once the rooftop was quiet and still again, the dark figure moved out of the shadows and made his own way to the street level below and from there, on to Yab M'vil's warehouse.

2

Ser Eglebon Dutte weighed up his guest's proposal carefully before reaching out to the goblet of wine that was on the table in front of him. His youthful looks betrayed his real age, indeed, Albron, the youngest of his four sons had already attained manhood and was a young officer in the marines of Tannaheim. The Count's fair hair was cut short in the manner of the Royal Court and his piercing blue eyes seemed to examine every inch of the exquisitely engraved silver goblet.

He raised the goblet to his lips, savouring the delicate fruity taste of the wine. It was from one of his own vineyards, situated far to the south of Tannaheim in his ancestral lands. When he finally spoke, it was in the calm voice that many were accustomed to hearing when the Master of the Privy Council spoke.

"You do know, if we fail, Anjoan will put us to death in the most gruesome of manner," as he finished his sentence, he raised his eyes to look at the man at the other end of the small dining table. Dressed in a drab, grey cloak that hid the man's true figure and size, he was the exact opposite of the Count.

Whereas the Count exuded jovial joie de vive, the stranger looked as if he dined with Kani, the keeper of the dead. His skin was pallid, and his snowy white hair was thin and receding. A black tattoo could be seen under the hair at the back of his head and Dutte could see it reach down the old man's neck and under his heavy woven cloak. From what the Count could see of it, it appeared to be a primal depiction of a wolf like creature. The stranger was old, and his eyes showed a certain type of weariness. Eglebon knew that look and had seen it many times. It was the look of an old soldier, one that not only knew Death, but diced and drank with him each evening. Eglebon didn't know much about the stranger, other than he was the envoy of the Cassalian war leader, General Karchek. When the Count had first met him, he had thought him a holy man from a far-flung country, an official of an inconsequential monarch after a trade introduction in the affluent Western Kingdoms. It had become evident that this Brant as he called himself was something more than that and had sought out Eglebon Dutte due to his ambition and faltering loyalty to the Red Throne of Danaria.

"Well, then you had better not fail. Success would be better for both of us." Brant spoke, his voice hoarse and rasping. Eglebon smiled, taking time to sip his wine again.

"Oh, I won't fail. But should this. . ." he paused, trying to remember the pronunciation of the word his guest had used, "this *knartvilder* fail? What then?"

It was the turn of his guest to smile now, the deathly looking skin on his face tightening as his lip curled, showing a mouthful of slightly yellowing teeth. His rasping voice seemed to reverberate around the room and the Count started, wary that the loudness would bring unwelcome attention from his household.

"General Karchek has commanded the Emperor's Host on

three dozen *knartvilder*," as he said the word 'Emperor' he clenched both fists in front of his chest, knuckles touching, as if saluting the absent man. "Not one has failed. Never! And this one will be no different." He slowly stood and the Master of the Privy Council was slightly taken aback by the man's height. He appeared to have grown a whole foot during the meeting and now would tower over Ser Dutte if he stood as well.

Eglebon regained his composure, helped by another sip of the red wine. He must really congratulate his vineyard manager, he thought to himself. Whilst his initial response to the stranger and his plan of treason had been slightly muted, he had been secretly pleased. If this succeeded, he would pull his family name back to the heights that it had been at before his great-grandfather had caused the Duttes to start to slide into the oblivion of minor nobility. He could be sitting on the Red Throne, King of the Western Kingdoms. True, he would be a vassal of the emperor of the old man now standing in front of him but he would have more power than any Dutte had ever had. And he would use it well, with Anjoan's runts paying for the sleight on his family's name done by Anjoan's grandfather so many years ago. It would have to be something slow and lingering to make up for the years of misery endured by his family in the lower echelons of the Tannaheim nobility. He would show them how to rule properly.

Another sip of wine and he had it! That was it! After Anjoan's death he would nail his little whelp, Garlen, to the Throne room doors so he could see how to rule properly. The daughters, he would take in front of him and then give them a quick death so Garlen would know he failed in protecting them. That just left Anjoan's wife, that witch Sarsi. He shuddered over the stories that he had heard about her. Better to kill her straight away, no need to take the chance that she really was a witch.

"Ser Dutte. Do we have a deal?" Brant's voice broke into his reverie, bringing him back to the present. Dutte looked up, meeting the gaze of his guest and for once, his eyes seemed to match the coldness of the impassive stranger.

"I assist your men in gaining access to the Palace – and you deal with King Anjoan. And when I am King, even though I swear fealty to your Lord Emperor, I will have complete dominance over Danaria?" he sipped his wine before continuing, "and I will have the Barstt line to do to them as I please?"

"Is that not our deal, Ser Dutte? Has that not been the basis of our agreement all along? Your help in ensuring Danaria crumbles with no resistance in return for Cassalian aid in elevating you to the Red Throne. Do not doubt me now." The Cassalian's voice seemed to rise a note as he spat out his words, clearly annoyed at the delay to seal the agreement. Brant continued, "I am sure I can always find another who wishes to warm the Red Throne?"

"There is no need for that. You know that. We have a deal. I just want to understand we have the same terms," Dutte replied, a slight blush colouring his face as he spoke. Brant was pleased to see a very minute tremor in his hand as Eglebon moved his goblet to his lips. By the Emperor's Hand, he thought to himself, would he ever grow tired of these negotiations prior to a *knartvilder*? He allowed himself a mental smile. No, he wouldn't tire of them. He enjoyed watching these worms bow and scrape as they promised his Emperor the world, quite literally, in return for the Emperor's blessing. In his time as one of the Adept Sinister, the Emperor's right-hand men, he had seen the so-called nobility of more than four dozen worlds prostrate themselves for the chance to rule their own worlds in the Emperor's Name. And not one of them had been worthy to even lick the arse of one of the Emperor's servants. He mental smile grew to a mental chuckle as his mind raced through the images of the *knartvilder* that had occurred before. The Adept's voice softened slightly as he replied.

"Yes, Ser Dutte, we have a deal. You will sit on the Red Throne and have dominance over Danaria. You will have Barstt's brood for your own pleasures. You will kneel in the Emperor's Name and take His Blessing. Agreed?"

Eglebon Dutte smiled, raising his goblet to his lips once more and draining the remainder of the dark fruity wine, savouring every drop.

"We have a deal. Do we need to do anything to seal it?" The common way in the Danaria to agree a contract was a signatory on paperwork, however the lower classes usually shook hands with either blood or spit. The Adept shuddered inside.

"No need, your word is as good as mine, Ser Dutte. Or should I say, Your Highness?" The mental smile became a physical smile as the corners of the thin lips twisted upwards slightly.

"Well, if you will excuse me, I have a plan to put in force and then Kingship to prepare for," Dutte broke into a small burst of laughter and stood up, indicating the audience was finished. The Cassalian studied Eglebon Dutte again. When this is over, he would deal with him. He despised the maggots who sold out their worlds, nations and kings and took great delight in showing them that betrayal was a lowly act not associated with the higher art of kingship. The Adept Sinister would never betray their Emperor, in thought or deed. Maybe Dutte would like to rule his new kingdom from within the slave pits until he ended up as ship fodder. Then he had it, Dutte was eager to rule and rule he will. He would allow him the satisfaction of sitting on the Red Throne, such a pathetic seat for a supposed king. He will have dominance over Danaria. Or what was left after the Emperor's Host had departed for their next *knartvilder*. He could rule over his land, the poisoned desolate wasteland that Karchek's forces would turn this shithole into.

The *knartvilder*, or *world plunder* would strip the land of any resource, fuelling the Host for its next campaign and filling the slave pits either for the Host or for transport back to Homeworld. He could rule over a land of nothing and no one. But maybe he would leave him Barstt's family for his revenge after all, or at least their corpses.

3

Bryn Kar had fought hard, his face matted in blood and sweat and his sword arm heavy. His unit had already been in combat with the enemy for two hours in a series of engagements as they pushed forwards towards the Palace complex. Dawn was still some hours away and the streets and buildings were illuminated only by the fires of the desolation that raged. The Black Serpents neither knew who the enemy forces were or where they were from, but the enemy kept coming. Bryn wiped his bare hand over his face, smearing the grime of war across his hardened features and making his appearance even more terrifying.

Caught by surprise by the invasion as he and his men were returning from a patrol exercise in the countryside, Bryn had taken the decision to fight his way through to the Palace; after all, the Black Serpents were part of the King's bodyguard. They found the city in flames and disarray. The invaders had arrived by ships, ships that flew in the sky and floated above the city crackling with a magical green energy. Several of the ships still sailed the skies above the rooftops, supernatural weapons sending blasts of light cityward destroying buildings and walls. Most of the ships however, had landed and had spewed forth hordes of invaders that wreaked havoc amongst the defenders.

He looked about him. There were just the five of them left from his original platoon of troops, the other seven dying as they had fought their way through the streets. Three of the others sat against the wall in the small, dark alley catching their breath in what seemed a surreal break in the slaughter that they had just experienced. The fourth man, Namot, a giant from one of the villages to the north, stood by the entrance and peered through the gloom towards the Palace. Bryn's mind wandered – Namot had enlisted in his cadre, what? eight...nine years earlier. By Tomnar, what was the name of his village. Bryn shook his head, exhausted.

He noted their battle-worn look, their chainmail stained in blood and grime. All had wounds of some sort and Tal, the youngster who had only joined his platoon a few days ago, was limping quite badly from a hammer blow that had landed just below the short hauberk of chainmail. He looked down at himself and knew he looked no different. His surcoat, once resplendent in the pale blue livery of the Royal House of Jacarna, was now tattered and blackened. He could just make out the silver horse rearing up on its hind legs. Namot had lost his surcoat altogether and Tal's was little more than a rag covering his chest. The youngster was in pain, his cheeks puffing as he caught his breath. Tal looked up and caught his eye, smiling as he did so.

"A fine time to join the Black Serpents, my Lord," he coughed as he spoke and held his side as well, his face contorting in pain. Bryn knew that the invader who had managed to hit Tal's leg with his warhammer had also managed another blow as well, maybe breaking the youngster's ribs.

"You only joined for the glory, Tal," he joked, trying to relieve some of the tension between the group. He knew the young soldier wouldn't be able to keep up with them when they moved next and wouldn't be any help in the next skirmish. Damn the invading scum, another of his men would be feasting with Kani tonight. The young recruit made it easy for him and coughed another laboured sentence out.

"I fear I would slow you down, my Lord. You go, I'll watch your back." Bryn clasped his shoulder and replied.

"We'll be back for you as soon as we can, Tal." Both knew it was a lie and both were aware the other knew it as well. Bryn reached down to Tal's dagger at his belt, drawing it and placing it in Tal's hand.

He called his men up and slowly they rose as one. Bryn admired them as he had admired all the men he had served with and led. They knew that this was probably their last day in the world of the living, yet they followed every command and decision he made without question. How appropriate, though, that their last day would be the Feast of the Dead. There was a great deal more souls walking the world now, and there would be many more by the end of the day. In the name of Sanda Sweven, he swore that he would send as many of the invaders to whatever Gods they served before he took his last breath.

Namot nodded to him and silently slipped into the street. As the others followed, Bryn hefted his sword in his right hand clenching his mailed fingers around the hilt. He gripped his war axe in his left, his mailed glove on that hand somehow lost several skirmishes ago. He followed the others and tried not to look at the bodies in the street.

They were only a few streets away from the Palace, home of the Royal Family of Jacarna. The building rose majestically above all others in the oldest city in the East. On a clear day, from the top it was possible to see the towers and spires of Jacarna's twin, the city of Tarim, some 30 miles away, across the

Great Oasis. The Palace was forty storeys high and was built with a lavish and opulent interior but with an oppressive exterior. The extensive site was surrounded by a wall the height of two men.

Bryn had noticed that the invaders seemed to be of different races and that there was a definite hierarchy amongst them. The race that seemed to be in control were tall, standing a foot taller than the average Jacarnan. Their appearance was terrifying, with images of dragons and demons adorning the breastplates and shoulders of their armour. Some wore half faced helmets showing the pallid skin of the lower part of their faces. All carried long swords, edged in a vicious serrated fashion, some curved, some barbed like obscenely sized arrows and others with a triangular head. This commanding race barked orders to the others. These were two castes – a warrior caste and a slave caste.

The slaves were held in check by mystic chains attached to great collars around their necks. Their skin was pallid and corpse like and their hair or fur was lank, matted and patchy. They wore and carried a variety of armour and arms, but they all had one thing in common. Their eyes were all black and soulless and their features betrayed a mental anguish that could only be imagined.

The other part of the invading army was made up of a range of races. Bryn had noticed both humans and other human like creatures including several light blue skinned warriors. At least one of the warriors his men had met in combat had been a towering reptilian humanoid complete with tail and scales. That one had taken one of his men down before it had fallen to a flurry of blows. The seasoned warrior shivered at the memory and murmured a short prayer to the warrior's God, Kani the hunter, that they wouldn't see another one of those lizards. Or anything worse, he added quickly. He looked up at the imposing figure of the keep and realised that they were minutes away from the man that they had sworn to protect. Bryn swallowed, his throat suddenly dry and urged his men forward. They crossed the deserted esplanade heading towards the rubble that was once the surrounding wall of the Palace Complex.

4

Radnak cursed loudly in orcish, goblin and the common tongue. As a half-orc he was fluent in all three languages and as a sword for hire, he had more than enough expletives and profanities in his vocabular armoury not to have to repeat any for several minutes. How he had managed to get himself into this mess was beyond him and he cursed everyone near him, blaming them for his predicament.

"*Sverd* Radnak, please do not use those vulgarities in front of the young Lords, a bodyguard does not need to use that sort of language to do his job," the tall goblin woman spoke sternly, admonishing him for his profanities. She used the archaic title 'Sverd' or 'sword', knowing full well that the sleight would irk him. As a half-orc Radnak was not entitled to rise higher than a listed soldier in the goblin army and so had chosen the only profession that would allow him to exercise his talents and skills but at his own discretion. The rank of *sverd* was now despised in the goblin world, an insinuation that the holder thought themselves above the basic tenant of the goblin world – to serve the tribe as one.

"Lady Iga, if it wasn't for you and your donkey brained idea to visit the great city and show the arrogant by-products of your job the sights and sounds of this mighty, opulent shit hole, then I wouldn't be here." Radnak glanced through the door into the bedchamber at the two young lords sitting on the couch. Another large explosion rocked the citadel and he saw both adolescent goblins jump. Igant, the older of the two, held a short sword out in front of him, pointing at the only door into the chamber. Janis, his younger brother was sitting slightly behind Igant and slowly rocking side to side, a terrified look on his face. His eyes stared at the door and window and, to Radnak, the already large eyes seemed ready to pop. He clutched a small hide bound book in his hands, knuckles turning slightly white where he gripped it tight. The half-orc continued, "I don't mind a whore needing to marry a rich client in order to safeguard a pension when she starts to sag, but maybe the Lady should have kept her legs together."

Iga blushed, the colour rising to her green tinged skin. The insult was unfair, she was still extremely beautiful. Tall and thin, she had very definitely not started to sag. Her dark hair was worn long with braids starting near her temples tied back above her ears and meeting at the back in a clasp of silver fili-gree. Ironically, her lightly tinged, green skin was more of a human appearance than the half-orc's dark green grey. However, her features were typical of a goblin, she had large eyes, rounder than a human's and her ears ended in soft points.

"Well, *sverd,* if this lady had kept her legs together then you would still be drunk in that tavern on the borderlands, doing whatever you were doing to pay for your next ale." She smiled sweetly looking direct at him. He returned the smile, displaying his large teeth and tusks. He knew she was right. Whilst good at what he did, there was a year when he had fallen on hard times, seemingly falling from one puddle of ale to another via numerous brawls and duels. That tavern on the borderlands had been his last stand. If he had fallen any further, then he would have disappeared into the wilds and would have ended up a distant memory.

He thought back to that day, when a small man arrived at his table and prodded his shoulder hard.

"Are you Radnak? Sverd, thief and mercenary?" The small man's voice had resounded deep into the foggy unconsciousness of his ale addled mind. As he stirred, he had noticed the two armoured soldiers behind the man, and he regarded them first. Their helmets covered their faces completely, apart from two small eye slits. The curved face of the helmet was blank and formless, giving them a chilling demeanour. Radnak recognized the helms and the armour as orcish and the long, curved swords that hung at the belts of the two bodyguards were very typical of his race. They made no move towards him, but he couldn't help but notice that their mailed hands weren't far from their sword hilts.

He sat up, his hand rising to his face to wipe ale from his cheek and took his time before setting his eyes on the small man. Radnak guessed he was about forty years of age though it was hard to be sure. His face was non-descript, hair greying about the temples and his eyes were dark pits sunk deep into his face. He couldn't tell whether he was completely human, there wasn't anything that indicated a part orc or part goblin heritage, but it was certainly possible due to the bodyguards. Not many orcs were employed as guards outside of their world.

"Who wants to know?" he slurred as his hand fell from his face and knocked his ale over. The dark brown liquid streamed across the wooden table as the leather flagon rolled onto the floor. From the corner of his eye he caught the look of disgust on the man's face.

"My employer wants to offer you employment," and he wrinkled his nose with an air of disdain as he added, "though Bolam knows why." That explains it, he had thought. The employer was the goblin, not this messenger. Radnak had chuckled, then slurred another reply.

"Tell your employer to come here and ask me himself," he reached absentmindedly for his flagon, placing it to his lips and then remembering he had knocked it over, before adding, "or the goblin can suck Bolam's cock." He waited, knowing what effect his words would have on the man. The messenger had sighed, and then he had closed his eyes and whispered his next words in an archaic language.

"Jorv man da irt."

The two guards moved as one, their swords making no sound as they were drawn from their belts, the only sound coming from the stomp of their booted feet as they started to lunge forward. When the envoy opened his eyes a full second later, he found Radnak's sword at his throat and one of his guards lying dead on the floor, a dagger stuck obscenely from one of the eye slits in his helm. The other was on his knees, hands clasped to his damaged throat, crushed by a powerful blow from the half-orc. As the messenger surveyed the scene the guard slowly started to over balance and fall forward until his forehead rested on the floor, a weird rattling sound coming from his throat as his last breath ebbed away. A wry smile flashed across his face.

"You are hired." Then he had smiled. Radnak contemplated him, keeping his sword at his throat before tilting his head and giving him an inquisitive glance.

"My employer, Lord Terek has requested that I obtain your service as a bodyguard for him." He calmly looked down at the carnage that Radnak had dealt out in a split second. "You seem qualified to take the post." The name flashed through Radnak's mind. Lord Terek? If he remembered correctly, Terek was a distant relative of the King of the Southern Goblin tribes and one of the few goblins to live above ground trading with the humans.

"How much?"

"Lord Terek will pay a fee of two hundred crowns a month."

Radnak had finally lowered the blade and turned to face the bar. The tavern was the sort of establishment where most of the clientele minded their own business and nearly all the customers had returned to their own conversations and drinks. He caught the eye of the bar owner, an old human soldier called Pedon, who was standing at the bar watching Radnak and the messenger whilst he wiped the inside of flagons.

"Hey Pedon, do you hear that! A job! I can now settle the tab – but first, bring more ale. Two flagons!" He turned back to the messenger, his big hand reaching out and grabbing the man's shoulder.

"Come, sit down and drink with me. And tell me more about this job." That had been a year ago and in the twelve months since he had organized the guards that surrounded Lord Terek and his household into a well-oiled machine maintaining the safety of the Lord, his wife Iga and the two young lords. Now, due to Iga and her desire to let her two sons experience the whole world, he seemed to be in the middle of an invasion. As guests of King Renta of Jacarna, the small entourage were quartered in the palace complex on the tenth floor.

Radnak moved to the large window in the outer chamber and edged the heavy drapes slightly to one side. He could see flames coming from most of the city, flickering high into the night sky. At some point he had thought he had seen a ship flying in the sky, circling the palace like a huge vulture waiting for its prey to die. He had shaken himself at that point, maybe the Jacarnan ale was stronger than he had thought.

"What do you see, Radnak? What is happening." Lady Iga glided to his side with all the elegance of a queen and the stealth of a footpad. Her soft voice and the light touch of her hand on his shoulder made his heart skip and his mind flicker momentarily from the events at hand. From the minute he had seen her he had known that she was no ordinary Lord's wife and that there were many secrets hidden behind the beauty. He had worked for many nobles over his career and known many more but there was something about the Lady Iga that was very different. There was not the aloofness that was prevalent in the nobles of many of the High Houses throughout Maingard, either human or goblin kind. She spoke to royalty and servants alike and never spoke ill of anyone. The banter they had shared betrayed the possibility of more to their relationship should events have not transpired against them. After all, she was a Lord's wife and Radnak was but a hired killer.

He turned, letting the drapes fall back straight, and took her arms. For a second they stood still, the lady in her long, flowing, white dress and the thickset warrior in his heavy, quilted cuirass.

"What shall we do?" the voice interrupted the moment. They both turned to see Igant standing at the chamber door, his sword still in hand. His younger brother stood behind him peering around Igant with wild, staring eyes. Radnak cursed inwardly but was also pleased with the interruption. He reached down to pick his gauntlets from the table and answered the young lord.

"Until we know the exact situation outside it would be foolish to try to leave the city. I need to know the extent of this attack. It may be that the Jacarnans don't come out on top in this fight." Igant looked at him, a puzzled look on his face.

"We can't stay here, Radnak. We will be found."

"Obviously. We move from here and work our way down. In the cellars of this palace there will be storerooms or culverts. We will wait this out there."

"You mean that we will hide and skulk around in the dark like rats." Igant sneered, raising his sword to point it at Radnak on the other side of the room. The myrmidon stopped midway through putting his gauntlets on and slowly strode over to the young goblin. As he approached, the sword wavered. His gloved hand moved up and slowly pushed the point of the blade away from him.

"Now, Lord Igant, you may call it hiding or skulking, but I call it keeping you, your brother and your mother safe. I am not being paid by Lord Terek to tell him you died a hero's death, bleeding your life away whilst you futilely endeavour to hold your guts in. I am being paid to keep you all safe and that is what I will do. We wait this out and I will scout out what is happening in this shithole of a city. If the Jacarnans win, then all well and good."

"And if not?"

"Then," Radnak paused. He hadn't thought much passed that. "I'll get all of us back to Lord Terek. We move in a few minutes. Grab whatever food we have here and something warm to wear. And don't forget that sword. I hope I am wrong, but there may be need for that before the day is done."

"Aye, *Sverd* Radnak. I will remember it and swear to prove to you that Igant, son of Lord Terek is not afraid to fight. . .. or die." The youngster turned away and started to collect some heavy robes for himself and his younger brother. Radnak stared at him, clenching his fist and silently simmering. He fought the urge to say something then turned back to the Lady Iga. As he pulled on his other gauntlet, he raised his eyebrows inquiringly.

"Son of? They still don't know?" he whispered.

"No, and they mustn't yet."

"But we could all be dead by the time the night falls again."

"Then it is even more important that they don't know. Igant is hot headed at the best of times." She paused, reaching out to rest her hand on his arm again. The slenderness of her fingers contrasted deeply with the thick biceps of the seasoned warrior. She looked into his eyes and with the utmost calmness carried on. "What you said earlier, about keeping us all safe. What are your orders from my husband?" A pained look shot across the half-orc's face.

"My Lady," he stuttered, "that is of no consequence now."

"It is, *Sverd* Radnak. I know them and wish to know that you understand them as well." Radnak winced again under the withering look aimed at him by Iga.

"My Lady, my orders from Lord Terek in the event of danger, are that my primary concern is the safety of the Lords Igant and Janis." He stopped, head tilted slightly as if daring her to continue and ask again.

"And his orders concerning myself?" she asked again.

"My orders concerning you are that you are secondary to the safety of the young lords, and that should any attempt to aid you result in any compromise of the lords' safety, then you are considered expendable." She smiled sweetly at him, her eyes only momentarily betraying a hint of sadness but then the Lady Iga that he loved was back, full of life.

"Good. You know your orders, now follow them." She draped a long fur cloak over her shoulders. "Now, shall we move?"

"Aye, my Lady." As she turned away to call her sons, Radnak slowly shook his head. I know my orders, but I understand them not, he thought to himself. Whether I follow them is only my choice to make.

5

Brant walked the near deserted streets of Tannaheim alone. He wanted to be alone, away from the soldiers that would bring desolation to this world and away from their victims – those that would fill the slave pits. He had helped to start this world's journey along the path of destruction and needed to be alone. Not that he felt guilt at what he had done. Far from it. World after world, the Emperor's forces had plundered and pillaged, and no one could withstand them. Not one race, nation, or world had been strong enough to stand against the might of the Emperor's power. And for that he felt nothing but pity for the inhabitants of this world. Pity for the fact that the only time that they would know what true power really was when it crushed them like a bug under a boot.

The cold night air made him clench the grey cloak about him tighter and he could see his breath form small clouds of steam as he exhaled. He passed the staggering forms of several drunken men muttering under their breath as they reeled like landsmen on an ocean vessel. A normal person would have felt some sort of apprehension at walking the streets of a foreign city, late at night, alone. However, despite plotting Tannaheim's downfall with Ser Dutte, Brant felt no worry as he strode hurriedly along the narrowing streets of the city's lower quarter. The lodgings he had taken were deep in the poorest area of Tannaheim, chosen so that he would become just another nonentity amidst the other denizens of the capital of Danaria. He shivered again, the cloak giving little protection against the hellish cold. Was it his age, he wondered? He had served the Emperor long past the span of a normal man's life. Was the weariness of condemning millions upon millions to death catching up with him?

"Hold on, old man." The voice cut through the moist night air and almost stopped him in his tracks. He slowed slightly but even the keenest of observers would have struggled to notice the slight turn of his head towards the alley where the voice had come from. A figure stepped from the gloom; a large stocky man who was a good head taller than Brant. A bushy black beard flowed down from the man's chin covering his broad chest. Brant saw the faint gleam of a blade in his hands as he spoke again, his voice soft and commanding.

"I said hold it, Old Father. There is no need for you to get hurt but it doesn't bother me either way." Brant halted, spying another form behind the big man. From the corner of his eye he could see another man step from the alley across the road and he guessed that there would be one behind him as well. The second man approached him. He was short and thin with a patchy beard and wayward hair, giving him a crazed look. His garments were threadbare, and Brant noticed that his left eye was glazed and unseeing. He carried a cudgel, connected to his wrist by a cord, which he twirled as he stepped out in front of Brant. One Eye opened his mouth in a toothless grin.

"Come on then, open up that purse, else I will open your head," he spluttered out, ending in an insanely hysterical cackle. Brant sighed, knowing it was futile to talk to them. The stocky leader had taken a few paces forward now and

Brant could see the way he held the long steel blade that he, at least, knew how to handle a weapon and would be the hardest opponent. Not that he considered any of them legitimate opponents. The man who had been behind the leader had slunk forward as well and now stood slightly nearer to Brant but to one side. He was young, Brant guessed at about fifteen years, but carried a small air of confidence as he looked at the old man, his hands held out in front of him, a serrated knife in one. Brant spoke slowly; the incantation was short and guttural, spoken in a language long forgotten except by the Emperor and his sorcerers of the Adept Sinister.

"Jakash min drorn tut." He could feel his head throb as the spell started to take effect and even though he had used this enchantment many times before, he started to double up as the pain wracked through his body. He knew that it would pass momentarily and that he could soon concentrate on an attack against One Eye who had started to raise his cudgel. The footpads paused momentarily as the foreign words came from his mouth. Brant started to glow with a ferocious light, blinding them for an instant. An instant was all that was needed.

The light grew more intense, turning through the blue spectrum to a pure white. Then out of the light a blur shot forward, a glimpse of fur and claws as the nearest of the muggers was bowled over. The leader didn't even manage to raise his sword point to the horizontal before the fast-moving form was upon the two of them, the younger footpad falling to the ground, hands clawing at his ravaged face. Brant looked away, knowing that the two men were dead already. He turned his focus to One Eye whose hand was still raised behind his head, weapon in hand. His gaze flittered from the old man in front of him to the large wolf-like creature that crouched above his companion, gripping the large man by his throat in its jaws. It shook its head fiercely; its maw buried in the stricken man's neck and with every shake his limbs shook heavily as if he were in the throes of a massive seizure.

Brant moved fast, his mind closed to the younger man's screams as he held his ruined face and oblivious to the sounds of bone crunching under powerful jaws. He lunged forward, his hand reaching into the voluminous folds of his cloak. One Eye's thoughts turned to running as the creature devouring his bandit leader raised its head and faced him. He was petrified as the blazing yellow eyes settled on him, the creature's snout dripping blood and viscera. It was as if a wolf had been crossed with a barbarous human, crouching down on its hind legs, its arms held out as if to balance. The beast's neck and shoulders were broad and muscular, the torso tapering down to slim hips. Its nose wrinkled as it caught the scent of terror.

Before One Eye could move, however, pain ripped through his chest and his head slowly tilted downwards, his one good eye settling onto Brant's hand, which was held about six inches from his chest. Brant was poised elegantly as if lunging with a sword, his arm held out in front of him. One Eye's confused mind staggered over the fact that the old man wasn't holding anything, yet his chest hurt, and he could see blood seeping from an open wound in the centre of his chest. A small bead of blood started to form at the corner of One Eye's mouth, and he trembled as he felt his life ebb away, the cudgel dropping from his hand with a thud to the ground. All he could hear was the whimpering of the young boy that had been hit first by the beast, the slow thud of his own heart that diminished in strength with every beat, and the snorting of the creature. He forced himself to look up from the wound in his chest and met the steel gaze of his killer, the old man they had tried to rob. There was no emotion at all in those dark orbs and no movement as the grey cloaked man held his posture. He looked across to the beast that had now stood up. It loped across the few yards in between them in a peculiar, hunched gait. The monster leaned in, his snout inches away from One Eye's face and it sniffed deeply. It bared its teeth, lips curling back revealing the yellowing daggers of death, flesh and blood still stuck in patches between them. Blood frothed as the beast breathed and One Eye felt his bladder give way and the slow release of the warm, acrid liquid down his leg as he felt the hot breath of the wolfish creature on his face.

A heavy boot stamped down onto the cobbles behind Brant and he started, pulling his hand back so that the invisible blade slipped out of the hapless, would-be mugger, releasing him from his agony. One Eye dropped to the ground like a sack of wheat, dead before he hit the hard stones of the roadway, spared from the teeth and claws of the beast. How could I have forgotten the last one? thought Brant, cursing himself. Twisting, he quickly turned, the hand holding his mystic blade up in front of him.

The giant stepped forward, taller even than the leader of the thieves. Whereas as the leader had been stocky, the figure that stepped out of the mist was immense. A waistcoat of furs covered his barrel chest, but his thick bulging arms were bare. The mist swirled around his legs, obscuring Brant's view of what he held in his right hand. A blackened iron collar sat round his wide neck and he was damp from the mist, his blond hair matted against his skin. He stood ramrod straight, his face expressionless until his mouth curled into a grin.

Brant lowered his hand, mumbling a charm under his breath, and then twisted his wrist slightly to withdraw the mystic blade into his forearm sheath.

"Oh, it's you." He waved a hand at the desolation around him. The wolf man was hunched over the body of One Eye and the only sound came from the laboured breathing of the young boy who had stopped whimpering but now tried to cling onto every second of life.

"I know you are fated to serve me, for as long as I desire to hold you in thrall, but sometimes you really are as much use as a eunuch in a harem. You were meant to be watching my back, you lazy dog." A pained expression crossed the giant's face and what could only be described as a soft growl escaped from his mouth. He lifted his hand until it was at shoulder height, extended straight out in front of him. Dangling in his grasp were two dead ruffians, held tight by their long, dank hair. Their feet didn't even reach the ground as the giant held them high. Brant nodded slightly and then carried on.

"Oh, so you did what you were meant to do? I hope you don't expect a promotion." He turned away and dismissed the giant with a wave of his hand. "Get rid of this carrion – and kill that one," he pointed to the young lad. He beckoned slowly to the wolf that looked at him, at first quizzically, then with a fearful hatred. The beast snarled at him with teeth bared. Brant stood with his arms held downwards at his sides, palms facing the wolf, as if to show the beast that there was no need to be scared. The creature stayed crouched on his hind legs and swatted at Brant with one of his arms. Due to the distance between them, Brant was more than safe. He slowly started to intone an incantation; his voice soft but with authority. As the charm went on, the words were repeated, and the tone increased until Brant was spitting out the words and almost snarling back at the beast.

"Dorshan, Dorshan. Jakash hor min wilvern. Dorshan, Dorshan. Jakash hor min wilvern!"

The beast whimpered and slunk to the ground, crawling to the old man. Its nose never left the ground, its arms like the front legs of a dog would be as it dragged itself to its master. Brant reached out and took the beast by the scruff of its neck and whispered one last word.

"Wolfernulf." As the words escaped the old man's lips both Brant and the wolfman started to glow. The light increased until any onlooker, if there had been any present, would have had to look away. When they would have looked back, they would have only seen the old man, face contorted in agony and nausea. If they would have looked in detail at the old man, they would have seen a tattoo on his head and neck, continuing down his back. And if they had looked really closely, they would have sworn on Bolam's name that the tattoo was moving slightly.

6

B ryn had lost two more men, leaving just himself and Namot to head on through the Palace complex. Hully had died when a blast from one of the circling skyships had brought a large chunk of masonry down from the palace as they crossed the courtyard. He had never stood a chance as the five-ton piece of granite had obliterated him. Okrad had fallen in a short but violent skirmish a few moments ago. Now the two men paced towards their destiny with a pessimistic urgency. Within a few hours they had seen their city brought to its knees and their comrades fall in a desperate attempt, at first, to save Jacarna then to take whatever vengeance they could.

Neither spoke as they moved through the war-torn passageways, overstepping dead bodies of guards and civilians alike. Every now and again they would see the bodies of the invaders, mostly the slave castes but a few of the warriors and even less of the leaders. They knew it was the end of their once great city state, there were far too few of the invaders lying dead in the corridors of the palace for the result of the battle to be anything but. Their only task now was to head towards the King, as they knew any of their colleagues would be doing. There they would form a shield wall for the royal family as their predecessors a century and a half ago did after the sacking of Jacarna by the Legions of the Mad King Androsiline. Then, the Black Serpents had been annihilated, their bodies eventually forming the wall that held the attacking hordes off until the relief force routed the attackers. It was one of the many battle legends drummed into all recruits of the King's Guard from the very moment the green soldiers marched through the barrack gates.

As they approached a corner in the corridor, Namot paused, holding up his fist clenched tightly to indicate to his compatriot to also halt. Bryn did so, understanding and trusting his colleague without hesitation. Namot's keen hearing had not failed them and Bryn heard the chatter of a foreign voice from around the corner. The tall soldier glanced at Bryn, a questioning look on his grimed face. Bryn took only a split second to make his decision – they would find another path to the throne room. Bryn picked his way carefully back the way they had come whilst Namot followed, edging backwards, his eyes all the time on the corner.

The two weary soldiers ducked into a side chamber. Surreally, the room hadn't been touched and looked as if a maid had just left. Heavy, velvet drapes hung against one of the tall, full windows that looked down on to the interior courtyard of the palace. Only the sounds of sporadic fighting and shouting that came through one the open windows gave any indication of the chaos outside their haven.

Bryn leant forward to Namot, who carried on watching the open doorway.

"That's the third time we have nearly come up against these bastards in the last ten minutes. We need to find another way through. We won't do any good if we die here." Bryn had made the decision earlier that they would only fight if they absolutely had to. There was no need for them to die here.

"We could go up a few floors and work through the Royal Tutor's suite?" Namot suggested. "That could be empty. Most of the bastards seem to be in front of us."

"That will bring us to the landing above the throne room. There are a few staircases down in that area."

"Hopefully we can then take vengeance for Tal, Hully and the others. My sword is practically crying with shame at this skulking about." As if to accentuate his point, Namot hefted his sword up, blade pointing towards the ceiling.

"You sent enough of the godforsaken dogs to Kani so far tonight, Namot." Bryn stood tall. He didn't like this either and would rather be there in a shield wall with his companions by his side, facing the invaders. But his companions, the men he lived with and trained with, those men that he had shared meals and drink with, as well as fighting skirmishes against bandits and marauders, were mostly lying dead in the city of his birth.

"Aye, my Lord, but not enough of them. Before I go to Kani, I want as many of them to curse the day they stepped foot in Jacarna." Bryn could see the guilt on the man's face and knew that his conscience was starting to eat him up. Similar thoughts had crossed his mind throughout the night. Why was he still alive? – Why not Okrad, or Hully? Why not any of the others? But whilst he had been able to shake himself back to the nightmare that they faced; he could see that the gentle giant could not. He slowly reached out to Namot's extended blade and gently pushed it to one side.

"And they will, Trooper." He purposely used Namot's rank, slipping back into using the official nomenclature. "When we get to the King, that is where we will engage the enemy, and that is where our blades will drink. Until then, we will avoid the enemy. But I think, Namot, before dawn breaks you will get your wish for killing."

7

On the other side of the palace complex, Radnak led Iga and her two sons downward, through ravaged corridors and past the servants' quarters into the storeroom levels of the bastion. These were situated on the first three storeys of the keep but were only accessible from above. Both the young goblins had followed every order that Radnak hissed at them, with the younger one helping his mother along. They had left behind the ornate corridors and stately rooms above and moved into darker passageways lit only by a few torches flickering here and there. The stonework of the keeps' foundations lined the narrow passages.

"What is happening out there, *Sverd* Radnak?" Igant, the older of the two asked as they hurried along. Three times they had to stop and hide as they heard soldiers. Whether they were guards or the invaders, Radnak did not know but he was unwilling to take any chances. He did not want to get involved in whatever was happening and the two young goblins were his responsibility. Orc kind were still not highly thought of in the human world and he didn't want anyone to make the wrong assumption as to why they were there.

"Shhh! boy." Radnak answered tersely, his mind striving to be alert to all around him. He still heard faint echoes of fighting from above along with occasional explosions and because he had avoided contact with anyone, he still did not know what was going on outside and on the floors above. And that worried him. Igant paused for a few seconds as if contemplating his next question.

"You should address me as 'my lord', *Sverd* Radnak. There is no need to be rude even in the midst of this chaos." Radnak spun about, grabbing the young lord's tunic and pushing him hard against the wall. He snarled straight into Igant's face.

"I have told you before, I am here to keep you alive. Not to be pleasant, not to be stately or formal, and not to address you as anything apart from 'alive'. Now keep your immature mouth shut and let me do my job." He let go, Igant sagging against the wall in humiliation rather than pain. Radnak turned his head to the figure of Lady Iga, who was still staring wide eyed at the half orc.

"Shut the little 'lord' up, Lady Iga," he emphasized the title for the benefit of Igant, "or I will cut his tongue out so he will be silent like his brother". He turned and walked away down the passage, a torch held aloft in his left hand and his sword drawn in his right. Lady Iga was already clutching her younger son who didn't look any less terrified than he had done back in the guest chamber. She reached out to Igant and gently squeezed his forearm. He shrugged her touch aside and advanced on, following Radnak.

A few minutes later Radnak found what he was after, a small doorway situated in the far wall of a main storeroom. The door was initially hard to see at first as it was hidden in shadow. He held up his hand to signify to the others to be quiet and rested his ear against it. Hearing nothing, he pushed against it. Years of disuse gave way under his shoulder and the hinges protested loudly as it slowly swung open. Iga spun about as the squeals echoed around the storeroom.

Radnak stepped forward into the room, sword first. The air was surprisingly fresh, and the half orc detected a slight breeze as the torch's flame flickered more than usual. Glancing up he saw the reason, the walls to the small room beyond were two of three feet higher than Radnak and set into them just below the ceiling were two small iron gratings. Pieces of presumably redundant, rickety furniture stood stacked to one side and several large crates were lined up against the opposite wall. The half orc grunted and turned to the others, beckoning them into the storeroom.

"This is our home for the next day, with luck we will know what the situation is in by tomorrow night and can make our move then." He noticed Igant screw his face up as he entered the cell like room. The young goblin lord opened his mouth as if to speak and then glanced at the squat warrior. Thinking better of it, Igant closed his mouth and reached out to his younger brother, helping him into the room.

"I have spent the night in worse accommodation, Radnak". Lady Iga glided through the doorway as if she was entering a ballroom. She moved to her sons, and clasped Janis to her warm embrace. "Come here, my boys. I promise things will be alright".

Radnak grimaced at the reassurance to the young boy but then realised as he looked at the slight doubt in her eyes that a reassurance was all it was. She was as scared as the two youngsters but was acting as a true mother should do, trying her best to protect her children.

He pushed the door until it was almost shut and then turned around to face his three charges. They stared at him apprehensively and expectantly and he suddenly realised that they were looking to him for inspiration and leadership. The Lords and Lady were looking at him, the *sverd,* for leadership.

He started to talk and found himself stumbling over his words and then he noticed the desire in their eyes, the desire to be led and the desire to live. He knew that he couldn't let them down and so he took a deep breath and then launched into a string of orders.

"Iga and Igant, take a quick look in the stores outside and check for food. It won't be luxurious, but we can't be choosers here. Be on guard for anyone approaching and don't be seen if so. Igant, can you snort like a kobold?" the young lord looked puzzled and then nodded, screwing his face up and letting out a weird, throaty, whistling noise. A kobold was a small dog-like creature that was semi-domesticated by many goblin tribes. Radnak hoped that the noise wouldn't be known by anyone stumbling into the main storeroom and would allow Igant to warn him safely if that occurred.

"Good, if you hear anyone approaching, find cover and snort like that. I'll come straight away. You," he pointed to the silent Janis, "you can help me move some of these crates so anyone looking into this room won't see us." He hoped the crates would deaden any sound they made as well as well as giving the illusion that the room had no other secrets.

By the time Iga and her eldest son had returned, Radnak and Janis had walled off the back of the little room, leaving a small gap at one edge to allow access to the void behind. There was just enough room for all of them to lie down, but at least the gratings above would allow some ventilation. Iga and Igant had got lucky, they carried several long rye biscuits and some salted beef. The stocky warrior had been right. It wasn't luxurious, but Igant suddenly realised how hungry he was and snapped a piece from one of the long bread-like sticks. He took a bite and handed the remainder of the portion to his younger brother, who immediately smiled and bit into it, his eyes lighting up as he chewed happily, rubbing his stomach with his free hand. Igant unslung a bag from over his shoulder and pulled a large red apple from it, handing it to his mother.

Janis finished the chunk of biscuit and then gesticulated to his brother, pointing at first to himself, then the floor and finally smiling. All the time he mumbled unintelligibly.

"What does he say?" Radnak asked. Over the last twelve months he had still not got used to the mute boy's conversations, indeed it only seemed to be Igant who understood them. The older brother dipped his hand into the bag again for another apple, this time passing it to his sibling.

"He says, 'It is good to be deep down again, this deep with the earth below you, feels like caverns, the caverns of home'." Radnak grunted.

"We are not down to the earth yet. We are close to ground, yes, but the humans tend to keep their prisoners as far from the sunlight as possible. There will be several more floors below us and we don't want to be visiting them." He busied himself checking that his armour was intact.

"I have been in prisons before, *Sverd* Radnak, with my father," the young lord protested.

"Have they been human ones, Lord Igant?" The half orc raised an eyebrow in the direction of the slighted lord as he once again unbuckled and buckled his heavy belt around his sturdy midriff.

"No, only the ones of King Mayak," Igant replied. King Mayak was the king of the southern goblin tribes, to which Iga and her sons belonged. The goblin world was split into kingdoms just like above in the human world. Mayak reigned over the southern tribes in the caverns of Moond. Moond stretched away under many kingdoms and principalities of the humans and was one of the biggest goblin kind nations. A few hours ago, Radnak would have chuckled at the young lord's ignorance and naivety but he caught himself as he looked up into Igant's eyes. He was trying hard not to show it, but the youth was terri-

fied. Over Igant's shoulder, Radnak could see the plainly fright-
ened look on Janis' face. He sighed inwardly; it wasn't Igant's
fault that he had grown up in a relatively peaceful decade. It
had been ten years since the Great War, or the Orc Wars as the
humans called it had ended. In that time there had been only
minor skirmishing mainly with the disorganized wild tribes to
the far south but on the whole humans and goblin kind had
lived an uneasy peace for most of his young life.

"I have had the pleasure of being in various prisons in my
lifetime," the warrior continued as he held his sword up and
examined each edge for damage. "Some of them have been
goblin ones, and other have been above ground in the human
realm. And yes, Igant," he looked across at the young goblin,
"some of these I visited and others," he shrugged and went
back peering at his blade, "well, let's just say that my journey
through life has not always been with both feet on the right
side of the law. The dungeons of Moond are a relative ease
compared to the ones up here under the sun." He looked back
up, at least the scared looks had vanished on the adolescent's
faces and had been replaced with a slightly shocked look.

"What have you done?" Igant asked.

"I am not sure that telling you is going to help. Let's just say
that what I have done in the past will be a great help in getting
all of us out of here and back to your father. And when we are
all safe, I can tell you my stories sitting next to a roaring fire and
good ale. Now, get some sleep – I will be back shortly."

Iga swept from her ever present vigil from next to her mute
son and moved to Radnak's side, catching his arm in her tender
grasp.

"You're not going to leave us, Radnak!"

The half orc stared at the slim, wispy figure that seemed to
throw herself at him. He knew that he only wanted to bed
down in their little hideaway with her and hold her but also

knew that would only end badly for them both, no matter who ever won the battle raging outside.

"I have to, Iga. I won't be long, I promise." He looked up at the two boys and addressed them all. "Don't leave this room and try not to make too much noise. I will be back before dawn." Radnak pulled the door open and stood so that his imposing figure was framed perfectly by the doorway.

"What if we are found?" Igant's question stopped him and he slowly turned to face the youth. He raised his sword so that it pointed to Igant's own weapon that the youth had left on the table.

"You have a blade there, I suggest you don't let it out of your grasp and if you are found, learn to use it quickly. I can only imagine I will need another *sverd* at my side if we are all to escape this shithole." With that the warrior turned away and left them without so much of a backward glance.

8

B ryn and Namot stalked through the eerily deserted corridors. Once they had ascended to the higher floors, they had encountered neither enemy nor friend. They were now in sight of the large, wide landing that encircled the throne room below but rather strangely they heard little sound of fighting.

Bryn stepped out onto the landing which was, in effect, a huge balcony overlooking the Throne of Jacarna. The cloistered area in front of him was wide, perhaps twelve feet or more across and the parapet of a waist high wall of white marble was punctuated by huge columns of the same bright stone rising all the way to the vaulted ceiling above. Due to the width of the promenade and the surrounding parapet Bryn felt invisible to those below.

As he felt the icy blast of the wind on his face, he looked to his right to see the once wondrous stained-glass windows that dominated the far end of the balcony area completely obliterated. He stopped dead in his tracks as he felt the light touch of steel against his throat and the urgent hiss of the voice to his left.

"Don't move and don't say a word."

Bryn's eyes strained in their sockets as he tried to see who had stopped him. The voice came again, this time showing a little relief and emotion.

"Tobes Tits! Bryn Kar?" He nodded slightly, trying to place the voice and he felt the coldness of the steel move from his throat. He realised he must have looked a state and have been nearly unrecognizable to many. Bryn turned slowly to face his ambusher.

The man was slightly shorter than himself with a gaunt face topped by a shock of blond hair, now matted with blood on one side. He wore a chainmail hauberk like Bryn's except one side was torn away and the jerkin underneath was stained a blackened red with blood. A small leather satchel was strung over his other shoulder. His tired eyes were fixed on Bryn as he stood straight with his chin lifted, the tip of Namot's sword digging into the soft underneath of his chin as his had done with Bryn's a few seconds earlier. Bryn raised a hand to Namot who slowly lowered his sword.

As the giant's sword was removed, Bryn stepped forward and clasped the man in an embrace. The man winced, his arms barely rising to return the embrace.

"Tarn! What in Tomnar's Name has happened? Where the fuck are the rest of the Serpents?"

Tarn stepped backwards and leant against the wall, his sword tip resting on the floor.

"It's over, Bryn. It's over," he repeated.

"What is?" Bryn shook his head, not understanding what his old captain was meaning.

"Jacarna! You dumb fuck!" Tarn reached up and grabbed Bryn's arm above the elbow before continuing, "Renta's throne has fallen and I never thought I would see the day when the Serpents stopped fighting."

"Stopped fighting? What. . . . my men have only stopped

fighting because they are dead, Tarn, dead! And even now I hope they are chasing these bastards down in the afterlife." Bryn shook the man's hand from his arm.

"Not your Serpent's, Bryn. But you need to look at this." With that the man crouched and loped over to the marble parapet and crouched down behind it, peering through a small break in the ornately carved marble. Bryn motioned to Namot to guard their retreat and then followed Tarn.

What he saw as he looked down into the throne room of his homeland sickened him. Renta still sat on his throne, though the old man looked closer to a seat in the Realm of the Dead. A crown of gold, a simple gold band, sat upon his balding head, wispy white hairs snaking this way and that. His hands gripped the arms of the throne tightly and it seemed to Bryn that he knew his grip on the reign of Jacarna was fading fast. In contrast to everyone else in the vast room, his white robes were unsullied, an island of purity in a sea of destruction.

It wasn't the state of his monarch that sickened Bryn as all Jacarna knew that Renta was on his last legs. Each month seemed to welcome another feast day in celebration by the amazed populous that the aged monarch was still breathing. Despite ascending to the throne later in life than many other kings of Maingard, he had still reigned for over forty years. Bryn Kar was not the only one who knew that Renta's long reign was rapidly approaching its sunset.

Bryn surveyed the rest of the throne room. To the King's right sat the queen, Rothanne. Some thirty years younger than her husband, she was still strikingly beautiful, her blond hair tinged slightly with the greying signs of middle age. She sat quietly, frequently dabbing her eyes with the small kerchief she held. Bryn could see that her eyes were red and her face puffy from tears. Renta's three children, the Princesses Rothannir, Rentanne and Ramene, lay prostrate on the marble floor in front of the thrones. Above each one stood an invader, a foot on their heads pinning each one to the cold embrace of the marble below.

A number of servants lay amongst the rubble and the dead, surrounded by soldiers of the invading force, a soft murmur of tears and distress coming from them. The blackness of the invaders stood out against the pale pearlesence of the polished marble, their armour bearing the signs of chaos and death. He could see a few of the tall lizardmen, similar to that that had killed one of his men and also quite a few other races. About a tenth of the enemy in the throne room were the master race of the invaders. These stood taller than most (apart from the towering lizardmen) and all wore ghastly helmets with a half visor modelled on the skull of a humanoid. All of this was over-shadowed in Bryn's eyes by the scene he saw to the side of the thrones.

Two dozen Black Serpents knelt in quiet solitude amongst a similar amount of palace guards. Each had their heads bowed, unable to look their king in the eyes. Behind each one stood one of the invaders and each one held a wicked looking blade pointed against the nape of each neck.

"They've surrendered?" The incredulity in Bryn's question couldn't be masked.

"Aye, a few minutes before you got here." Tarn sat with his back against the marble wall, his breathing slightly laboured. Bryn looked across and saw that he was holding his hand against the wound in his side. Tarn caught Bryn's glance and nodded slowly.

"One of the bastards got me, caught me right in the ribs. I think one of them is broken, maybe more." Bryn returned to his vigil on his king and the companions who had betrayed him by laying down their arms.

An excited howl went up from the victorious soldiers below and Bryn saw several collapse to their knees. The soldiers guarding the captives did not move. At first Bryn couldn't see why they were howling, but then a figure moved into sight from below his vantage point.

This figure was half as tall as Bryn again and his armour was blackened steel. A trio of skulls surmounted each shoulder pauldron, one each facing forwards, sideways and backwards. A great helm sat upon his head, and as the figure raised his arms high, he turned saluting the crowded room. Bryn saw several of the captives flinch as they looked upon the terrifying individual. The giant warrior was surrounded by several guards in black armour and scarlet capes along with a solitary old man in a grey robe. The old man appeared as old as King Renta, though he moved a lot less stiffly than the arthritic king.

The red cloaked guards were armed with halberds and one smashed the steel shod butt of the shaft against the marble floor. As the echo reverberated around the throne room, he hit the floor again and again, and then called the room to order.

"Silence! Silence for The Almighty Emperor's Lord Commander of the Host, His Excellency, General Karchek." The room indeed fell quiet, the silence punctuated only by the occasional sob from one of the captives. The tall figure swept forward until he stood in front of the prostrate princesses. Due to his immense height his eyes were almost level with the eyes of King Renta despite the several steps of the dais that his throne sat upon.

His hands reached slowly to his helm and with a deliberate motion, he unclipped the face visor so it fell to one side and then lifted the great helm up and over his head. His skin was a pale grey, the colour of dull steel and his short-cropped hair was close to white. The General turned to one of his guards and handed him the helmet. As he did so, Bryn could see his face. If the leader of the invading force had to be described in one word, it would be, Bryn decided, ugly. If further words were needed, then perhaps killer, murderer or a demon would suffice. His face was a criss cross of scars showing a lifetime or longer fighting. His lips were thin and bloodless, almost indistinguishable from the rest of his skin. One ear was missing, a hardened mound of scar tissue covering the spot that it once occupied, and his nose had been broken a number of times. He turned back to face the throne.

"I shall dispense with the time-consuming pleasantries. I have far more important tasks to complete ere the day is out. Your lands and throne are now under the dominion of the Almighty Emperor and as the Lord Commander of his forces on this plane I now present you with this choice. Willingly swear fealty to the Almighty Emperor and you shall continue to sit upon your throne and rule your people. You will cede your military forces to my control and the industry of your people will feed my war machine in the rest of the subjugation of this plane." The giant's voice was harsh and cutting. His last words were delivered with his front foot on the third step of the dais and he leant forward with his elbow resting on his knee. "Swear fealty, kneel to my Emperor, or die."

Bryn had expected a similar ultimatum, but even so the callousness that the enemy leader had displayed caused him to take a sharp intake of breath. He sensed the room below fall even quieter and found himself staring at his King and knew that every other eye in the throne room below was on the frail old king.

Renta rose, every bone in his body shaking, not with fear but with age and the frailties of his exhausted body. As he spoke, Bryn felt a short stab of pride. Renta's voice was every bit as authoritarian as Karchek's but with a softer tone, one that would inspire others to follow rather than intimidate them.

"Three hundred and twenty-seven years ago, my ancestor made a similar speech to the Dukes of Karame. Frentarn the Holy decided that he needed to bring the dukes into line to strengthen our borders and to reduce incursions by bandits.

The armies of my ancestor marched on the dukedoms and displayed their power, bringing the dukes to the treaty table.

"Frentarn gave the same speech that you have just given. Three out of the six dukes rejected him outright. Their heads sat upon spikes in the market squares of their towns that evening. Their lineage was obliterated, and their goods and chattels confiscated. The families of Manto, de Vanirt and Toresk ceased to exist overnight. The other three knelt in fealty to Frentarn and their families live on to this day as an important and integral part of Jacarna.

"The occupant of the throne of Jacarna has kept journals for the last four hundred years. Apparently the Maesters here like memories recorded for prosperity. The King's thoughts, written down to give reasons for choices made so that future Kings will learn and understand what has gone before. Four hundred years! Can you even imagine that, Karchek? Can even your barbaric mind comprehend the written thoughts of four hundred years?" The immense figure of General Karchek did not rise to the slur but just turned and slowly walked the small circle of space in front of the crowd.

"Four hundred years, Karchek! Do you hear me?" Renta's voice rose an octave and he started to shake as he vented his anger. "Do you know what Frentarn the Holy wrote? He had admiration for the bravery and courage shown by the dissenters. The bravery to shout out and the courage shown as they walked to the axeman's block. He despised the submitters and their cowardly deeds. In his eyes, they had failed their towns. For seventy summers I have served Jacarna and I will not fail her!" Spittle bubbled at the lips of Renta as his rant rose to a crescendo. He raised one arm and punched the air as he repeated his plea.

"I will not fail Jacarna! I will not fail her!" he collapsed, shaking, into his chair his cheeks red from the exertion. He carried on mumbling the words over and over, ignoring the sobs of his family and the buzz and murmur around the throne room. General Karchek circled the room again, his eyes burning into anyone who locked eyes with him. He marched over to one of his soldiers who kept guard over one of the princesses and shoved him viciously in the chest. He fell to the floor with a clatter losing grip of his sword. Karchek reached down and grabbed Princess Ramene by her long blonde hair and lifted her effortlessly. In his tall grasp her feet kicked a foot or so above the marble floor. She wailed like a cat in a trap, her hands grabbing at her hair. He raised his mailed hand and slapped her across her face. The sound of the slap cut through the throne room like a knife and Ramene stopped screaming, her eyes wide and terrified and the side of her face already a scarlet patch.

"Who entered the palace first?" The question echoed around the throne room, repeated once again by Karchek as he held the terrified princess aloft. A warrior stepped forward; his skin almost bright against the darkness of his armour. An old scar jagged its way across his face like a chaotic bolt of lightning and a black leather patch sat across one eye socket. He knelt in front of the towering figure of Karchek, his head bowed and hands clasped in front of his head. After a few seconds he stood and announced loudly.

"Luciani of *The Dark Flame*, Sire. We were first into the palace."

Karchek nodded and addressed the crowd again.

"Does anyone disagree with this?" he challenged his soldiers. He took the absence of a reply as read and spoke once more.

"As your Lord Commander and the Emperor's Voice, I am empowered to reward your courage and servitude. Take this for the soldiers and crew of *The Dark Flame* and use her as you will." With that he flung the girl at Luciani's feet to a chorus of cheers. She rolled onto her back, cowering, her gaze darting left and right desperately seeking an escape route. The soldier grabbed her hair and dragged her back into the crowd towards his men.

Bryn bristled with anger, the humiliation of seeing his men kneeling captives and the treatment of the princess made his blood boil. He snarled and went to rise but Tarn grabbed his arm.

"Stay, fool. Can't you see? It is over." He reached for the satchel and winced as he lifted it over his head, before holding it to Bryn. "Take this, this is Renta's last letter explaining what has happened here. You need to get away and warn Danaria. They can't fall the same way we did. Make sure they are warned so that they take more of the bastards than we did."

"But..."

"But nothing, I am your superior, Bryn. It is an order. Already a messenger has been dispatched to the Eastern Ports and one to Turikstal to warn them. I should have been away to, if it wasn't for one of those cursed bastards!"

Bryn turned back to see Karchek throw the second princess, Princess Rentanne to another one of his commanders. He reached down for the third and last one, Princess Rothannir. He held Rothannir by her neck, her toes barely reaching the floor as she struggled on tip toe. Karchek grabbed her long plain dress by the neckline and tore it away leaving the young princess naked. The litheness of her hips and waist were in stark contrast to her large breasts that hung, round and full. Karchek licked his lips, maybe he would keep this one for himself. His gaze wandered down to the soft down between her legs and he had very nearly made his mind up when she lashed out a kick into his own nether regions and wrenched herself free from his grip. He winced slightly; the area was heavily mailed but it was still the hardest knock he had taken in the invasion.

He smiled. He certainly would keep this one for himself. He

liked a little bit of fire in his women and this one had that. But for now, he had to keep her quiet whilst he dealt with her mother and father. Karchek stepped forward and she feinted another kick to his waist and then snapping the leg back again and upwards with all the grace of a desert Padstan, one of the elegant but deadly martial artists from the desert nomad tribes.

But Karchek had not stayed alive through so many *knartvilder* without being a capable fighter, and the Commander of the Host during thirty-six *knartvilder* was not going to let a mere princess end his day. His hand flashed upwards and blocked her kick, the wrist rolling back over and then under her leg, trapping it under his arm pit. His warrior's mind sensed her posture shift in order to gain balance for another strike and he shifted his own weight forward, confusing her balance. As she started to fall, he punched downwards with his other hand, the mailed fist connecting with the side of her knee with a resounding snap. She screamed once then fell to the floor as Karchek let go, her hands clutching her shattered leg and bile blocking her shrieks.

Karchek stepped over her without a second glance and marched up the dais steps to Rothanne. As he approached her, she stood. Her eyes welled up with tears, but she stood tall, her back straight and faced her fate.

"This one is too old. I wouldn't insult one of my command by giving them this old hag. Take her to the slave pens or for ship fodder." A soldier stepped from behind the throne and took Queen Rothanne by her arm and led her away. She was resigned to her fate and never made a sound or protest.

Tarn shook Bryn's arm and urged him again to leave.

"Bryn Kar, Follow my orders."

"Why me? Why not you?" Bryn knew the answer to that as soon as he spoke. He took the satchel from Tarn's outstretched hand and lifted the strap over his arm and head.

"Because I will be dead before I left the palace. Look at me . . ."

"So why not Namot?" Bryn indicated his giant compatriot.

"Because you are the son of an Earl. You will carry sway at the court of Tannaheim. Myself and Namot?" he winced as he spoke, his hand moving to his side to hold his aching wound. "We are only good for two things. Is that right, Namot?" he looked at the giant warrior.

Namot paused and looked quizzically back at him.

"Killing and dying, killing and dying. Is that not so, Namot?" He coughed, a little too loudly and a dribble of blood spluttered from the corners of his mouth.

Namot grinned, hefting his sword.

"Killing and dying, is good, Bryn Kar! Time to go, I will give you time."

Bryn stared into the eyes of his companion, a companion who had served under him for several years, never flinching. He nodded, unsure of what to say and still crouching, grabbed Namot's shoulder in a display of friendship.

"The Gods be with you, friend." Bryn took off on a crouching run around the upper tier of the throne room making sure he kept far enough back to avoid being seen. Tarn whispered a prayer and then looked at Namot.

"Let's do this. See you in Kani's Hall, trooper." The giant made his way silently to the staircase and started to descend.

As Bryn reached the far side of the balcony, he heard a tremendous scream from below followed by the instantly recognizable tone of Namot shouting as he lashed his way through the throng of soldiers. He kept low and moved to the balcony edge to see his friend's last moments. There were already two fresh bodies behind Namot, and his sword was fresh with blood.

"Come on, you whore-sons! Fight for Jacarna!" the giant howled as he shoulder-charged a soldier out of his way. The black armoured man went sprawling, his sword clattering across the marble floor. One of the towering lizard men moved to intercept him and he directed a huge upwards swipe of his sword, both hands gripping the hilt tightly. His opponent tried to dodge backwards but the ferocity of the strike surprised him. The tip of Namot's sword cleaved through the lizard man's jaw and snout cleanly. Blood sprayed from the cloven wound as the invading soldier breathed his last. Two more soldiers blocked his path to the throne, naked apart from fur trews. Their lightly blue tinged skin was woven with scar tissue tattooed a darker shade of blue. Pieces of skin and bone that were hung from the bindings of their spears, just below the long steel head, matched similar totems woven into their long dank hair.

"Up, you yellow bellied whores!" Namot called to the Black Serpents that still knelt as hostages.

Tarn had staggered to his feet and now stood on the far side of the circular balcony to Bryn. He was still unnoticed due to the commotion below and had hefted a piece of masonry the size of a skull up to his shoulder. Watching the scene below he gauged the trajectory he needed and let fly. A small groan escaped his lips as the exertion hit his pain wracked body and he clasped one hand to the dark stained hole in his armour.

The blue skinned barbarians held their spears high, as if ready to propel them into Namot. The impromptu missile caught one unawares and smashed into his bare shoulder. There was a sharp crack that even Bryn heard from the other side of the auditorium followed by a yelp as the warrior dropped his weapon and gazed at the wound with a surprised look.

Namot took his chance, a quick two-handed stab at the armed opponent to put him on the defensive and then a backhand slash into the good arm of the injured warrior. As he collapsed screaming in agony Namot turned back to the other one who looked nervously to and from his fallen comrade and the crazed berserker in front of him. Several of the kneeling Jacarnan guardsmen took their chance to rise up and attack their captors. Unarmed, they struggled against their guards, trying to wrestle their weapons from them.

As Bryn watched Namot despatch the second blue skin, he saw several other soldiers run to the stairs to reach Tarn. He was torn between his orders from Tarn and his loyalty to his King, throne and regiment. He thought of his own men now all dead except for Namot who was sure to follow them to the Halls of Kani very soon. Bryn ducked down behind the balustrade, needing to watch Namot's sacrifice.

From his vantage point he could see two of General Karchek's red cloaked guards intercept his friend. Several of the Black Serpents and palace guardsmen who had tried to fight back were still struggling with their one-time guards, however four more lay unmoving on the floor. Karchek himself took a long withering look at Namot as he closed down the red cloaks and started to climb the dais.

Namot swung a heavy overhead blow against the first soldier, a blow that crashed down on the clumsy block thrown up by the guard. The second guard attacked with a low sweep to Namot's left, catching his leg below the hauberk and cutting into the Jacarnan's flesh. He winced and jumped backwards. Too late he realised his predicament. Releasing the first guard from the block now left him with two opponents and he was now injured. He managed to beat the next few blows away but took another cut to his waist, his chainmail opening up under the heavy thrust of the polearm. He blindly parried another blow from his other opponent and reached out and gripped the polearm that had just cut him. Namot willed his strength into one last attack and pulled the weapon, a loud exclamation escaping his mouth.

The yank caught his opponent unawares and he fell forward off balance. The giant took his chance and swung ferociously with his sword in a one-handed club. The huge blow landed across the shoulders of the red cloak and Namot shouted in exhilaration and triumph as the soldier was decapitated.

He desperately tried to recover in time to block the oncoming thrust from the other soldier, but his sword was inches away from the parry when the sharp spear head on the polearm pierced his armour covering his ribs. He felt the long cold steel rend the small links of chain apart and slip into his skin below. The blade grated against his ribs as it dug deeper and deeper. Even as his hand let go of his sword, his legs were giving way underneath him and he met the oncoming floor with a thud. He looked up at his King knowing that he had failed him and his City.

Another thud silenced the room and his view of the king was obscured by something hitting the floor in front of him. It took a few seconds for his gaze to focus on the dead body of Tarn. The scene started to blur and then it went black.

Whilst Namot was spared the fate of witnessing his King's end, Bryn was not so lucky. Karchek was face to face with King Renta, the giant bending low to look the old man in the eye. Hate emanated from both of them, but it was the old king who spoke first.

"Unsheath your sword, dog. Let us get this over with." His hands trembled as he held the arms of the throne and he tried to spit on the usurper in front of him. The globule of phlegm just bubbled on his lips and started to dribble on his chin. Karchek grinned.

"No sword for you, old man." And he pulled the king from his throne and stood tall, his hand clasping the front of Renta's robe. He spun the old man round so that he stood behind Renta, his left arm wrapped round the king pinning his arms to his side. Karchek's right arm reached over the old man's head, dislodging the gold band of the crown slightly. His hand rested against the left side of the white-haired king and Karchek felt the old man tense himself ready for the twist he thought was coming.

Instead the General started to grip tighter, his fingers digging into the parched old skin under and slightly behind Renta's jaw. Karchek's forearm bulged as he dug his fingers deeper, feeling the skin start to tear as the thick fingers started to bury into the old man.

Renta struggled, his legs kicking aimlessly as he was lifted from the floor. He gritted his teeth as if willing his body to stand strong. Karchek started to snort as he ground his fingers deeper and his eyes bulged as his rage grew. Renta stared blankly as the giant gripped him tighter and then his eyes rolled into the back of his head as first one, then two of Karchek's fingers burst through his skin and into his neck. The pain spread quickly from his neck, running down the side of his body in spasms as Karchek searched for a grip under his jaw and the base of the skull. Blood seeped from the wounds in Renta's neck as Karchek tensed his muscular frame and in one movement tore the old king's head from his body. As his feeble heart carried out its last few beats, Renta's arterial spray jetted upwards covering the screaming and leering face of Karchek, obliterating any last vestiges of humanity in the Commander of the Host.

He let the body fall to the floor and it slithered down the few steps of the dais to a collective groan of all the Jacarnan's in the throne room. As he held the torn head aloft, he received the rapturous cheers of his men. Karchek tossed the head to one side and sat down in the throne he had just won.

"Carry that around the city so that the occupants know they have a new king. Start clearing out the city, you know what to do by now. The Pen Masters, Slavesmiths and Quartermasters are going to be busy." The General addressed one of his commanders who now stood attentively at the foot of the dais.

The old man in the grey robe had slowly climbed the steps and now stood at the new King's side.

"Shall I take these captives to the Quartermasters, Lord Commander?" The officer who spoke had obviously seen combat that night. His armour was battered, and his face splattered with blood. He was slighter and a lot younger than Karchek. The Lord Commander of the Emperor's Host looked upon the kneeling captives. There were, perhaps, two dozen left, Black Serpents and palace guardsmen alike. All knelt, their gaze upon either the floor in front of them or the torn body of their king. All those who had tried to fight when Namot had made his charge were dead, their bodies adding to the many that were lying in the rubble.

"Neither, Lord Remoh. Take them to the pens and tell Soshin to add them to the quotas for ship fodder. Lord Remoh hesitated and Karchek spoke once more.

"You think I make a mistake, Lord Remoh? What are your thoughts?" He sat back, his huge frame only just fitting into the throne. His expression was now calm and relaxed, a complete juxtaposition to his terrifying visage and appearance.

"They are, well, good soldiers, Lord Commander. Lord Albermas will look on them as good additions to the Host."

"If they were good warriors, Lord Remoh, they wouldn't be kneeling there. If they were more like him," he waved his hand at the fallen figure of Namot, "or that crazy old shit of a king, then there would be more of us lying in the rubble than there are. Take them to Soshin."

Lord Remoh bowed and indicated to the guards to move the captives out. Other soldiers started to drag away the palace staff accompanied to the sobs and screams of the weeping Jacarnans.

Bryn made sure that all the soldiers who had come upstairs to the gallery to get Tarn had gone before looking to move out. Before he went however, he mouthed a silent prayer to Kani,

God of hunters and warriors that he would avenge Namot and his king and one day take Karchek's head. He estimated the time and thought there was maybe two hours to dawn break. He hoped to be outside the city walls by then on the way to Tannaheim.

9

It had taken Radnak all of two hours to find out what he needed to know. He had spoken to several Jacarnans including a couple of palace guards who could now be classed as deserters. It was from these that he got the best information. They told him of the flying ships and how the Jacarnan forces had been taken by surprise. From their information along with the garbled rantings of the few palace staff he found, he managed to piece together a timeline and details of the forces he faced. He knew also that Jacarna was falling and would cease to exist in its independent state by morning. He made his way back to his charges and was careful to avoid all contact with the invading forces. As he entered the large storeroom that their small hideaway was situated off from, he knew something was wrong. He drew his sword to accompany the dagger that he had held unsheathed since he had left them two hours earlier.

Crouching, he moved silently from one huge stone pillar of the vaulted ceiling to another, his senses straining to pick out what was troubling him. As he made it to the centre of the room, he saw them. Two figures approaching the door to the small room the Iga and her sons hid in. From the distance they were at, Radnak couldn't tell a great deal about them apart from the fact that they were armed and harnessed and both held aloft a burning brand. That was why he couldn't see them clearly earlier, the lights from their torches merged into the light cast by the brands fixed to the walls in their iron sconces.

He quickly looked about to check whether they were the only two and then when satisfied that was so, moved swiftly to the next pillar. He was close now and surprised that they hadn't picked up on him, though he imagined that they thought that any resistance was already broken and all they would find down here maybe a good wine or a wench to release some of their pent-up aggression on. That thought caused him to think of the Lady Iga and what would happen to her if she fell into their hands. There was nothing for it, he thought to himself, but to draw their attention to him before they opened the door. He poked his dagger down the inside of his boot and reached for a small stone at the foot of the wide pillar.

He cursed as the taller of the two invaders reached for the door handle before he could pick the stone up, but then cursed even louder as the door sprung open to reveal the figure of Igant silhouetted in the doorway. The soldier stood transfixed; one hand extended as he reached for the door. What was the little runt thinking he was doing, Radnak thought? If either of them managed to get out of this, he added to himself, he promised to belt the young lord into next week.

Things now seemed to happen nearly simultaneously. As Radnak leapt forward, his sword aloft in his hand, Igant also lunged forward, his sword stabbing the soldier in his arm. As Igant hurriedly withdrew, shocked at his own bravado, the soldier stared at the wound in his arm for what seemed like an eternity.

Radnak expelled an oath as he charged forward, and the second warrior turned flailing his sword outwards in a hurried parry. He was slightly taller than Radnak though not as stocky. What he had taken to be the soldier's hair was in fact fur, his features that of a feline though he was well adapted and practised at walking on two feet. The snarl of the soldier and the bared teeth surprised the seasoned warrior only slightly, but it was enough for his late swing to collide heavily with the cat man's sword. As they readied themselves to attack each other, Radnak was aware the first soldier was over his shock at being stabbed by the young goblin.

Radnak cursed his luck at being saddled with looking after the two young lords. For all Igant's bravery and the surprise attack all the young lord had managed to do was deal a flesh wound to the invader. The soldier now stood straight, all his attention focused on Igant who stood stock still in the doorway, his sword held down at his side. This warrior was humanoid and would have passed for an inhabitant of Maingard if it was not for his burning yellow eyes. His sword was still in his sheath, the only means to defend himself or to go on the offensive was the lit torch in his hand. He decided he didn't fancy being stabbed again by the young upstart and thrust the burning brand straight into Igant's chest. Igant dropped and fell backwards into the room, his sword clattering to one side. The tall soldier slowly drew his steel and took a step forward.

Radnak cursed again and doubled his efforts against the man cat, his sword flashing in the torch light. He over exaggerated a swing that seemed to leave his defences open but when his opponent darted in, sensing an easy victory, Radnak quickly shifted his weight and kicked out high, driving the ball of his foot into the cat man's jaw. The half orc didn't stop to see whether he was out of the fight completely but turned his attention to the other soldier. Lady Iga had grabbed Igant's sword and held it out, very unconvincingly, in front of her as the soldier crossed the threshold to the room.

The stocky half orc bodyguard leapt at the man threatening

his charges and shouted as he felt his sword slide through the man's armour and into his body. He hit him with so much force that the point of his sword exited through his chest. Radnak crashed into the doorframe as the soldier staggered a further step forward before sinking to his knees. As his eyes rolled backwards he coughed, a dribble of blood seeping from the corner of his lips down onto his chin.

Dazed slightly, Radnak made to retrieve his sword from the man's body when he heard a sound behind him. Spinning he managed to catch his original opponent's attack just in time, his arm jarring upwards into the cat man's wrist as he swung a mighty overhead blow at the orc. His heavy mailed fist jammed into the cat's chest stunning him for a split second. For a stout figure Radnak could move fast. He skipped behind his attacker, his left arm snaking out across the cat man's throat trying to catch him in a strangle hold. Even though his attacker was stunned slightly from Radnak's punch, he managed to get his hands up swiftly and struggled to stop the brawny arm from closing around his neck.

Radnak gritted his teeth, his face straining as he tried to squeeze the life from the feline soldier. He noticed Iga step forward lifting her sword as she approached the wrestling pair.

"Keep back, he's mine. Keep back!" he screamed at her in orcish and then let out a yelp of pain as the cat man bit down on his arm. One needle-like incisor managed to find the unprotected skin between the cuff of his hauberk and the mail of his gauntlet. The pain hit him as it penetrated his skin and the cat man thrust backwards knocking Radnak into one of the many stone pillars supporting the low vaulted ceiling. Radnak's face contorted in agony as his arm burned from the inside. Pinned against the column he was able to lift his leg without losing balance and drew his curved dagger from his boot. As he grimaced in pain, one of his tusks bit into his skin and drew blood.

However, the half orc's arm and the position of the cat man's hands obscured the blade from his enemy, and he felt the cat go limp as he slowly stuck the blade into the soldier's throat. The pressure on his arm relaxed and he was able to move his arm away from the cat man's teeth. He bent down and wiped his blade clean on the dead soldier's clothes and the sheathed his dagger.

As he took a couple of steps towards Lady Iga, he spoke out. "Are you okay? Are any of you hurt?"

"I'm so sorry, Radnak. I have no idea where they came from." Lady Iga sobbed as she grabbed Radnak by his arm. He winced in pain as her hands came close to his wounded wrist. Noticing his reaction and wound, she added, "Here, let me see to that."

"There is no time, we must leave immediately. Jacarna has fallen." As he spoke, Igant stepped out from the room, his silent brother behind him.

"Radnak. . ." the young lord started. The half orc waved his comments away.

"You did well, lad. What you did was very brave." As he spoke, he felt sick and nauseous. He managed to catch himself before he coughed bile and stopped speaking. He looked on their faces as they stared open mouthed at him. Their faces started to blur, and he felt as if the room was starting to spin. Radnak looked down at his wrist where the cat man had managed to bury one of his long incisors. The skin was a dark purple around where the tooth had penetrated and a thick, mucus-like discharge seeped from it. He watched as the darkness spread along his veins making them rise like old scar tissue.

Two thoughts leapt into his fuddled mind as he dropped to the floor. The first was 'poison' and the second 'failure'. Before he could dwell on either, merciful unconsciousness removed the fire like pain from his body.

10

"What in Tomnar's name does your brother think he is doing?" Anjoan, King of Danaria crumpled the note that had been brought to him by one of his pages. The young lad flushed as red as his tunic and was relieved when the King waved him away. He hurriedly fled the chamber. Anjoan was tall and big in stature. His immense frame was pure muscle and there was probably more fat in one of the small songbirds that sat on their perches next to his wife than in his body. His lower face was covered in a bushy beard, a House Barstt tradition no matter what fashion was in trend in the kingdom.

He flung the crumpled note onto the small occasional table near the open balcony that looked over the Royal Harbour. He reached out for a goblet on the table and drained it in one gulp, the dark wine making him feel ever so slightly better. He turned back to his wife, Queen Sarsi, who sat brushing her long, red hair. She turned away from the dressing table mirror to look directly at her husband.

Queen Sarsi was in her forties but every bit as graceful and striking as she had been when she first met the then Crown

Prince Anjoan's eye. Since then she had sat at the side of his throne and served him well. Danaria was ruled as a patriarchy just like the vast majority of Maingard however Sarsi had always been integral to Anjoan's rule. Not only had she abetted his legitimate claim to the throne, but she had also protected their position by any means. She had also borne him four children. The two youngest, Ingren and Moren were asleep next door whilst Garlen could have been anywhere. The twenty-four-year old Crown Prince was a disappointment to her. Once a helpful, talented and delightful child, Garlen had changed that fateful day when his twin, the Princess Antht had died. She sighed, perhaps they had all changed that day.

"My brother, my dear, is his own man. Who knows what he thinks?" she replied dutifully as she continued to brush her hair.

"Don't patronise me with that crap! And why do you insist upon tending to yourself. You are a Queen; we have maids for that."

"I tend to myself because I can. The day I can't is the day I get to hold my darling Antht again." Anjoan knew better than to pursue that argument and returned to the matter of his brother in law.

"I sent him to the North to deal with that pirate scum whilst we finalise the trade contract with the snow walkers. I have lost count of the number of ships that have been lost between Worte and the Isle of Winds. It seems every day there is a complaint from some merchant that the Throne is not doing enough to protect their pretty arses!" The King poured himself another goblet of wine from one of the finely crafted crystal carafes and raised the goblet to his lips. He didn't drink but lowered the wine and carried on.

"And now, as if the syphilitic runt couldn't mess things up anymore, I hear that he has been dallying with the wife of the Jarl of the Isle of Winds. The wife! Unless the Jarl has an intelligence network of an orc then he will know about it and that is going to make this trade deal awkward. The Jarl reaches Tanna-heim in the next few days and I can only imagine that these negotiations are going to be tenuous."

"What would you like me say, dear husband. It was you, after all, that sent him there. You know exactly what he is like."

"Yes, I do know, but I don't expect him to lay with every woman he walks past and especially one who is the wife of an ally to be." He raised the goblet again to his lips and this time he drank deep, wiping the back of his hand across his beard afterwards. "If he makes it out this time, I have a good mind to geld him."

"And where has this news come from, Anjoan? A reliable source?"

"Yes, of course. Though you probably know where the information is from already. You have more spies in this palace than our enemies do, my Queen." Anjoan smiled and took the Queen's brush from her and placed it on the table.

"I prefer the term 'eyes and ears'. 'Spies' is such a horrible word. My 'eyes and ears' just bring me the information that I need to provide you with."

"Gossipmongers, you mean," Anjoan laughed. They duelled like this quite regularly, Anjoan understood the trials of state more than the petty squabbling of the court. If it threat-ened the Crown and Danaria directly, he knew about it, if it didn't – then did he really need to know? He had enough to think about with the rule of Danaria, along with several small and often fractious duchies and city states that the incumbent of the Red Throne was overlord to. His family, House Barstt had ruled over the kingdom for the last 113 years, since his great-great-grandfather had led a virtually bloodless coup against the inept reign of Harnyak II.

"It's not really power is it?" he teased her again.

"Oh, dear husband, gossip is knowledge, and knowledge *is*

power!" she stressed the last two words and reached out to caress his face just above his beard line. He harrumphed and turned away.

"Oh, but it is, Anjoan. I know exactly who owes what to whom in the court, along with who fucks who and in what position. I know which Lords like their pages a bit more than is normal and I know which Lady of the Court prefers to lay with her dog than her man."

Anjoan refilled his goblet and took another sip. He stood resplendent, despite the early morning start and the troublesome news about his brother in law. He wore hose of a dark grey colour that clung tight to his tree trunk like legs, but he was bare-chested as he had only just awoken. A thin scar ran across his left side just below the rib cage, a result of a wound during a skirmish in a border dispute some fifteen years ago. How Sarsi had thought that she had lost him then, seeing him carried back home swathed in bandages.

"Go on," he prompted in between sips.

"I even know the names of every maid, page and whore who sleeps with any Lord of the Court." Sarsi spoke as she walked to her husband and then trailed her fingertips across his bare back as she added, "My Lord." Anjoan paused before replying and placed the goblet back onto the table.

"And what power does that knowledge give you?"

"It gives me the power to know which cards to play when I deal with anyone in the Kingdoms. It gives me the power to make deals and to break deals. And it has given me the power to help you when you have needed it." Anjoan turned back to his wife and gently took her hands in his.

"And I am eternally grateful." He raised his wife's hands to his lips and kissed each knuckle before continuing, "So, do you know where my information has come from?"

"I know the name by which he is known. He is known as the Phantom or Tikar Welk in the old language, Anjoan's Phantom.

But I, like everyone else versed in the intrigues of the court, do not know who he is."

"And I would like it to stay that way. Not even Magus Vent knows who the Phantom is."

He sat down on the vast canopy bed, sinking down into the mattress covered with a luxuriant red and gold velvet bed sheets. He beckoned her to him, and she shimmied across to stand in front of him. As the sunlight streamed into the bedchamber for the first time that morning, he was more aware of her beauty than ever before. Anjoan reached upwards and slowly and deliberately untied the small bow that secured the lacing to her bodice. Her dress was low cut, the neckline of her bodice starting just above the nipples of her tiny and pert bosom. As he pulled the lace through each eyelet on her bodice, he asked a question, timing each word as the lace cleared each golden ring.

"Do you want to see real power?"

As he spoke the last word, he revealed her tiny breasts and the golden, sheer dress slipped from her thin frame to display her totally naked body. His rough hands slipped over her skin to rest on her breasts. He felt her body react as the palms of his hands rubbed across her nipples and realised that his own body was reacting too.

"Of course," she replied her face melting to a seductive smile which was totally superfluous. His eyes were already taking in the sight of her nakedness and their lips met in a fierce kiss as her fingers started to untie his hose.

11

N arbek drank alone in the Scalloper Inn, a small but crowded ale house in the dock area. The clientele was loud and rowdy, shouting and carousing as only dockers and sailors can do. In the corner an old minstrel played a shanty on a small lyre, the melody only just escaping through the volume of the nearby drinkers. Narbek was deep in thought, eyes down upon the flagon he held in both hands on the table in front of him. The figure seemed to appear next to him, a voluminous grey cloak wrapped about him with the hood thrown up over his head.

"I hear you can help me." The voice rasped from inside the hood, the stranger's face obscured by the shadows thrown by the heavy folds.

Narbek had glanced sideways at the figure who had sidled up to him in the booth. He had been contemplating visiting the little whore again, the small dark girl from Thesh in the south. She rented rooms not far from the dockside and the gold he had earnt from the sale of those stolen gems was burning a hole in his purse.

"I think you have the wrong man." He bluntly shoved away the stranger's statement and went to stand.

"I hear you can help me." The stranger said again, his hand reaching out from the cloak and grabbing Narbek's wrist as the smuggler braced himself on the table. The skin on the stranger's hand was grey and stretched over the gnarled fingers, the nails blackened and talon like. Narbek winced, not with the strength of the stranger's grip but from the icy cold touch. It was as if he had plunged his hand into a bucket of ice and he swore he could see the skin around the claw like grip tinge blue. "Sit." The stranger commanded.

Narbek sat down, his right hand slowly reaching for the short dagger he carried at his right hip. The stranger released his grip.

"Do I know you?" the smuggler asked.

"No, but I know you." The dark figure chuckled, a dark, macabre sound muffled by the hood.

"Your name has come from a mutual acquaintance. Narbek the smuggler, the fencer, the transporter. Narbek is the man to come to when you need to get something in or out of the city." Narbek nodded inside, the stranger was right. He was one of the best in the city, anything could be moved in or out of the walls, by ship or by land and he had the best knowledge in order to move it.

"You can draw your knife, but my man behind will kill you before you can strike," The muffled chuckle came again. Narbek sighed and moved his hand above the table again, taking his ale flagon and taking a huge draught of the strong, malty beer.

"I need something getting beyond the city walls, two bags. Each one the size of a batch of furs and about eight bars in weight." The stranger described a pack that a trapper's mule would carry from the North, a sizeable bundle of furs held on either side of the mule. "I will travel with them, and we would need to go to the North, about ten miles from the city. There I meet my companion who will take them from there."

Narbek knew better than to ask what would be in them. His mind was already starting to ponder the situation and work out how he would move them.

"My fee. . ."

The stranger interrupted him, throwing a small purse of coins on the table.

"I know your fee. That is fifty pieces of platinum from the Far Isles. The equivalent of two hundred of your gold crowns." Narbek knew the value of the coins even before the stranger had said. Platinum was quite sought after by the want-to-be-elite of the city. Two hundred gold crowns would more than cover his normal fee. He snatched the purse of the table, afraid that any unscrupulous character in the Scalloper Inn should see it and get any strange ideas of relieving him of his new wealth.

"There will be another two hundred pieces when we meet my companion." The stranger rasped. More! thought Narbek, a thousand gold crowns would be more than his normal monthly operating profit. Whatever the stranger wanted moving was definitely expensive.

"Two more things; bring no one else. Only yourself must see this through. Secondly, if you shy from this job, I will take you down and hand you over to that captain of the trader currently on the South Pier. I understand he wants to know who has been lying with his wife whilst he has been sailing to and from Norheim." The stranger had slowly stood, his hand once again gripping Narbek's wrist and once again the coldness had spread through his flesh.

The pay for the job already seemed to weight his purse down as he reached for his ale again, a slow smile starting to form on his narrow lips.

"Speak, grey one, tell me more."

They talked for a while and a cold feeling of dread spread slowly from his heart as he listened to the stranger's plans. Finally, the grey cloaked man stood and left leaving Narbek staring at his ale in silence, a worried look on his face. He was no longer interested in finishing his ale, and all thoughts of the little whore from Thesh had disappeared from his mind. He rubbed his wrist, the cold ache had seemed to settle in his bones and when he looked down, he noticed that the skin on his wrist had faded from the icy blue to a corpse like grey.

12

The Hawk studied the young girl as she sat in front of him, her hands reaching across the Arda board as she pondered the next move. She was at the most 10 years of age, but it was hard to pin-point an exact age due to the raga-muffin look. Her brown eyes looked out from under the thatch of mousey brown hair with a mix of world weariness and sadness but also an air of confidence that was often missing from the street urchins of Tannaheim. A street urchin she was, her clothes torn and her skin dirty. She looked well fed and healthy which gave the indication that she was under some-one's protection whilst out on the streets. If the Hawk hadn't known better, he would have said that she was under the protection of a pimp or one of the nefarious criminal guilds.

As soon as she had darted past him and his guards as he walked through the Middle Quarter and then slipped the dark purple head of a field rose into his hand, he knew who she was, or rather who her patron was. It would be the Phantom, the shadowy figure who fed his king information that seemed crit-ical to the prosperity of the House Barstt. He knew better than to chase her as she would turn up again when she decided the time was right. He had even given up hope of following her from the meeting place as each time he had done so and pursued one of Tikar Welk's urchins they had led his troops on a merry dance around the rat runs of the Maze and then disappeared into the culverts of the extensive storm drains and sewers under the capital.

King Anjoan had forbidden him from pursuing his investigation into the Phantom and that only rankled the old soldier. As the King's Marshall, Magus Vent was the second most powerful man in Tannaheim and Danaria. He was responsible for guarding the king's reputation and life so seeing the king place so much trust in a shadowy figure and then for Anjoan to protect him irked Vent. Yet he had sworn to uphold the king's orders and rule and vowed he would serve out the rest of his term, and maybe leave the court then. Eleven long years he had held the position of Marshall, normally the position favoured a term of two years but Anjoan had personally appealed to him each term to stay.

Behind his back, and on the streets of the city, he was known as the Hawk. The name suited not only his looks, his nose pointed and hooked and his eyes were piercing and close together, but also his manner – he was merciless in carrying out the orders of Anjoan, no matter what they entailed or who got hurt on the way. But eleven years was a long time and he deserved a retirement on a smallholding towards the remote corners of the Kingdoms, anywhere as long as it was away from the bustle and sounds of the city. He wondered whether Anjoan would find a more trustworthy and dedicated replacement and then snorted as he imagined the ghostly Phantom in his role.

The snort brought his opponent's attention back to him and away from the game board. She looked up, her small fingers holding one of the pieces, a carved piece of bone depicting an archer.

"It's a good move, ser Vent. You shouldn't be disparaging about your opponent's position until you have won." She spoke with the roughness of ten years on the streets, fighting every day against the system and the other denizens of the Maze just to survive. He smiled, casting a glance about the crowded plaza before answering.

"I'm sorry, it was not you. Just a thought about someone."

The small girl tutted then continued to ponder her move. After she had darted through his small cordon of guards and left her flower in his hand he had not seen her for another few minutes, not until they had reached the edge of the market area. Here old men played Arda and drank while they regaled each other with stories from their youth. Small children played games, dashing in and out of the many people streaming into and out of the market. It was here that she waved to him and beckoned him over to play a game whilst they talked.

His guards kept a respectable distance, now used to this strange intrusion into the normality of their routine. So, the young girl and the old man could play in peace, and even the slight refinery of his tunic didn't draw attention from the locals.

"What is your name, girl?" he enquired in an authoritative tone which he seemed to favour most of the time.

"You don't expect me to give you my name, do you, ser?" she replied, her fingers still holding the archer.

"Why not, you know mine."

She sighed and then played the archer into one of the squares of the board containing one of her towers. The pieces threatened several of the Hawk's own. As he puzzled over the board she added, "Call me Yanna." The Hawk closed his eyes for a second and breathed slowly. There must be thousands of Yannas in Tannaheim, it was one of the most common names for a girl.

"Anjoan won't like it if he hears you are still trying to find out who the Phantom is, ser Vent."

"Who taught you to play, girl?" he changed tack, knowing he was going to get nowhere in tracing the true identity of Tikar Welk. "Was it your father?"

"Never knew him, my mother always said that he only stuck around long enough to squirt me into her and then left. I think he was a sailor." Magus Vent blanched slightly, and he was suddenly aware that the young girl's brashness was unsettling. He had a young granddaughter who was a year or so younger than Yanna and hearing the young urchin talk how she did, made him feel glad that his young Marsy was growing up in the richer quarter of the city.

"So who did?"

"Tikar Welk. He taught me when he took me in and made me one of his men."

"You have seen him?" The Hawk leant forward with an incredulous look on his face. Many people claimed to have been approached by the Phantom, yet all confirmed it was only one of his agents. And now this ten-year-old was saying that she had met him. He cast a glance across to one of his men, trying to gauge the distance between them and wondering whether Yanna's escape could be blocked.

"I wouldn't get your hopes up, Marshall Vent. There are two crossbows trained on you right now. One funny move and Anjoan is looking for a new Marshall." At the girl's words he took a final look round but saw nothing. He didn't want to take the chance that she might be bluffing and so turned his attention to the game. He moved his king behind a carving of a warrior holding a spear and a full shield. This was one of his Phalanx pieces, a figure for attack and defence.

"Speaking of your notorious employer, I take it he has a message for me. If I wanted to play arda I could have stayed at court and played in comfort, and against a more, shall we say, substantial opponent."

Yanna threw him a bitter look and wiped the back of her

hand across the end of her nose. He couldn't help but see the smear of moisture cause a streak in the grime on her hand as she reached for a piece. She moved a Cavalry figure dashing across the front of his Phalanx to attack one of his Skirmishers. She knocked the base of the horseman against the head of the light archer making it fall over. She placed the horseman on the hex and handed Vent's taken piece back to him.

"He does. Something big is about to happen. He doesn't know what but there are ripples running throughout the Kingdoms. He also states that this might be an attempt against the king's life."

"Is that all? Maybe I should have stayed at court. The information is as mediocre as the game. There are plots against the king made every time he makes a decision. The vast majority turn out to be hot air." His hand hovered over his Phalanx and he moved it a space forward, turning it to attack the victorious cavalry. Over jubilant and over enthusiastic as most cavalry, they fell to the well-oiled machine of the phalanx and he smiled as he handed her the dead horseman.

"My mother always told me not to be rude to other people, Marshall Vent. I take it my mother and your mother never ate at the same table?" She looked crossly at him before snatching a Light Cavalry piece and moving it in behind the Phalanx, threatening not only its rear but also the king. The Phalanx would be taken if attacked from the rear, its tightly packed spearmen unable to manoeuvre except in a forward direction. The Hawk knew though that she wouldn't bother with that move next as his king was also threatened. Having now charged, Yanna's Light Cavalry could only move one space in the next move but would still reach the king ending the game. His eyes perused the game board as Yanna continued.

"The king will receive a message from Lord Shales tomorrow morning requesting a further squadron of ships to be sent north to aid in his campaign against the pirates. Tikar

Welk advises against this and urges you to double the guards in the palace for the foreseeable future."

"But the Queen's brother is close to routing the pirate scum. This could be the chance that we have been waiting for, a safe sea between Tannaheim and the Isle of Winds. And a show of strength, especially with the Jarl of the snow walkers here will help these trade negotiations. I will not advise this course of action on the supposition of a spy, and a spy who passes on information purely for his own benefit at that." He reached for his king and moved it a space away from Yanna's cavalry piece. He went to release but had second thoughts and moved a further space away giving him more time for his army to regroup.

"I shall pass your comments on to my employer, Marshall Vent. But like you, I wish I had stayed in the lower maze today," Yanna referred to the maze-like underground slum that stretched under the city using the sewers and drains for movement. Her tiny hand flittered over the board before resting on a piece. All too late Magus Vent saw his mistake. "The conversations and companions are better there and the arda games are slightly more challenging." Yanna's archer moved out from the comparative safety of her tower to within a couple of spaces of the Hawk's king. On the arda board, like the real battlefield, an unprotected man in the open close to enemy archers never stands a chance

"I think that is game over. Your king is dead, ser Vent. Make sure this is the only king you lose this week." With those chilling words, the girl who called herself Yanna turned and dashed off into the crowd before the Hawk could call to his guards.

13

The approach to Yab M'Vil's villa had been easy. With the slaver and trader working late in the offices at the warehouse, the guards he had left behind were not as vigilant as they should have been. Within minutes of reaching the outer limits of the villa's grounds, Bex was balancing on top of a high boundary wall just a few feet away from her planned entrance. Yab's villa was large, as one would expect from the self-styled richest man in the Kingdoms. The stonework had been rendered with a pale, sand coloured plaster reminiscent of the large houses in the merchant's native country far to the east. A walled garden and courtyard joined the back of the property whilst well maintained lawns surrounded the rest of the property. This wall, about the height of a man's reach, was what Bex found herself on.

The tall, lithe thief leapt for the window ledge above and managed to grasp the edge of the plastered stonework. Hauling herself up she wriggled around so that she perched sideways, one buttock on the ledge and one leg braced against the recess that the window sat in. Her other leg dangled below the sill.

She was dressed completely in black with a hood pulled up over her head which caused her face to be hidden in darkness.

Over the top of her outfit she wore a tight-fitting web of straps, known through the thieves' guilds as a spider's web or a spider. Upon these straps were small buckles and rings, each individually wrapped in felt to minimise the noise, enabling the burglar to carry several tools and pouches easily to hand. It was into one of these pouches that she reached and pulled out a small folded scrap of blackened paper, blackened not with soot or burning but thick, gloopy tar. She carefully opened each fold until the paper measured twice her handprint, and then pressed it against one of the leaded panels in the window, smoothing it out until she was sure that it was stuck well. Bex drew her only weapon, a shortsword known as a greck. Its blade curved slightly, and it had a leather-bound handle and a pointed steel pommel. It was this steel point that she drove against the tar paper stuck to the glass. With a satisfied smile she felt the glass give way with no sound except the dull thud of steel on paper.

Peeling away the paper and glass left a hole big enough to get her arm through and open the window catch from inside. Laying the paper on the windowsill, she broke a couple of shards that still clung to the leaded frame and reached in. When she was sure that there wasn't any alarm wire or trap stretched between the jambs Bex opened the window and climbed through.

As well as the surveillance of Yab M'Vil at his warehouse in order to learn his routine, she had also spent several days gaining as much information about the villa as possible. She had managed to track down a man who had been a paid servant of the merchant and for a few crowns he had drawn a small map of the building and described every room. She was relieved to see that it had been crowns well spent. The information was correct, the room was indeed a storeroom, mainly old bric-a-brac and furniture, some covered with dust sheets and others with cobwebs suggesting that this room had not been used in a while.

She crept to the door, throwing her hood back to reveal the black hair running down the centre of her scalp. The hair cascaded to one side, covering intricate tattoos of two wolves inked over her skin. On the other side of her scalp was tattooed a diving hawk. A scrap of black felt was wound over her face, across her eyes, with slits cut so that her black eyes glared through. She leant against the door slightly, her ear cocked against it. Once again, her fingers rummaged through one of her pouches, drawing out a piece of stiff leather, trapezium in shape. Listening at the door her fingers quickly rolled the leather into a cone shape, placing it between her ear and the wooden door. Silence, no movement. Her left hand dextrously replaced the leather into a pouch whilst her right silently and smoothly opened the door.

She peered out onto a landing where rich woven rugs from the Western Isles covering the oak floorboards. Candles flickered on silver sconces along the walls in between tapestries and paintings in ornate frames. Elsewhere on the wall hung decorative swords and animal skins, trophies bought with ill-gotten wealth. She noticed a white wolf skin from the far north along with several animal skins that she had never seen before. Statuettes and small busts made from alabaster and fine marble were spaced along the landing.

The low light put out by the candles was a thief's blessing. Long shadows danced along the landing cast by drapes and statues that adorned the route. On one side of her the landing opened out onto an ornate staircase leading down to the hall below. A similar landing ran alongside the opposite side of the villa, leading down to the same staircase.

If her memory served correctly, and if once again the information was correct, then the merchant's chambers were to her right at the end of the corridor. From below she could hear a few of the guards chatting as they waited for Yab M'vil to return from his offices. She crept towards the banister and peeked between the alabaster columns to see two men in banded mail. They stood close to one of the roaring fires that lit and warmed the great hall below, whilst a third stood near the main door looking out onto the courtyard outside. 'No doubt waiting for the fat merchant's return', Bex thought to herself. She estimated that there would be another three sleeping somewhere, and she had slipped past two or three patrolling the grounds outside when she had broken in.

Silently she crept down the corridor, keeping to the plush, thick pile of the handwoven rugs until she came to the double doors at the end. As she neared it, she could see that the fastenings were heavy iron, and that there was a lock fitted. 'And if M'vil had fitted a lock, then it would be locked' she thought. Within a few steps she was there, with a set of lock picks open in front of her. She chose the two she needed and inserted them into the keyhole, feeling and listening to the tumblers inside. It took her twenty heartbeats until she felt the last tumbler click and the door open. She stepped inside, and softly shut the door behind her.

Now she knew exactly how opulent the merchant was. The chamber was large, very large with windows down one side only. They were covered with near transparent silks hanging from gold rods. Heavy, velvet drapes hung from the same rods, ready to be drawn and plunge the room into darkness. A fire raged in a tall fireplace in the centre of the near wall. A large four-poster bed occupied the end of the room closest to the doors. Bex noticed that heavy iron rings were set into the posts of the bed, set at the right position to cuff a person to. Whilst she had witnessed his treatment of certain slaves at his offices, she knew that his tastes ran into stronger perversions than that. She had heard tales amongst the city's underworld about how his captains reserved certain types of girls for him from their shipments and that they seldom survived long once they had made the short trip to his villa. She blanched, trying to drive obscene imagery and unpleasant memories from her mind. But despite the splendour laid out in front of her it was what she saw at the far end of the room that stopped her in her tracks.

A set of large drapes hid something as if another four-poster bed was situated in the middle of the room. She approached the curtains slowly and silently. As she crept forward, she drew her short blade and held it ready. Even though she had not explored the room fully she was sure this was 'it'. Behind these drapes was the thing that M'Vil's men had found in the forest and within a few feet of her was the thing that M'Vil thought would make him a fortune. Her mind worked overtime wondering what it could be – could it be a large diamond? an animal? Or some magical artefact left behind by one of the early men many generations ago? The black-haired burglar was apprehensive as her left hand reached out for the curtain.

Waiting no longer she swept the curtain to one side revealing a cage about eight foot in all dimensions. It was made from vertical bars about the thickness of a man's thumb, with a solid base and top. Connected to the roof of the cage was a chain, possible about 4 feet long that hung down to a collar. It was the creature that sat; head bowed forward that made Bex gasp. It was her size, female in shape yet not human. Her skin was a patch work of black and a dull red and it smouldered. She was naked and hairless, but two twisted horns sat on her head just above the temples. As she lifted her head to see the intruder, Bex could see the colours on her skin move and shift and the creature's eyes stared lifelessly and dark at her.

Bex did not speak but moved back until she stood about six

feet from the cage. A question formed in her mind '*Who are you?*' yet she didn't utter it.

'*Who are you?*' the question rose in her sub consciousness again, and it was then she realised that it wasn't her mind asking the question, but the creature itself.

'*I am dying, help me please.*'

Bex answered out loud "My name is Bex, what can I do to help you?"

"Ahh, how sweet!" a high-pitched voice, almost effeminate, behind her spoke. She spun round, cursing as she did so. In the doorway stood Yab M'vil.

'By Tomnar! What is he doing here?' she thought to herself.

"A spider returns home early to catch a delicious looking fly in his web" Yab carried on.

Up close she could now tell that he was almost as broad as he was tall. He wore clothes in the style of the Eastern Ports, despite the colder weather here. Long, loose trousers gathered at the ankle, with a long robe, in a horrible garish blue. He was bald and even from this distance Bex could see the heavy make-up that he wore. Flanking him to either side were two of the guards from downstairs and she could hear more on the landing outside the room. The guards were Northerners, tall and muscular, wearing mail made of steel horizontal bands that were tied with leather at the front of the chest. Curved plates were fitted at the collar to cover the shoulders and allow their arms free movement. Their armour reached the top of their legs where hinged plates protected the groin and hip area. They wore short greaves made of hardened leather with short fur boots. Bex noticed that they carried shorter swords than most North men, who normally favoured huge hand-and-a-half swords, or even larger axes. She hoped that this might give her an advantage if she had to fight her way out. Her eyes glanced to the windows opposite, but she now noticed that they were barred as well.

"Just as you have been watching me, I have been watching you. My reach stretches far and wide into every court and palace in the land. How a simple thief could think she could meander into my world and not come to my attention is plainly insulting. Now that you have broken into my home and found my secret, the question is what to do with you?"

14

If Ser Eglebon Dutte was showing the pressure of arranging high treason, then he was hiding it well. He had arrived home from his Privy Council meetings and had enjoyed a very late, light supper of herrings and eggs on toast.

At the second bell of the cat he had risen and left his large townhouse, engulfing his tall form within the folds of a dark, voluminous cloak. For the first time in a while, he had taken not only a sword for protection but also a long dagger, that he had added as a precautionary extra. That hadn't been the only protection; as he left the gated courtyard, one of his trusted guards fell in step with him, garbed in a similar cloak.

Walking confidently from the Palace quarter along the Street of Coins, where many moneylenders and banks had their premises – because of which, was one of the safest places to walk in Tannaheim after dark, they moved into the Merchant's quarter. Within a few streets they turned into Black Street and thence into Fish Lane. The areas became less affluent with every turn and soon, by Fish Lane, Dutte was holding a slightly perfumed kerchief under his nose. Meanwhile, Sato, his guard, kept a tight grip upon the hilt of his sword.

The streets were deserted, apart from some elements of the city guard but these were only evident in the richer streets. By Fish Lane, they passed no-one but instead felt the eyes of many. They soon came to their destination, a small non-descript brothel called the Red Tart, tucked between a brewery and a tar warehouse.

With a furtive glance left and right, Dutte knocked on the tatty door, three short raps, pause, and then the three raps repeated. There was an uneasy pause before the door cracked open with a creak and an older woman peered out.

"Yes?", she enquired, displaying uneven, yellowing teeth.

Dutte had rehearsed the lines that the paid thug, Murf, had told him a myriad of times in his head whilst they had walked to the Red Tart. He was now at the point of no return, up to now it had been just talk; an idle notion. If he proceeded now, it was something more; a betrayal, treason. A path to riches and power – or one to failure and death. He cleared his throat and began.

"I am but a poor nobleman from afar looking for an ale and a wench with fire in her heart and in her loins. I have been recommended to see Harsti."

The brothel madam narrowed her stare and eyed him up and down.

"Harsti is unwell. I can recommend Fferyll instead." It was the reply he had hoped for, the one that Murf had assured him would be given. He nodded, and the woman stepped back from the door and ushered him in. His guard warily turned to survey the road either side of the brothel before following him in.

The room they walked into was dark, with all manner of fabrics hanging from the walls in a half-hearted attempt to obscure the dinginess and the sorry state of the building. Several padded couches and chaises were set about the central fireplace that housed a roaring fire. Half a dozen naked women lounged on them, two of them in a passionate embrace. As the men entered, two others stood and begun dancing together, their swaying hips mesmerizing Dutte's companion.

"Fferyll is upstairs. Follow me." The brothel madam walked through the dancing women, not bothering to look to see if Dutte was following and made her way to the stairs at the back of the room. Dutte turned to his guard.

"Get a drink and stay here, Sato. Be ready to leave when I return." He could see the annoyance on the guard's face, now aware that he could only look but not touch. The stairs creaked as Dutte stepped foot on them.

At the top, the madam indicated the first door. As Dutte stepped forward, she held her hand out, barring his way.

"The fee." She hissed.

He looked down at her, disgusted that someone like her should lay hands upon him but then remembered where he was and what lay at stake. He reached into his cloak and pulled a small purse from within, placing it in the older woman's hand. She nodded as an acknowledgement and lowered her hand, the purse disappearing faster than the eye could see. Dutte glared at her retreating back and then slowly opened the door to the room.

Two candles flickered and struggled to light the room past a dull gloom. The absence of a fire was extremely noticeable and Dutte shivered. It may have been the cold, or just the thought of his actions ahead. The whore on the bed looked up as he entered, and he drew the mantle of his cloak up higher to obscure his face. When he saw her eyes, milky white and sightless, he realized it wouldn't matter and relaxed slightly.

Despite the cold air that pervaded the room, she was naked apart from a long, sheer headscarf with one end thrown seductively over her shoulder, the other draped down her chest and pooling in between her crossed legs. She wasn't who or what he had expected.

"I'm here to. . .‟ he stammered before she cut him off.

"I know why you are here. Speak not!" she admonished him and gingerly rose from the bed. She made her way to the window and opened it. The pungent odour of fish washed in from the docks and strangled the sweet incense that was burning on the bedside table.

"This way. Quick!" She beckoned in his general direction. As he approached, she moved to one side but stumbled and fell against him. Dutte reached down and grasped her forearm, lifting her to her feet. Her fists clenched as she slightly shook.

"Thank you, good Ser," she mumbled and lowered herself to sit on the edge of the bed, one hand outstretched behind her to feel for it. "On the balcony outside, you will find a ladder to the roof. On the far side of the roof is a board that will take you to the neighbouring warehouse. Who you wish to see will see you there. On your way back, tap the window and I will open it."

"Thank you," he stepped through the window, then lent back in. "Are you sure you are okay?"

"Yes, now go, he won't wait."

With that, Dutte turned and made his way along the balcony, another step towards the ultimate treason. Whilst back in the room, Fferyll closed the window and unclenched her fist, revealing a small razor-sharp blade and a piece of dark cloth that she had cut from Dutte's cloak as she had fallen against him.

15

'*Fire*', a single word formed in Bex's mind.

"What?" she replied, assuming her fighting stance, her hand holding the short scimitar rising to her chest, the point seeming to aim straight at the fat merchant's gullet. Her other hand reached out in front of her as if to deflect any blow from her opponents.

The fat merchant thought she was speaking to him and answered as his two men moved into the room, one angling towards the windows in case she made a break for it in that direction, the other keeping himself between her and his employer.

"We don't know what it is. Some of my men came across it in the forests to the north of here a few days ago. It killed three of them by the time they subdued it. And by all means talk to it, it doesn't answer. So, my dear . . . Bex, is it? Why have you come to visit? To see this . . . thing? To kill me? It has been a while since a woman came voluntarily to my rooms." He smiled and gave a little hearty chuckle that seemed forced. "Maybe you wish to entertain me tonight? Keep me warm throughout this winter night?"

"Over my dead body, you miserable scum!" Bex snarled, lifting her blade higher. Her left hand wandered over one of the many pouches attached to her spider, dipping in and out so fast that either guard did not see it.

'Do not speak, Form your words in your mind. I will hear them.'

'Like this?' she tried it.

'Yes! But quick, I am dying. Fire, bring me fire.'

'Fire?' Bex formed the question in her mind, looking about the room. Yab had placed a candelabra on one of the side tables next to the bed, and a third guard stood outside the bedroom door with a lantern in his hand. Her eyes settled on the fire crackling in the marble fireplace between where she stood and the open doorway. This, she decided, was her best hope.

"Over your dead body, well, my dear; that can certainly be arranged, though I would prefer to hand you over to the guild myself. Have you seen what they do to your sort, my dear? As a warning to other lone wolves? They might even let me watch you squirm in their torturers' hands. You are a lone wolf, I take it? Even the Guild wouldn't be so stupid as to bite the hand that feeds it." Yab referred to the slang term for those who operated without the Thieves' Guild blessing. He chuckled to himself and beckoned his guards forward. "Kill her!"

The two guards inched forward, wary of her blade she kept pointing towards each in turn. They were confident that they would take her, but neither was certain that they would both be unharmed by the end of the skirmish.

"When I have killed your pets, Yab, I will come for you." Bex spat out, her dark eyes focused on the corpulent merchant. From the corner of each eye she could make out each guard.

"Oh please, you thieving bitch." Yab's falsetto voice whimpered in sarcastic joy and he raised his fists into the air and screamed at his guards, "Now kill her! Gut her now!"

This seemed to spur the mercenaries on, and the one by the windows stepped forward. Slightly smaller than his companion, his eyes gave a hint of nervousness about him. Maybe this was the first time he had been in proper combat, maybe his service so far with Yab had just been as a hired thug putting the frighteners on to some poor sap of a shop keeper. The other guard was another matter, his face and arms a hotch potch of small scars that bore witness to many fights and skirmishes.

Bex weighed up her options. One of them would need to be taken out straight away; she wouldn't be able to put a prolonged defence up against two opponents especially if one of them was a fairly experienced warrior. Which one though?

'*Hurry, I am . . .*' the thought interrupted her.

"I know!" Bex shouted her response, forgetting to think inside her head. "If you can see, I am slightly busy here!"

Her shouting distracted the younger, smaller guard whose eyes flickered bemusedly between his companion and her. She directed a slight lunge towards him as a feint, her front foot moving towards him and her blade following suit. He took a great step backwards, lifting his sword clumsily to ward off a blow that would never come. As Bex thought, the other guard charged forward, his sword coming up in an overhead swing. She paused her feint perfectly and twisted her torso to face the on-rushing guard, her left hand rising towards her face. Too late he saw his predicament, as she leant forward and blew across her open hand, the small scrap of wax paper flat on her hand and the small pile of dust now hurtling towards his face like sand blown up in a sirocco. It was the last thing he saw as the dust hit his eyes. He raised his free hand to his face and screamed. His sword hand came crashing down in a clumsy arc on the spot that a fraction of a second before Bex had been as his eyes erupted in a stream of tears and agony. Before his sword had even clattered uselessly to the floor, his eyes were nearly swollen shut and Bex noticed small flecks of blood in his tear ducts. The tall thief had danced lithely between her attackers and followed up her attack with a spin towards her blinded opponent, her arm outstretched. The razor-sharp blade cut through three of his fingers and into his face as he held them up in front of him. From the pain that ravaged his eyes he didn't seem to notice as his severed digits fell to the floor.

Bex had paid handsomely for the contents of that wrap of paper. A blend of peppers, chilli and spice ground down to a fine dust, mixed with some interesting minerals from a little alchemist's shop in the poor quarter of Tannaheim. She made a mental note to visit his shop again and buy more.

She finished her move to stand behind him and her eyes took in his weak points in his armour. His back and shoulders were all armoured but below the banded mail he only had a skirt of thin leather straps. She plunged her sword through this and down on to his unprotected thighs, cutting deep into the flesh. He sank to his knees and then collapsed on the floor face down.

'*Nice*' she felt the thought in her mind.

'*Thank you*' she silently acknowledged.

She now found herself near the open fire and, sensing that the other guard was still far enough away not to be a threat, she bent down and grasped a blazing brand of wood. She danced back into the room waving both weapons in front of her as another two guards entered the room. Time seemed to stand still as she could see one raise a shortbow, a black feathered arrow already notched. The younger guard had moved to cut off her route to Yab, who was screaming at his men to kill her.

She turned and lunged towards the creature in the cage, her hand holding the brand outstretched. She noticed the creature was now kneeling up, arms thrust through the bars towards her.

Bex suddenly felt her arm explode in a ball of pain and she turned and fell onto her back. Her blade fell from her hand and skittled across the floor. She looked across and saw the arrow point protruding from her bicep. She felt nauseous from the sight and pain, her mind groggy. She could see the two guards moving towards her and the third stringing another arrow. She turned her head to the other side and saw that she still held the burning brand.

Mustering as much energy and power as she could she rolled towards the cage and held the brand up to the creature. She seemed to black out for a fraction of a second, her whole arm awash with agony, but she could see the creature stretch more and finally grasp the brand, its fingers grasping the burning flame itself, whilst its other hand reached out to hold her bare wrist just above the glove. As she did so she felt one thought.

'*Trust me*' and then another, slightly fainter, '*I'm sorry*'.

She watched in amazement as the flame on the brand crackled with renewed energy, and the whole thing burst into flame, engulfing first the arm of the creature and then its body. Bex struggled to free herself from the grip of the creature as the flames raced down the other arm towards where the creature held her fast. She looked on, face aghast, as her wrist and forearm blistered and ignited. She screamed, unable to escape the blaze.

The two guards stopped dead in their tracks as they saw her now completely engulfed in flames. She could hear Yab screaming and laughing and calling for more guards. The pain that the arrow had brought her was nothing to the searing agony of the fire. For a few seconds she was conflagrant with the creature and they locked eyes together. The creature smiled, her eyes were balls of fire and flames danced upon her head in a mockery of human hair. She now looked like a human chiselled from living fire, her skin patterned with move-ment like molten lava flowing from the earth, as she sat phoenix like surround by the licking flames.

And then, abruptly, the pain stopped and she felt cold. The

creature had disappeared, the floor of the cage scorched black from the heat and now she seemed odd. Her whole body ached, as if she was being crushed. Her skin was now red and flames still writhed over her skin, yet she felt nothing from them.

'*I am here with you now, relax*' the voice came again in her head, this time clearer and louder than before. As she relaxed the ache seemed to diminish.

'*Now, I ... we... can kill them.*' The voice spoke again.

'*Yes, but the fat merchant is mine to kill alone!*' she responded as before, placing her hands on the floor before her and slowly rising to her feet.

'*That may be difficult.*' She heard the reply and then heard and felt the laugh that accompanied it.

She spied her blade on the floor and slowly staggered towards it. Something wasn't right and she felt almost drunk. An insane thought came to her and then the situation was almost clear to her.

'*You are here, inside me?*' she asked in her thoughts.

'*Yes, it was the only way for me to live and for me to help you,*' as she bent to pick the blade up from the floor the creature's thoughts paused. '*Now we must fight, and there will be time to talk later.*'

Bex turned to face her opponents. Four swordsmen now faced her, along with the archer that had shot her. There may be more downstairs or outside.

'*Seems like a fair fight,*' came the voice again, and she could almost see the smile.

She could hear the younger guard swear continually as she raised her blade.

"By Oric's Grave, By Oric's Grave!"

She swept forward, almost gliding across the floor, making the distance between the first guard and herself within a heartbeat. It was his last. Her hand closed against his on his sword's hilt, pushing it to one side. She brought the curved blade up until she pushed it against his bare throat before slashing it back across, seeing the whole blade slice through his skin and seemingly not make a mark. As he fell to the floor a thin beading of blood appeared along the cut. She plucked his sword from his hand and hefted it up, feeling the weight.

The next guard was shaken from his reverie and swung hard at her. Breathlessly she flung the heavy sword up to block his attack, and then she thrust forward with the hilt into his nose which split under the punch. As he staggered back, blood pouring from his nose, she swung downwards and the tip of the blade bit into his leg just above his knee.

She felt she was moving faster than she had ever moved before, and she noted, definitely stronger. The wound in her arm wasn't slowing her now and as well as faster and stronger, she seemed to have a newfound awareness.

Her right arm jerked upwards, and she felt the arrow strike the blade and ping harmlessly wide.

'*Thank you again!*' she thought her gratitude to her new companion.

'*This body is amazing. It feels good to be this alive.*'

'*We have a way to go before we are sure we are staying alive*' she replied. Bex realised that she had to get rid of the archer as soon as possible. She might not be able to block the next shot and at this range, he would not miss. There was however the case of the other two guards between her and him. She noticed that Yab was running from the chamber as well.

The two swordsmen attacked together, and she used the guardsman's sword to parry and block, and her own blade to dart forward and counterattack. She could see the archer now, moving to try to get a better shot off. She stepped back and to the right, hoping that the opponent to her left would step in towards her, helping to block the archer's view.

As her opponent on her right swung his sword, she strongly

parried it forcing it downwards – at the same time thrusting up over the crossed swords with her own blade, watching the point sink deep into his throat. Without pausing, she pulled the blade free knowing that he was completely out of the fight and advanced to the next guard. A flurry of blows and swings with both swords forced this last swordsman backwards towards the door and the archer. She ducked under his flailing blade and swung the heavy sword hard at his leg. Despite the stiffened leather greave she could hear the bone snap as the heavy steel blade crashed into the side of his shin. He crumpled under the blow, dropping his sword in order to clutch at his wound. Bex allowed herself a small glance as she swept on towards the archer. She grimaced as she saw the glint of bone protruding from the bloody mess.

Desperately the archer grasped for a dagger from his belt as he raised the bow up, sideways to block Bex's attack. The steel blade came down in an arc over Bex's head and cut straight through the bow and his hand. He fell to his knees holding his shattered hand and then died as Bex's sword swung again, this time against his neck.

She ran to the top of the stairs, her footprints leaving smouldering marks on the ornate carpets on the landing. Bex stared down only to see the crumpled form of Yab M'vil laying at the bottom of the stairs.

Bex slowly descended the flight of stairs, as she did so she felt the anger and rage drain out of her. Her skin tingled and she noticed that her flesh was returning to normal, and she was astounded to see that there was absolutely no effect from the fire. Not even a blemish out of place. She felt tired as she approached the misshapen form of the fat merchant and the heavy sword dropped out of her hand, clattering to the floor, though she was able to keep hold of her own thinner, lighter blade. Crouching next to his body she was aware that he was still alive, though he probably wouldn't see dawn.

His legs were folded at an obscene angle and blood seeped from his nose and the corner of his mouth. With each laboured breath, more blood seeped and foamed from his nostril splattering over his fat jowl. He turned his eyes towards her but despite the events of the last few minutes they showed nothing but contempt for the woman that had brought about his end.

"Kill me, demon!" he spat the words out with a cough, blood again stemming from his lips.

Bex lifted his robes with the point of her sword and saw the damage the fall had done to him. His left leg was bent forward just below the knee, his shin bone poking through the flesh. She gently pushed the tip of the blade into his leg above the knee and saw the point sink into the fat, fleshy thigh. Yab made no sound at all, with no recognition that he had been cut as he stared at her.

"You can't feel that, can you? You can't move either."

He coughed again, his eyes straying down his immobile body to see Bex's sword sticking into his leg. He moaned and his breath became a strange rasping sound as he realised the horror that he faced.

"You are paralysed; probably a broken back and your legs are broken. Possibly something injured inside as well. You won't live to see the dawn break, pig. Just a slow and painful death."

She stood up, towering over him then turned her back and walked away.

'You are an evil one.' The thought sprang into her head.

"He deserved it." She replied out loud, the adrenaline seeping away from her leaving her tired. "Now leave me alone."

16

Dutte reached the roof and made his way towards the next warehouse. The moon illuminated his way to the edge and the narrow gap between the two buildings. As Fferyll had said, a short board made of planks bridged the gap and he gingerly tested it by tapping it with one foot. Despite it looking older than the city itself, it seemed to be strong enough and he gulped heavily before stepping forward.

He swore as a small gust of wind caught his cloak, causing him to hurry the few steps across. Dutte reached under his cloak and touched the bulging purse double tied to his belt, to reassure him that it was still there. He crouched on the far side as he jumped down from the low parapet and surveyed the rooftop. There was a small shed that possibly allowed access to the roof from the warehouse below, and this cast a shadow across the wooden boards. There weren't a lot of overlooking roofs nearby, making it a perfect site for clandestine meetings. No doubt, there were several escape points at either edge.

However, Dutte was alone. He rose and stepped forward towards the centre of the roof. He slowly made his way circling the shed took centre stage, his hand on the hilt of his sword.

Still no-one, just a few tattered tarps and a pile of old boards, tied down against any wind. He sat down and waited, cursing Brant, Fferyll and the lineage of House Barstt under his breath. Twenty minutes passed, twenty long minutes that might have been hours as he waited for his meet. Finally, he stood and turned to make his way back down.

As he did so, a shadow seemed to rise from the pile of tattered tarpaulins. The dark shape shifted into the figure of a man, taller but more slender than Dutte. He took a step forward and Dutte saw that he was garbed in black leather armour, segmented in bands about the torso and shoulders to allow more flexibility. A stiffened cowl that came forward in a short point covered his head, whilst a half mask obscured the lower part of his face.

"There is no need for your sword, Client." The figure whispered, standing his ground and holding his hands to out to his sides to show he wasn't bearing a threat to Dutte.

"I am not your client yet. We haven't a contract." Dutte took umbrage at the figure almost immediately, especially at the length of time he had waited and that he had been there all along.

"Then we do not need to be here, Client." The figure turned to walk away. Dutte cursed and started forward after him

"Wait! I have the fee." The leather clad man turned back to face Dutte, now face to face.

"Good, then we talk. But a warning. Do not approach a member of the Brotherhood of Karnast like that again. Should you wish to disrespect the guild then our retribution will be swift and ruthless. We address you as Client out of respect of your anonymity, but we do know who you are."

Dutte stepped back, annoyed at himself for being so reckless. What was he thinking? He had no doubt that this man, a member of the guild of assassins, would be able to best him even without a blade. He didn't think words would carry much sway with the figure that faced him, so acknowledged his comments with a nod.

"Show me your coins, Client. I have other work to do tonight before the sunrise."

Dutte slowly moved his hands to push his cloak back and then unlaced the purse from his belt. Relieved to be shed of its weight, he held it out and the assassin reached out and took it. He slipped it into a bag strung across his back by a cord over his shoulder and looped back under his belt.

"Aren't you going to count it?"

"As I said, Client. We know who you are, not many people double cross the guild." He held out his hand, having palmed a small vial from the bag when placing the bag of coins there.

Dutte took it and held it up, the vial was the size of his first two joints of his little finger. As he peered at the contents in the light of the moon, he noticed it was a little under a quarter full.

"It isn't a lot for a thousand gold coins, is it?"

The assassin harrumphed, knowing that the purchaser knew the value of the vial and its contents but was just acknowledging the power encapsulated within.

"A thousand coins gets you whatever you get following your enemy's death, Client. That is the most potent toxin known to man. Cultivated from a flower in Thesh, that small vial represents a thousand hours of work and has cost several lives so far.

"It is a contact irritant that kills within seconds of touching bare skin. I would recommend gloves whilst administering it. It will stay potent in the air for an hour before becoming ineffective in its primary use."

Dutte tucked it inside his belt pouch and nodded his acknowledgement.

"Thank you."

He turned and crossed over the plank bridge, looking back when he had jumped down the other side. But the figure had already gone, melting back into the shadow world.

17

C hurt had wondered what the commotion was and had sneaked from the kitchen area below to find out. He soon wished he hadn't. Three of the master's guards ran past heading for the stairs. The last one, a tall northerner called Marn, paused and spoke to him.

"Get back, boy. Nothing for you to help with."

Marn was one of the more pleasant guards in Yab M'vil's villa. Of course, he was surly more often than not, but he had never laid a hand on Churt or given him any abuse. Not like the others. 'Horse-brain', 'pig shit', 'idiot' and 'dolt' were the normal names he was called, often accompanied with a slap or swift kick. The young boy had grinned and nodded and made as if to close the heavy kitchen door. Marn turned and followed his compatriots, notching an arrow to the string of his short bow as he loped off.

Churt however, had no intention of hiding. His employer, his real employer that is, had asked him to gather certain information on the merchant's business dealings and in particular, information as to what the merchant's men had found in the forests nearby. His attempts during the last few days to gain access to the upper chambers of the merchant had failed miserably and his attempts to speak to the guards and men that protected M'vil were fairly non-productive. Only Marn had spoken to him about what that they had found. He had called it a '*Lampanyx*'. He had never heard of the word before and guessed it was from the northerner's own language. Not wanting to press it too far he had grinned inanely at Marn and waved his arms around, then had mimed a large stalking creature. Normally Marn would have laughed at his antics but the tall mercenary just shook his head and had then walked away to his bunk room.

He knew they were badly shaken as three of the men had not come back that day. One of the northern mercenaries had died along with two of the local thugs that M'vil employed. Their badly burnt bodies had been brought back to the villa where their temporary storage in the garden had caused an argument between the old mercenary leader, Dag Harnik and the merchant's major-domo. The stand-off had been won by the long-haired warriors and the major-domo had run to Yab M'vil like a dog with its tail between its legs. Unsurprisingly with the mailed soldiers in such an uncompromising mood, Yab had taken their side, allowing a burial ceremony at the far end of the grounds and that commonest of sweeteners for paid thugs; a pay rise.

Now Churt made his way up the staircase hugging the wall and keeping as low a profile as he could. As his eyes drew level with the top of the stairs, he saw Yab M'vil running towards him, a look of abject terror in his eyes as he flung a glance over his shoulder towards the bedchamber. Churt could do little to avoid him and only by dropping to his knees and covering his head with his arms did he manage to keep himself from being seriously injured. Yab M'vil however, was not so lucky. His front foot struck the young lad in his shoulder and the fat merchant somersaulted over Churt rolling down the stairs like a rag doll thrown by an angry child.

Churt heard the sickening snap of several bones as Yab landed in a crumpled heap. He raised his head to see and then turned in the direction of the bedchamber as he heard a loud yell of pain. The cry was loud and drawn out and it brought a slight chill to his bones. However, he was not prepared for the sight that he saw next.

Marn was kneeling on the wide landing, frantically trying to notch another arrow to his bowstring as he looked at the apparition in the doorway. Churt's stomach churned at first when he saw the horned woman, her skin the colour of coals in one of the large kitchen fires, a swirling pattern of red and orange and black. Flames licked from her head where hair would normally be, and he noticed the carpet was smouldering from the touch of her feet. In each hand was a blade, one a heavy, broad-bladed weapon, the other a long, thin, curved sword.

He saw Marn give up with the arrow and drop it, instead reaching for his dagger as the fiery woman swept towards him. He threw up his bow in desperation to block the blow that he knew would come as she swept the heavy blade back up over her head before crashing it down to earth in a shiny arc. Churt watched mesmerized as the steel blade fell, snapping Marn's bow in two and cutting through his hand. Everything seemed to be in slow motion as he watched the fire demoness snuff out Marn's life. There was a perverse serenity as the events that unfolded before his eyes seemed to happen in complete silence. He saw his friend slowly hold what was left of his hand up in front of his face as if to inspect the damage. The peace was shattered as the heavy blade thudded home into the floor in front of Marn. As the burning woman started to raise the sword again, Marn screamed. It was a horrible, terrifying scream that seemed to call for the mystical grave maidens that attended the deaths of warriors of Marn's culture. It certainly wasn't going to prevent Marn's death as Churt saw the woman hold the sword over her head again, and he hurriedly ducked under the relative safety of the top of the stairs, knowing that there was nothing that he could do to help the stricken northerner.

He slid down the stairs and then ran, four stairs at a time and hurdled the body of Yab M'vil, barely noticing that the slaver still breathed. He briefly contemplated the safety of the kitchens to hide but wondered whether the monster above would hear the door open or close. Instead the young boy chose the tables that adorned the hall of the villa and were draped in heavy velvet cloths that reached to the floor, and he dived under one and sat, arms clenched around his knees and his eyes and mouth firmly shut. As he prayed to all of the Gods, in particular Tobes, the Goddess of Luck and Chance, he could hear his heart pound like a drum.

For twenty long minutes he sat there, praying every second for deliverance from an unearthly fate. The silence and the closeness of death amplified the terror that he felt and at one point his nerve failed and he felt his trousers dampen as he relieved himself.

As the thudding of his heart subsided, he chanced a look out from underneath the tablecloth. Once he could tune out the sound of his heartbeat, he realised that the villa was in silence. He crept towards the doorway and once he felt the calming, cool air on his face, without a backward glance he ran to Tannaheim.

18

B ex looked up at the sign of the Inn of the Black Dragon, an intricately carved wyrm in full flight. The colouring was worn, but she could see the flecks of black paint on the dark, mottled wood. One of its eyes was missing, which led to the inn having the soubriquet "Ol' One Eye". The other eye shone in the morning sun, a small piece of stained red glass.

They had left the villa some hours earlier, walking a mile into the surrounding forest to a small clearing. There Bex stripped off the tools of her trade, recovering a pack from under some ferns that threatened to creep into the clearing. From the pack she drew a large black cloak and boots, and then stuffed the spider with all its tools into the pack, covering it with the black garments she had worn to blend into the shadows.

She stretched, reaching upwards and outwards. She stood about six-foot-tall, which was tall for a West Coaster woman. She was lithe and toned, but also had a very feminine shape to her figure. Whilst in the past this had caused her more atten-tion than she wanted, she had now learned to use her figure when she needed to. Apart from the tattoos on her scalp, she had no others bar a small moon on her left hand.

Although her criminal activities were over for now, she still favoured dark clothing. Her outer garments had come away to reveal a tight leather bodice that finished at her midriff. She still wore the same trousers as before, again black leather, tight to her legs. Down each side, leather thongs drew them tight. Over the tops of these she pulled knee length boots that were favoured by the west coasters before finally buckling a scabbard to her belt and slipping the curved blade into it.

As she stood up straight, she found herself rubbing her arm where the arrow had struck. Although she still had a dull ache throughout her upper arm she was amazed to feel and see the wound healing well. If she hadn't had known that it had only happened a few hours ago she would have guessed that it was two weeks since the wound occurred.

'*Is this your doing?*' she asked the voice inside her head. Since leaving the villa it had been quiet, not responding to her thoughts and she had made no conscious attempt to direct these to it. It was obviously respecting her last comment.

'*Yes – my surplus energy can go to making your body stronger, faster and your body – our body, will heal faster now.*' The demon was clearly still getting to grips with the situation like Bex. '*I am not used to this either.*'

'*You could always leave.*' Bex replied dourly as she lifted the pack on to her shoulder and started the walk back to the city.

'*Alas, no. Now we have joined we cannot separate without us both dying*'. Bex noted the lack of humour and understanding in the demon's voice.

'*So, we are stuck with each other until we die?*'

'*Yes.*'

'*A lifetime with you in my head. Great.*'

'*Not just your head.*'

'*What do you mean?*'

'*The villa and the merchant and his men. What happened there....*' The demon started. Bex sort of understood and shuddered as she remembered the transformation that she had carried out and the horror of the bloodlust that she had had.

'*You mean I can change again?*'

'*Well, it's not strictly you. I had heard my people could do this, but have never spoken to any who have, they are only stories from my youth.*' The demon's voice seemed to show slight emotion for the first time. '*If I understand it correctly, we occupy the same space. Because it is your world, your body has preference and I cohabit. If you travel to my world then the reverse would happen. But I can push my physical manifestation to take over in this world, but it does exhaust my energy. Did you feel that in the villa? An outside feeling?*'

'*Not really, the whole thing was quite disturbing.*'

'*Do not be ashamed as to what we did, we had to extinguish their life-fires. And each change should become less painful to both of us.*'

'*I know – who are you and what are you?*'

'*My name is Ishtara, of the Qoi people.*'

'*Qoi?*'

'*I am not of your world, Bex. I have crossed the planes to come here.*'

'*Crossed the planes? Is that possible?*' Bex had heard of some conjurors who had reputedly summoned creatures from other worlds but had just thought of it as folklore and legend.

'*Well, I am here.*' Ishtara replied.

The demon kept silent for the rest of the walk back to the city. They passed no one on the way to the gates. Bex was still struck by the high walls of Tannaheim – even after living there several months. They were reportedly the highest of any of the civilised cities in both the West and the East. Towers rose above the walls to add to the impressiveness and the Kings of Tannaheim had reigned long over the area, safe from invasion or siege.

She pushed open the door to the Inn and strode inside "Ol' One Eye". The Black Dragon Inn was one of the largest coaching Inns in the city due to its proximity to the East Gate. Many travellers sampled the hospitality offered by Mon Baxt, the owner. It wasn't just the finest food (at reasonable prices) or a range of ales from across the West Coast that had led Bex to take a room there, but its locality. To the north of the Inn was part of the lower quarter of the city, a maze of streets and alleys inhabited by the poorer denizens of Tannaheim. A place to offer many pieces of gossip and hearsay for a young thief along with almost every unsavoury weapon and tool of the trade sold without any questions asked. That, and a rabbit warren of escape routes should the law come calling. The Inn stood on East Street, the main land route in and out of the city via the East Gate, a prime source of rich merchants and unsuspecting travellers all desperate to 'mislay' their valuables.

The tall thief strode inside, her cloak billowing outwards as she did so. The interior was large, with a stone hearth taking centre place. Four stone pillars stood at each corner, originally bleached white but now dusted with varying layers of soot. Across the top of these rested a copper mantel, crudely beaten into shape. A young boy tended the fire dwarfed by the size of the fireplace.

Ale soaked tables with their simple stools and benches occupied the centre of the room in a haphazard manner. Around the walls were stalls, some with chairs and stools whilst others had fixed benches, all separated by slatted walls of various heights. A bar reached across the whole of the back wall, and beyond that were the quarters of the landlord, Mon and her staff. A narrow flight of stairs led up to a gallery above where several more stalls were situated, a rickety handrail protected those too inebriated from a painful fall to the area below. A narrow hallway led to the guest rooms, one of which was Bex's.

Despite the early hour there were a dozen or so patrons in the main room, though most were keeping to themselves. The air was still filled with the aromas of last night's customers and Bex wrinkled her nose in disgust as she made her way to a stall near the foot of the stairs, gesticulating to one of the serving girls and then sat down with her back to the bar. The barmaid acknowledged her with a raise of the hand and started to pour a flagon for her.

Bex closed her eyes, suddenly exhausted by the events of the night. From touch she felt out the two copper crowns from her belt purse and placed them silently on the table. A few moments later she heard the approach of the staff with her order. It wasn't Kilde though, the serving girl she had motioned to but someone more cumbersome. She knew who it was even without opening her eyes.

"Hello, Landa"

Landa placed the flagon down in front of Bex, and she felt a little of the ale splash onto her hand.

"And how is our very own dragon lady this fine morning?" his voice was toadying and irritating. If there was one thing that she would change about the Black Dragon Inn it would be Landa. The man was a letch. Everything about him annoyed her beyond words. She despised the way he took liberties with the other female staff and female clientele of the bar, patronizing words, ogling eyes and wandering eyes. She wasn't sure whether that annoyed her more or the fact that most of the women fell for it, got used for quick pleasure and then discarded whilst he worked his charms on his next victim. There had been quite a few times in her tenancy at the Inn that she had been tempted to beat him black and blue and only her respect for Mon had stopped her.

She declined him the liberty of a reply, turning her head ever so slightly to face him and opened her eyes. He stared down at her, fixated upon the curve of her cleavage that threatened to overspill from her bodice. He was her height and of indiscriminate build, his blond hair and blue eyes betraying his Northern heritage. She wondered if he had come from the same tribes that the men she had killed earlier had came from.

She slid her hand over the two copper coins and slid them towards him. As she did so, his gaze lifted to meet her eyes and his mouth dropped. A slight panic showed in his face as his pupils widened and he appeared petrified. Landa seemed to want to speak but couldn't find the words. Finally, he tore his gaze away from her and turned and fled back to the rooms behind the bar.

Bex smirked, though somewhat perplexed by his reaction.

'Maybe he is a mind reader, though he would have to be a simpleton if he thinks I actually find him attractive,' she thought.

'Oh, he seems quite good looking by your world's standards.' Ishtara broke into her thoughts.

'Tobe's Tits.' Bex swore back. *'Will I ever have any private thoughts again?'*

'Maybe,' came the reply, *'maybe when I get bored by your world and your ways.'*

Bex couldn't be sure whether the demoness was being serious though Ishtara hadn't displayed many signs of humour so far in their brief coexistence.

'Though, to be honest, you humans intrigue me. So many emotions I can sense and so many feelings. So many new ideas and sensations for me to experience. I have caught glimpses of some in your mind. You humans are far more complex than us Qoi.'

'We are? We are born, we live, we die.' Bex grunted and raised the leather covered flagon to her lips, supping a deep mouthful of the dark ale.

'Mmmm', their thoughts came together and they giggled together, Bex laughing out loud.

'What is this?' Ishtara asked,

'Dark Sceptre, it is brewed locally here.'

'Brewed?' Images flashed through Bex's mind and she realised that it was Ishtara searching through her consciousness to work out what the word meant, as if she was rummaging through a drawer. 'Ahh, I see. But why?'

'You don't have alcohol on your world?'

'No, we do not need to sustain ourselves as you do. Our Inner Fire is kept burning by the power of our sun and world. We have no requirement for food or drink. Though if it all....' Ishtara sought the right word again, 'tastes? If it all tastes like that I can get used to it.'

Bex laughed, lifting the flagon once more.

'No, our food and drink here does not all taste like this.' She thought of the days where she had struggled to survive, living on stale bread and vegetables discarded from some of the poorest kitchens in Samak. 'Though you probably wouldn't want to drink too much of this!' She drank deep and wiped her mouth with the back of her hand.

'Why?' the inevitable question from Ishtara, followed by the imagery as her memories and imagination were shuffled by the demoness. Scenes of drunkenness involving hangovers, uninhibited behaviour and more flashed before her eyes. She could feel the puzzlement in Ishtara's voice as she asked again, 'Why? Why drink this if it leads to this?'

Bex shrugged, mentally and physically. Another image clicked on in her mind. Two figures writhed naked on a capacious bed, silhouetted by candlelight through the drapes. The voile canopy moved in the breeze from an open window. She recognized the room as that of Yab M'vil's. She saw and felt the heavy curtains sway at the side of the windows as the wind picked up and the gossamer drapes on the bed billowed to give her a glimpse of the occupants. A couple laid together legs entwined, the man on top, rhythmically moving together. The man's short blond hair contrasted with the woman's dark hair. As the man looked up, Bex became aware of his face, it was Landa. The woman reached up and grasping Landa by his shoulders pulled him down close to her. They rolled over and the woman sat up, legs straddling the naked form of Landa, back arching in ecstasy. Bex recognized with horror her own tattoos. She was the woman with Landa.

'*Stop it!*'

'*This is procreation here in your world?*' Ishtara asked.

'*Yes....I mean no,*' Bex stammered a reply.

'*Is this a memory, or a wish?*'

'*Neither! Now please stop.*'

'*It looks animalistic. And very fun. Will I get to experience this?*' Bex ignored her question.

'*Sometimes it is and sometimes it isn't.*'

'*How do you mean?*' Bex felt the now familiar searching through her mind.

'*Don't!*'

The imagery reappeared, this time Bex recognized herself straight away. The room and bed were the same, but this time she was on her knees, her arms pulled out in front of her, iron cuffs circling her wrist. Chains fixed to the cuffs reached out to the bed posts, holding her fast. Her back was a criss cross mess of welts, some broken and bleeding – the blood and sweat dripping down her side. Behind her knelt the corpulent, gross form of Yab M'vil one hand holding a short cat and the other gripping her hip. Every thrust he made rippled his rolls of fat, and after every thrust he lashed out with the cat, striking her back. As Bex recoiled in horror he started to change. His skin changed from a fleshy tone to a pallid grey. Now with each thrust forward he grunted and coughed, blood splattering from his nose over her back as he grinned, grey lips pulling back to reveal his teeth, each one lined in blood.

'*Stop!*' Bex screamed inside her head.

This time Ishtara obeyed. The vision cleared and Bex was left with emptiness. A small tear started to collect at the corner of her eye.

There was a minute or so of silence before Ishtara broke it.

'*Sorry.*' The apology came in a soft voice, almost tearful. She knew she had overstepped the mark with her host.

They now drank in silence, Bex staring ahead of her oblivious to the comings and goings as the bar started to get busier. The exertions of the night had left Bex exhausted. She sat back and rested her head against the back of the stall and slowly closed her eyes, drifting off into an uneasy sleep.

19

Yuthie Longhand stirred, but if truth was to be told he hadn't slept well since he had first seen the 'lights in the sky' several days ago. It was before dawn but close enough for him to throw back the heavy bed covers and stand up, stretching his arms wide.

His thoughts crept back to that night. He had been woken then too at the middle of the night, his chickens squawking as if a fox or wolf was near and Luka, his hound, growling. The rain had been lashing down, and he had almost thought to himself, that whatever predator had been out in that weather was welcome to whatever pickings it could get. Still he had taken his spear from the racking by the door and left the sanctity of the house, carrying a lantern in his other hand. The big, black hound bounded out ahead of him, his fur blowing chaotically in the storm and Yuthie followed. He had instantly regretted it; the wind had been icy cold, and the rain matted his hair against his head within seconds.

The flame of his lantern had struggled manfully against the howling wind and several times between the house and the chicken run it had threatened to die and leave him alone. He had cursed whatever was frightening the brood through gritted teeth but had been both relieved and disappointed to find no intruder. The birds had been squawking loudly and jumping from roost to roost, but he had been unsure why. He had made one last circuit of the area, and then had turned back to the house, calling Luka to him. When he noticed that the dog wasn't at his heel, he turned back to look at the roost. Luka was looking out into the countryside, staring away to the Asken Forest, growling – a low, long drawn out growl. What seemed like a low rumble of thunder had washed over them, seemingly in answer to Luka's growl, and had brought his attention up to the night sky. And then he had seen it. A storm over the Asken Forest, perhaps even further away than that. A storm of immense magnitude, but one that emitted an eerie green glow. The edge of the forest was nearly a hundred leagues distant, the twin cities of Jacarna and Tarim nearly double that. Both man and dog stared transfixed at the glow for several minutes, rain soaking through their cloak and fur. Massive cracks of lightning split the night sky in two and shattered their reverie. Luka threw his head back in a mournful howl and had then turned and slunk back to the farmhouse. Worried and slightly afraid, Yuthie had followed him back to the sanctuary of his farmstead.

That had been four nights ago, on the Feast of Sanda Sweven. The next night he had checked the horizon again, but the green lights were gone. Luka though, had acted the same each night since. Bounding out to sit and face the Eastern Cities and howl mournfully, head thrown back and muzzle pointing to the sky.

The rise of the sun was perhaps an hour away. Yuthie staggered downstairs and into the main room of the farmstead. Even though he was up earlier than normal he started his morning ritual of tea and bread. Always tea, not the ersatz herbal teas of his own country but the stronger tea from the mountain sides in the far south. It cost him an arm and a leg, but the feeling of wakefulness and strong taste was worth it. He always visited the tea merchants when he was in the capital and always made sure that he had enough silver for a small caddy of the dark green leaves. Yuthie sawed at the loaf eagerly, hacking off a thick wedge of the coarse rye bread and contemplated brewing another mug of tea.

As he prepared this second mug, he noticed Luka raise his head from his slumber and prick his ears back. The hound stared at the door and started to rumble a low growl. Yuthie knew at once what it was. Someone or something was near to the farmhouse, and something out this early, this close to the Hinterlands, was generally bad news.

This time he picked a onehanded billhook up, a vicious looking tool with a wide flat blade ending in a hook. He thrust this into his belt and strapped a small wooden shield onto his arm. Finally, he picked his long spear up and opened the door. Luka bounded out, starting to bark wildly.

The shield and spear were from his old soldiering days, now only used when he had to face down wolves coming down from the Hinterlands, or for protection from brigands on the two-day journey to Tannaheim.

Yuthie could now see a lone rider on the path to his homestead. He called Luka to him and the big dog obeyed, running back to where he stood. Ears pricked up, he took his guard next to his master and watched the rider attentively. The old soldier braced his butt of the spear against his back foot and fronted his shield towards the horseman.

As he got closer, even in the gloom of oncoming dawn, he could see the blue tabard of a guardsman of Jacarna. His old eyes were still keen, and he picked out detail as the rider steered his horse towards the waiting pair. What he saw troubled him.

The guardsman was riding light, no packs were carried by

him or his horse. He was also helmetless and unarmed. The
City Guard of Jacarna normally carried lances and a heavy
sabre. He had neither. His hands gripped the reins tightly and
his scabbard was empty. Not only had he ridden light but also
hard. His horse, a big bay was lathered in sweat. Its dark mane
matted against its neck.

Yuthie wasn't sure what this all meant, but he changed his
guard a little, lifting his spear point so that it pointed to the sky.
An unarmed man wouldn't charge him. Still, he kept his shield
facing him.

"Watch him, boy", he murmured to Luka under his breath.

The rider pulled up, the big brown horse skidding to a halt.
He looked haggard, but when he spoke his voice still carried
the authority of one who was used to policing citizens.

"Good Farmer, which way to Tannaheim and how far?"

Without taking his eyes off the soldier, Yuthie raised his arm
and pointed with his spear westwards.

"Keep to the west road until the village of Durnsk, and then
turn south. That will take you towards the East Gate of the
city."

The guardsman took a hand of his reins and raised it to his
face in acknowledgement, but addressed Yuthie again, this time
more impatiently.

"And how far?"

"I make it in two days" Yuthie answered then, sensing the
soldier was aggrieved, added "with a wagon. You could be there
long before the day is out."

"The earlier I get there, the better", the guardsman replied,
reaching to his wineskin at his side and taking a short swig. "If
you had any sense you would follow me as well."

"Why?" Yuthie asked.

"Because Jacarna is fallen, Tarim will be soon and then they
will be coming this way. Leave now, good ser, take your belongings and run."

"Nay, ser." Yuthie retorted. "This is my farm. I paid my life savings to buy it and I will be damned if I am going to leave it." The old soldier-turned-farmer spat into the ground in front of him. "By Bolam, I have fought wolves and bandits here, and have fought for my King in the northern wastes. Whatever evil you ride from, I will fight here, and they will find that Yuthie Longhand will not flee."

"Then Good Farmer Yuthie Longhand, you are an idiot and here you will die!" The guardsman threw his empty wineskin down and wheeled his horse around and cantered away. As he left, he turned in the saddle and shouted to the defiant farmer.

"I hope you know how to use that spear, Yuthie Longhand. It won't be long before they reach here and drain the very land of life as they have done with my city."

Yuthie watched him until he was a speck in the distance, and then with the rising sun he turned and walked back to the house.

20

"Father, can we hunt later?" The young girl sat at the table and bit into a red apple.

"Oh no, Ingren. That isn't fair." Moren was two years younger than her sister and still at the age where she was a little princess whereas Ingren, in her thirteenth summer had transformed into a tom boy. A beautiful tom boy but a tom boy all the same. Whereas Moren was still into sitting with her hand maidens and wiling the days away, Ingren was into riding and hunting with some of the young Lords of the court. Moren preferred dancing to Ingren's sword play, and singing to her older sister's partying.

Despite their differences in attitude, they were very similar in their looks. Both had the dark hair of their father though Ingren's was a little longer. Neither had developed into young ladies yet but their father and mother knew that it would not be long before Ingren entered adulthood.

They often took breakfast together, whilst their mother, Queen Sarsi attended her own appointments. Rather than the great hall, they chose a small ante room to break fast in which made their meal more personal and allowed them to be a normal family, if only for a small part of the day. There were six chairs around the table, one each for the immediate Royal Family and Anjoan took a brief moment to think back when all six chairs were taken every day.

Those days had been almost perfect, the sound of the children laughing and arguing had been, as he now realised, wonderful. The smile on his wife's face and in her eyes had been magical and as common place as gems in the Royal Treasury. Now those days were past and though Sarsi still smiled, her eyes remained dark. Since the death of their daughter, the Princess Antht, five years ago the whole dynamic of the family had changed. Her twin, Prince Garlen, who had been riding with Antht when she had fallen from her horse that fateful day, had become more reckless and swashbuckling. At fifteen years of age, losing a sibling, yet alone a twin would affect anyone dearly. Garlen had become destructive, so much so that Anjoan had enlisted him into the army early as a lowly sergeant just as Anjoan's father had done with him. Two months later what started as a border skirmish with the Orcs from the south had turned into a full-scale military expedition and Garlen spent two years fighting in the mountains.

The death of their older sister had hit the two young princesses hard at first, yet they seemed more resilient to the loss with each passing day. They did occasionally pass furtive, longing glances at the seat of their sister at the family dining table but on the whole had accepted Antht's passing.

"I am afraid not, Ingren," her father replied. "Master Tarnal will be waiting for you. And I have important work today. I have trade discussions with the Jarl of the Isle of Winds to prepare for." He reached across the table to pluck an orange from a platter and started to peel it. His daughters groaned.

"But Master Tarnal is so boring, Father." Moren sighed. "He drones on and on about wars. Do princesses need to know about that?" Her older sister laughed.

"Wars are fun, Mori," she used her pet name for Moren, "lots of heroes!" As if to accentuate her words she swished an imaginary sword over the table towards her sister.

"They are not! They are boring!" Moren sulked, glaring at her sister.

"Now, girls. Wars are not boring, but neither are they fun. As both myself and your brother can attest to." Anjoan tried to quieten the two princesses. As he spoke, he pulled segments from the orange and ate them, droplets of juice coating his beard. Ingen finished her apple and lent forward with her elbows on the table.

"Have you killed a man, Father?"

"Every decision I make as King leads to people dying or living, Ingren. Some die and some live. My decisions make it my responsibility," he skirted about the question. How else could he tell his young daughters that yes, he had killed. He had charged into battle leading his men and yes, he had taken lives, sending his enemies to sit in Kani's Hall or whatever place their damned religion sent the dead. Right now, there were sons and daughters taking breakfast with an empty seat at the table that their father once sat in because of him. Maybe Antht's death had been in recompense at the slaughter that he had carried out, not only by his orders but by his hand as well. But at least his son had returned from the war in the south alive, if not a little darker than when he had left, and he thanked Tomnar for that every day. Anjoan shook his head slightly, he was sick of war and killing and hoped he would not have to order men to war again.

"War is not fun and being King is not fun," he added.

"Then why do it, father?" asked Moren, popping another grape into her mouth. Thankfully Anjoan realised that she had already moved onto new thoughts and did not require an answer. The young princess crammed another couple of grapes into her mouth, her cheeks stuffed like rodent pouches.

"Father, why are the snow walkers called so?" she asked, quoting an epithet for the people of the Isle of Winds.

"Why do you think, buckethead," her sister interrupted. "Don't you pay attention in Master Starnsen's lessons?" A stern look from her father stopped Ingren from adding to her outburst.

"Well, anyone can walk on snow. And don't you call me a buckethead!" Moren stormed back at her elder sister.

"Well, Moren, you are right. Anyone can walk on snow – the snow we get here in Tannaheim. We seldom get snow deeper than a man's ankle and only once in my lifetime have I seen snow as deep as my knees within sight of Tannaheim's Walls. And we walk on that snow, or really, we walk in it. On the Isle of Winds, the snow is deeper than a man is tall all year round. A man would sink in that snow and be up to his waist in snow in no time. A snow walker though, they skim across the top of the snow, gliding over the surface and can move faster than you or me on normal land."

"How?" A puzzled look crept over Moren's little face.

"They wear special shoes, shaped like large bowls. It spreads their weight over the snow, according to Master Starnsen." Ingren answered for her father. He nodded and then went on to expand Ingren's answer.

"That's right. I am glad you pay attention to our Masters, Ingren. The snow walkers are also taught to do this from an early age as well so that it is second nature to them." Moren pondered for a while before answering.

"I would like to see that one day."

Anjoan stood and ruffled his daughter's hair. Smiling, he gave thanks to Tomnar for such wonderful daughters before speaking out loud.

"We will see that together, young Moren. It would be something to behold, wouldn't it?" He bowed slightly to his daughters and added, "Good day my princesses. Bid Master Tarnal good day from me and pay attention in his lesson. I look forward to seeing you this evening." The two young girls stood and curtsied as he walked towards the door. Ingren looked up.

"Father?"

"Yes?" He stood at the door, poised to open it and turned back to face his daughters.

"Can we go hunting soon?"

He laughed.

"Of course. I will speak to Master Smit and Marshall Vent to leave a day free as soon as the Jarl of the snow walkers' leaves."

A young page stood the other side of the door, his face flushed with embarrassment at having to disturb his king so soon after breakfast.

"Your Majesty, Marshall Vent awaits you in the Great Hall." Anjoan nodded in response and walked the short distance down the hall to the open door of the Great Hall, the home of the Red Throne. An older man awaited him, dressed resplendently in a long, dark red coat, silver mail visible underneath. His hair, once black but now speckled with grey, receded at his temples. He stood with an air of authority and turned his steely gaze upon the King as he entered.

"Magus, what can I do for you? It is not like you to bother me this early." Anjoan grinned, his white teeth breaking out through the dark beard.

Marshall Magus Vent bowed slightly. Second to the King, he was the most powerful man in Tannaheim. His position was to ensure that the King's orders were carried out and to protect the King, person and reputation. The rank was normally assigned to one man for a period of two years, yet Magus Vent had held the position for eleven years now. Behind his back, and on the streets of the city, he was known as the Hawk. The name suited not only his looks, his nose pointed and hooked and his eyes were piercing and close together, but also his manner – he was merciless in carrying out the orders of

Anjoan, no matter what they entailed or who got hurt on the way.

Anjoan often found Vent cold and calculating but could never doubt the Marshall's position in defending the interests of the Red Throne. Now he could see that something troubled him, and his tone became more serious.

"Magus?"

"I had an encounter with a young girl in the marketplace yesterday. She identified herself to be in the employ of the Phantom and gave me a message." Anjoan mounted the steps to the throne and slowly sat in the great red chair. Magus paused before continuing.

"According to the Phantom, there is a threat to your life."

"There will always be threats to my life, Magus. You can't sit on the Red Throne and not make enemies, no matter how hard you try. However, last night, I too received the same message."

The statement cut into the Marshall like a knife, although the King didn't notice the effect of his words on Vent. No matter how hard the Marshall tried, it seemed he was unable to rid the court and the kingdom of the influence of Tikar Welk. He took it as a slight against his power that there were agents, as he saw it, of an enemy power at loose in the palace.

"You will have no problem with me increasing the guards at the palace, Your Majesty?"

"As you see fit, Magus."

"Did your message last night also mention your brother-in-law?"

The king rested his elbows on his knees and pressed his fingers together in front of his face. He stayed immobile, statue-like for a few seconds and Vent could see that indeed the message had included information about the request from Lord Shales as Yanna had known. He could see the dilemma that the message had imposed upon his liege.

"Has Shales requested more ships? Are you going to send another squadron?" Vent added.

Anjoan took a second before replying, standing as he did so and walking down to stand face to face with Vent. The King did not trust his brother-in-law, but he could not doubt the man's ability to get results. For this reason, the problem of Lord Shales was a double-edged sword. If Anjoan kept him at court, any stifling of his ambitions would bring a divide between himself and the Queen; but sending him away on perilous missions only enhanced his reputation and allowed him to burrow deeper into the court's administrations.

"Too late, Magus. I have already sent the Fourth Squadron under Ser Visney to the Isle of the Snow Walkers. It is too good a chance to rid the seas between here and there of the pirates."

"Very well, Your Majesty." The older man bowed his head forward again.

"Something I need to ask, Magus. After the negotiations with the Jarl has finished, I need a day to spend with Ingren."

21

A slamming door brought Bex back to the land of wakefulness with a start. It took a second or so to realise her surroundings, her normal stall in 'Ol' One Eye'. From the number of people now occupying the filling lounge of the Black Dragon Inn she guessed that she had slumbered for some time. Her sleep had been filled with troublesome dreams of fire demons and flying ships and her bleary mind struggled to comprehend them. A single word, spoken in her mind, brought her from her reverie.

"Hello."

In a flash the events of the night came back to her. As she hurriedly searched herself for visible signs of the possession she fired of thoughts to her new inner self.

"So, it was all real, last night I mean."

"Yes", Ishtara replied with a slightly smug tone to her voice.

"And Yab? He is dead?"

"Yes, I am not sure of your way of dying here, the others died fairly easily, but the one called Yab looked like his fire was going out."

"His fire? Is that what you call your life force, consciousness?"

"Yes."

After what seemed an eternity Bex phrased a question to Ishtara.

'Why did you come here and why choose me?'

'Choosing you was easy. I could sense that you and I were simi-lar. We both want the best for us and for other good people around us. We were also both in danger of dying before achieving our goals.'

'And why did you come here? I gather this world is not like your own?'

'I came here as I have a message for your leader, your chief?" She looked in Bex's mind for the right word. *"Your King, I need to see him urgently.'*

'Our King? You just can't see the King. But why?'

'There is an invasion coming.'

'There's an invasion coming?' the voice that Bex spoke in her mind sounded incredulous, so much so that she repeated the words softly under her breath. They didn't seem any more believable as real words than as thoughts.

'Yes' Ishtara replied.

'But who would invade Danaria? We are one of the most powerful states in Maingard.'

'Not just your land. All of your world.'

'Absurd' Bex couldn't believe her mind.

'Believe me, Bex. Please! Your world will be brought to war and I have to warn your king.'

'Who will do such a thing?'

'The Cassalians.' Ishtara spat the word out with venom.

'Who?'

'The Cassalians, they come from another world, another plane. They are able to travel from one world to another with ease.'

Bex struggled with what she was hearing, her hand caressing the half full flagon in front of her.

'They devastate any world they invade, taking warriors from the populace to fill their ranks and then enslaving the rest. They render each world impotent, raping the natural world and the weak of that

world alike. When they have finished, the dregs and remnants of that world are ripped from the slave pits and sacrificed in order to power their magicians and demonic allies. With that power they sail the astral planes searching out new worlds to plunder and destroy.'

'And they are coming here?'

'*They are here! Now it is the turn of Maingard, as it was once the turn of my world.*'

'Your world?'

'*Yes, Qoi was destroyed by them. I am the last of my people.*' Her voice seemed to reach out to Bex to implore her to warn her world and to. . . . . do what? To fight back and avenge Ishtara's world? Could that be done? Was there any hope for Maingard?

'*There is always hope, Bex.*'

'True, Ishtara.' Bex thought back. '*What did they do to your world?*'

'*I will show you. Relax your mind and body.*' With that Bex sank back against the padded couch. In her mind she saw herself, standing in a field of snow, or so she thought at first. What it was, was nothingness, a complete and endless void. She found she had feeling and all her senses in this dream-world. Although there was nothing there, she seemed to be on the ground.

Abruptly, Ishtara appeared in front of her, gliding above the invisible ground. She stood a little taller than Bex and she radiated energy. Her fire was bright and alive, flames flickering across her body, her arms widespread as if she was flying. She reached down with her hands, holding them out for Bex to take hold of.

Bex was shocked to hear her voice, shocked in that the words spilled from Ishtara's mouth and didn't seem to form in her mind. Her speech was articulate but seemed gravellier than the feminine, sing-song voice that Ishtara the parasite had.

"Come with me, Bex of Samak, and see my world, as it was and as it is now. Do not be afraid as nothing can hurt you here, the only hurt that can be done here is to me as I remember my people, my land and the All-Giving Fire of Qoi. Come with me, but do not cry. I have shed a million tears for the soulfires of my people and I feel I cannot shed another until I have my vengeance upon the foul hordes that did this."

Bex reached up and took her hands. As she touched the red-hot hands, that void seemed to shimmer and blur until it burst into life. Mountainous ranges erupted from the nothing-ness. The ground rendered and tore to reveal streams of magma and in the distant Bex could see forests of strange mushroom type plants. The sky brightened to an incandescent orange as a sun blazed fiercely. The sun took up most of the western sky which accounted for the high temperature. Bex could feel herself sweat and rivulets of moisture ran down her face and back.

"Ishtara!"

"Is that you?"

A chorus of voices came from behind them and they spun round to face one of the weird forests. Bex could now see that the mushrooms were the size of mighty oaks on Maingard. The biggest man in Maingard could stretch his arms around one of the trunks and not reach halfway round. The trunks were grey, but the tops shone different colours that seemed to fade and sparkle alternately.

Coming from the forest were three Qoi, two females and one male. The male was muscular and big. He stood a good foot taller than the two females and the horns on his head were taller and longer, bending backwards. All three blazed with the same flames as Ishtara, their skins reminiscent of the molten lava flowing in the streams nearby.

"Pira and Moh! Jascek!" Ishtara let go of Bex and ran to them, calling out to the three with what Bex took to be their names. They met and held hands, standing in a circle. The four started to move round, slowly at first, but then gradually faster with each rotation. They seemed to float as they spun. As they did, they chanted:

"Welcome, Brother and Sisters of the fire. I bid you welcome and praise the All-Giving Fire."

A small twister of fire grew between them, the single flame growing until it looked solid, a pillar of heat carved out of superheated air. As they finished the chorus, they released each other's hands and slowly came to a halt. The pillar between them gradually died down first to a flame and then to smoke.

"It is good to see you, Ishtara." The male Qoi, Jascek said.

"And you!"

They walked together, friends together in a carefree world. It became apparent to Bex that she was there in an incorporeal state only. The other three Qoi seemed to take no notice of her, as if she was invisible. At the crest of a nearby hill Bex was met with a wondrous sight. They stood above a canyon carved from the land below, formed by a steep cliff on the side they stood. To one side the valley ran away into the distance. To the other, the cliffs from either side met to form a basin. Cascading from that were numerous cataracts of molten magma, pouring down into a lake of liquid fire below. The lake fed a river flowing away through the canyon. A river of molten rock.

As if the sight was not impressive enough, the opposite face of the canyon was terraced. Carved into the walls of the terraces were ornate buildings that seemed glazed and polished. As the rays of the huge sun hit them, they flashed and radiated in a brilliant multitude of colours.

Ishtara said one word and Bex noticed a feeling of elation and happiness in her voice, though tinged with a hint of regret.

"Home."

22

Bryn Kar pulled up his horse. The big, brown horse was lathered in sweat and the soldier reached forward and patted the muscular neck. He had not let up since he had left the farmstead just before dawn. The horse had done well but he didn't want to push it too far and have it collapse in a heap under him. Not that he considered the fate of the horse more important than the fate of Maingard itself. He just needed the horse to keep going until he reached the gates of Tannaheim.

After escaping from the palace at Jacarna, he had made his way on foot through the city until he had reached the cavalry barracks near the Gate of the Sentinels. There he had killed another of the invaders before saddling one of the fast horses from the Lancers. His escape plan had been worked out in his head when he had lain in the rubble watching Karchek's regicide of King Renta. He felt it that it had would be safer to make his way on foot to the city walls. He had chosen the Gate of the Sentinels as his exit from the now conquered city due to the proximity of the cavalry barracks to the gate. Less than an hour's ride away on the other side of the city walls was the

Asken Forest, a great swathe of oak and ash that ran north to south on the western side of Jacarna. Although the King's Road ran through Asken Forest, Bryn felt that if he encountered any invaders, he could evade them by making his way into the dense undergrowth on either side of the highway.

That covered his route from the palace to the wall and from the wall until he left the territory. The danger point of the plan involved breaking out through the gate. He had climbed to the top of the stable area in the barracks yard and from there he had been able to see the gate. He couldn't believe his luck. The Gate of the Sentinels stood open. The tall, wooden gates hadn't been closed, either the invaders were complacent or lacked intelligence. He had checked himself at that point, whether they lacked intelligence or not was irrelevant – they had taken his city overnight.

From his vantage point he had been able to see about six of the invaders standing guard. Three were from the slave caste, he could see the collars around their neck. Two of their controllers had been seated on masonry that had been jammed up against one of the large gates. That was why the gates had been left open, one side had been unable to close. Bryn had looked up to the towers on either side of the gateway and saw massive damage to the ornate stonework, no doubt caused by the mystical blasts from the flying ships, he thought.

The enemy were complacent, feeling that the city was under their control and that further resistance from the vanquished Jacarnan's was unlikely. Bryn though, was a gambling man, after all he was a common soldier, despite being the son of an Earl. He hadn't fancied his chances of getting through the gate unscathed.

With a heavy heart he had clambered back down to the ground floor of the stable and swung himself up onto the horse he had chosen. He had sauntered forward knowing the light dirt of the stable yard would mask the sound of the hooves of the steel shod horse. There he had waited, out of sight of the gate guards whilst he caught his breath. He had raised his blade to his mouth and nudged the cold steel with his lips, muttering a short prayer to the Goddess of Chance.

"Lady Tobes, grant me luck in battle today and all days." Bryn had nudged his horse forward with his boot so that he now stood in the gate of the stable yard in full view of the men who guarded the gate and obstructed his path to safety. The gap between him and their swords had been about fifty yards and he had watched as one of them spotted him and excitedly pointed him out to his companions.

The six enemies had faced him as his horse impatiently pawed the dirt. The leader of the six had barked out orders, reinforcing them by waving and gesticulating with his sword where he had wanted his men to be. Bryn studied him closely. He was un-helmed, his grey skin almost translucent as he snarled orders at his men and grinned at the solitary rider who faced them. His plate armour was a crudely beaten relief of a skull hung over his chainmail, and his long white hair was tied back, woven with black leather straps from which dangled two small, bleached white skulls.

The two controlling the slave warriors had been from separate races, one was covered in matted fur, his features only just visible. The other had been one of the blue skinned warriors that Namot had faced in the palace throne room. At a guttural shout from the leader, they snapped their chain handles up, the magical glowing links disappeared, and the three slaves started forward, their short swords ready.

Bryn had waited, wanting to string the invaders out so he could fight them at better odds and then the unexpected happened. The cold night air had been split with a huge crack. Part of the right-hand tower, already weakened by the damage done earlier in the invasion, fell away. Perhaps Lady Tobes was looking out for Bryn after all.

The chunk of masonry plummeted earthwards striking part of the wall above the gateway as it fell and shattering into several parts. Several of the guards threw themselves aside to avoid the death from above. One of the slave warriors and blue skinned guard stood petrified as the stones hurtled downwards. Both were struck and fell dead, pulverised by the falling masonry.

Bryn kicked his horse forward and she burst into a strong gallop. He closed on the remaining soldiers as they righted themselves on unsteady legs. The great, brown warhorse stormed forward, emerging from the cloud of dust thrown up as the chunks of masonry had smashed upon the ground. The furry warrior was doubled up, coughing as the dust invaded his lungs and he was soon sent sprawling as the half-ton of horse smashed into him.

The leader of the troops had recovered faster than the others and had thrown his sword up in anticipation of Bryn's downward slash. Bryn had the initiative still, because as quick as the whitehaired warrior was, he was still dazed from the change in circumstances and the near death of the avalanche. Instead of smashing his blade downwards, Bryn arced his sword in a backward motion, following through in a clean sweep that left the point of the blade into White Hair's chin. The tip cleft through the man's chin throwing his head back and lifting his feet of the ground with the impetus of his attack.

And then he was gone, the strong legs of the cavalry horse carrying him away into the darkness of the night. He had ridden on, not wanting to look back at the city that had been his only home. The city that he had deserted and let down. He had carried on riding, torn between the love for Jacarna and his duty to follow his orders from Tarn. Deep down, his heart bled for the men of his regiment, the Royal family and for his own father who was by now dead or captured, he had no doubt. But it was the ordinary people of Jacarna that had seemed to affect him most, the citizens of the city he called home, the life blood of Jacarna. As he thought of them, let down by the city they knew as the Jewel of the East and facing whatever horrors that were in store for them, he wept.

But now he was near his goal. After five days and nights of riding with little sleep and all too infrequent stops, he was close. He looked out over the crest of the small hill at one of the wonders of Maingard. If Jacarna had been the Jewel in the East, then the vista offered to him was surely a treasure chest in comparison.

The rolling hillocks and knolls undulated downwards, turning to lush pastures and fields dotted with farmsteads and mills. To the north the fields returned to pastures as they met the slopes of the Wolf Mountains rising high into the clouds. The vast mountains were the highest in Maingard. To the south the fields met the seemingly impenetrable wall of the Danner Forest. This huge expanse of old oaks and thorny underbrush was really the western most prominence of the Great Asken Forest that separated the east and west of Maingard.

It was the central part of the vista that awed Bryn more. The walls of Tannaheim stretched for leagues. It took him a few seconds to register the scale when he realised the distance he still had to cover. The outer walls must have been the height of twenty men and were interspersed with towers that protruded outwards. He could see that the walls were topped by a dull black roof and guessed that underneath this were the battlements and their crenels. Beyond that outer wall was a taller wall, again topped with a protective roof and then beyond that still were the towers and spires of the city proper. Tannaheim dwarfed his own city of Jacarna and its neighbour Tarim, and he wondered at its magnificence.

The whinnying of his horse awoke him from his thoughts, and he snorted himself as he kicked the horse on in a slow trot. He gave a cursory glance over his shoulders for pursuers but nervously at the sky rather than the ground behind him. He grimaced as he thought how smug and safe the Court of Tanna-heim and their subjects felt behind their strong fortifications. The walls would be strong against an army that walked or rode, but one that flew?

23

The image of the wondrous Qoi town and its shimmering walls faded and blurred into another. Bex and Ishtara were back in the forest of strange trees again. Even though the great mushroom heads of the trees shaded her from the sun, she could still feel the intense heat.

'Is it always this hot?' she asked Ishtara.

'Yes, beautiful, isn't it?' and then she cryptically added. 'It will happen now.'

'What will?'

'You are watching my memory, Bex. In a way, we are in a lifetime away, literally another world. But we are also here in the past, seeing, feeling, experiencing what I felt at that time. Not only that but because we are together, you can sense my emotions now. And right now, this is or was the worst day in all of my being.'

Bex could sense the despair and sorrow in Ishtara voice and mind but before she could answer an ear-splitting noise rent the air. An echo rolled through the forest like the drawn-out rumble of thunder from a distant storm. Ishtara looked up startled, and then more thunderclaps like the first noise, six in rapid succession.

Ishtara flew from the forest, her feet gliding across the land. Bex was whisked along with her, attached psychically but was glad to recognise the landscape from the first image. This was where they had met the Pira, Moh and Jascek. Ishtara was heading to the Qoi town, her home. They reached the crest of the hill where she had first seen the magnificent houses of the Qoi.

Ishtara clenched her fists and threw her head back, screaming loud.

"Nooooooo!"

As she looked out over the canyon though, she was met with a terrible sight. The Qoi town was in ruins. Smoke poured from the terraces and several of the houses had been pulled or blown down. Rubble was strewn across the area. However, the most shocking parts of the image were the seven large ships above the terraces. A green mist seemed to emanate from the ships and every now and again frightful bolts of green lightning crackled along the hulls, arcing to the ground. They were like the dragon ships of the Northmen in her own world, with either one or two masts. Each had a great leering dragon head at the bow of the ship, facing forward as if it was about to sweep some terrified prey up into its craw. Some of the ships had settled upon the esplanades below and the Qoi were engaged in a confusing melee with the crews of the ships. She could make out the fiery forms of the Qoi, but they seemed to be outnumbered by the dark figures.

From two ships that were still flying came a devastating bombardment. She could make out figures on each deck that were able to generate pulsing bolts of blue light that they directed downwards. Each one struck the ground with shocking explosions, blowing huge chunks of stone and masonry in the air.

As one of the houses exploded, a piece of rock the size of a horse cannoned upward and struck the side of one of the ships, tilting it sideways as if it was about to capsize if it had been at sea. As it continued to tip, Bex saw several of the crew swept overboard to plummet to a horrific, fiery death below in the lake of molten rock. The mast, tipping perilously close to the magma, ignited sending rigging whipping away. Bex and Ishtara watched the ship slowly slide into the lake, breaking apart and disappearing in a flash of fire sent rising from the surface.

Ishtara plunged over the edge of the cliff, down a steep but well-trodden path. Bex leapt after her, unable to move separately. The path headed straight for the place where the river of plutonic fire plunged over the cliff edge. Even though she was intangible, Bex shrunk away from the inescapable heat. As they neared the firefall she noticed that the path disappeared behind the torrent. Ishtara followed and Bex found herself dragged along.

Bex felt she was melting from the heat of the plummeting volcanic rock, the temperature even higher than the outside. Within seconds she was through, heading down the path to the terraced esplanades where the Qoi were putting up their last stand.

Three of the enemy had spotted the lone Qoi and had moved to cut her path to the terraces off. The two nearest to her were slender and pale skinned. They wore ornate plate armour that had seen better days. Gouges covered the steel and dents and even tears were evident. Once proud and shiny the steel carried rust patches and blood stains. The figures were stooped and hunched in stature and carried short clubs and nets.

Their pale skin seemed nearly opaque in places and Bex was certain she could see a slow pulse of blood where veins stood close to the surface. Their hair was long, lank and matted against their skin. Around their neck they wore a heavy collar of black steel that even to Bex's eye, untrained in the ways of magic as they were, seemed to emanate with a dark sorcerous power. As they approached, she could see into their blank soulless eyes and she was reminded of an age ago when she had stood over her first dead body, that of her pimp when she had been young.

Behind these two stood a third, different creature. Again, humanoid in form, he stood a foot taller than the others and Ishtara. Where the first two enemies wore armour that was once proud and eye catching, there was nothing glorious about his harness. It had been predominately black but now had the brownish red matt of dried blood. Instead of eagles and fleurs decorating the steel like the first two, his armour` had demonic faces covering it. Around his neck, hanging across his breast plate was a string of bones. In one hand he carried a long, black sword with a serrated blade ending in a barbed head, in the other, a short sceptre. Every now and then Bex could discern the movement of thin chains of psychic energy that linked the sceptre to the collars of the first two creatures. They were slaves, held in check by the master behind.

His hands were more like talons, long and bony fingers tipped by sharp black nails. The skin was parched and grey, stretched across his bony features.

He spoke, a grating harsh sound, and in doing so he whipped his hand holding the sceptre up and down once. His thralls moved forward to attack Ishtara.

She accelerated, the burst of speed catching the first one unawares and ducked under his clumsy swing of his club. She dropped her shoulder, barging into his midriff and sent him sprawling towards his accomplish. The two collided and fell to the ground perilously close to the edge of the lake. As they tried to stand, their limbs entangled, she moved on towards their master.

He raised the sceptre, pointing one end towards her and he grinned. A small flash of flame burst from the end of the weapon now pointed at her and Bex felt the projectile hit

Ishtara in the stomach. She watched as she flew backwards, rolling across the ground as the agony spread through her body. Ishtara came to a rest, face down laying parallel to the lake edge. Bex looked on, helpless in her non corporeal state as the being moved towards her.

As his two minions righted themselves, he struck them hard with his open hand and snarled at them in his guttural language. Bex's vision became blurry and she realised that Ishtara's memory was affected at this point due to her injuries or perhaps lack of consciousness.

The invader came close to her and she raised her head slowly. The vision became shakier and blurrier but Bex found Ishtara focusing on the scene some distance away. She could see lines of her people all being herded onto several of the ships, all the time harried by blows and shouts from the invaders. Around them smoke billowed in the wind from the ruins and she could see bodies of other Qoi lying immobile on the ground.

The creature standing over her snarled again at her, then with his heavy boot nudged her over the edge into the fiery lake below. Ishtara fell without a sound and Bex's sight went black.

They awoke on a ledge close to the lake edge sometime later.

'*This is what will happen to your world, Bex*'

Bex was silent for a while.

'*I am sorry for what happened to your people, Ishtara.*'

'*It is worse.*' Came the reply and then Ishtara was silent ignoring any further questioning.

They climbed up from the ledge to the esplanade above. The ships were gone but the devastation was still there. Bex could feel the sorrow that Ishtara felt as they sought amongst the ruins. Bex could see now how the rock buildings glistened in the sun. They were covered in a hard crystal glaze, and the face of the stone underneath was studded with quartz and gems. Even now the sun's rays caught the precious and semi-precious stones and shone bright despite the horror that had happened here hours before.

Each time Ishtara came across a body she cried and bade each one goodbye by name. Finally, she knelt by the side of one Qoi and wept for a long time. It was Pira, one of the three that had 'met' Bex before. Slowly Ishtara laid Pira flat on her back and folded her arms across her chest. She left her hands holding Pira's and slowly chanted.

'Farewell, Sister of the fire, Farewell.' She stayed kneeling for some time until a noise distracted her. Someone was still alive in this destruction. She searched the rubble until they came to the source of the sound. It was one of the invaders. He was lying on his back, his legs crushed by a block of masonry. He was whispering in his own language, the words interspersed by long drawn out breaths.

He saw the Qoi woman standing over him and he reached out with his right hand for his sword. As his hand scrabbled about for the hilt, Ishtara stamped down hard on his wrist. She smiled in satisfaction as she heard bones crack under her foot as she ground down hard. He grimaced with pain and his eyes betrayed fear. Ishtara knelt by his side, her foot still on the wound she had just inflicted.

Her hands reached out for his head and she shuddered as she touched his cold skin. As she held his temples, she felt her anger rise and her bodyflame begin to blaze ferociously. The flame leapt down her arms and enveloped the invader's face and head. He opened his mouth to scream but no sound came out. Ishtara held his head tight as the invader writhed in agony. The vengeful Qoi still held him even after he stopped moving, even after his eyes had burst in the heat and his skin had started to peel off. Finally, she let go and turned away, tearful and retching.

Bex opened her eyes and found herself back in the Black

Dragon Inn. She stared silently at the empty seat of` the stall opposite her.

'I am sorry, Bex. I had to show you what awaits your world.'

'Can we stop them?'

'Maybe, I don't know. No one has so far.'

'What can we do?'

'Well, first we need to warn your King. When can we see him?'

'I don't think he will see us. He can be unapproachable, especially to people like me.'

'It is literally a matter of life and death, Bex. You have seen that. You must make him see us.'

'We should go to the palace.'

Outside, East Street was now packed with the flow of people ebbing to and fro. Merchants, drivers, guards and citizens thronged in the street, like ants. Bex pushed herself through the crowd making her way towards the Palace. Several times she found her way impassable by sheer weight of people but found that hard glares seemed to melt away the blocking traffic.

'How did you get to this world, Ishtara?'

'After my village was destroyed, I journeyed towards some of the bigger towns. I found where the invaders were based and saw more horrors that I dare not divulge now. I watched how they operate and saw ships leaving my world through a planar gate. When I noticed that more ships were getting ready to move on, I presumed that they were possibly scouts or spies ready for their next target. That night I managed to creep on board one of their ships and journeyed with them to this world. I jumped ship as soon as I could.'

'And then Yab M'vil's men caught you?'

'Yes, I felt bad at killing them then. The Qoi are quite a peaceful race. Before them, I had only killed in anger. The rage inside of me at my village after the ships had left, let me kill that invader. Your fellow men, I killed them to survive.'

'They weren't my fellow men. Not them. And you will notice that death through violence is commonplace here in Maingard.'

'I noticed.' Bex thought she could hear the smirk in Ishtara's voice. 'Being away from the sun for so long tired me. It was so dark and cold between the planes. They managed to overpower me fairly quickly. And then you came.'

24

Bex approached the Palace of Tannaheim and felt an exclamation from within from Ishtara. The Palace itself was situated on a large rocky mound that was separated from the rest of Tannaheim by deep gorge. In front of them the ground fell away gradually for about twenty or thirty feet before plummeting downwards in a sheer drop. Some of the small houses or dwellings on this side of the chasm had small terraces that faced the palace and in between the terraces and balconies wild gorse clung onto the rocky ground.

In front of them now was a gatehouse, two large squat concentric towers joined by the gate and topped with a tall foreboding central tower. It looked to Bex that it was something a child might make by balancing building blocks on top of each other. The gap ahead was crossed by a double drawbridge. A bridge of solid, oaken planks, each one a foot thick and supported by crossbeams underneath the same size reached out from behind the gatehouse to meet another lowered and operated from a gatehouse on the other side. This gatehouse was the exact twin of the first. Great iron chains held the bridge in place, stretching from the point the two met back up into the central tower above.

As Bex stood in the road facing the tower, she could see through the gate. The Palace soared high into the sky completely overshadowing the tall gatehouse towers. It was said that the Queen could reach from her chamber window and gather clouds. Looking up at the spectacle that the palace created, Bex didn't doubt the story. The palace and accompanying towers were built from the same buff stone as much of Tannaheim. Whilst this was one of the two bridges that crossed to the outcrop where the Kings of Tannaheim had made their fortress, entrance could also be gained from the Royal Harbours on the other side of the promontory.

'Legend has it, thousands of years ago when man and the Gods walked Maingard together, King Harward and his people were chased by an army of giants. They came here and with their back to the sea below they faced their death at the hands of the monsters. King Harward's wife, Gruenwild prayed to Kani the Hunter who fired an arrow here, cleaving the ground apart to form this chasm between them and the giants. Harward and his people were safe and they built this palace here, on Gruenwild's Rock in thanks to Kani for saving them.' Bex projected the story to Ishtara.

'Where are the Gods now, Bex?'

'There aren't any. At least, I don't think so. The priests just speak lies.'

'So, it's just a story?'

'Yes.'

'But a good story. A very good story.'

'Yes, but still just a story.'

"Hey!" a loud shout woke her from her reverie. "Get away from the gate!" A soldier in chainmail and red livery gesticulated wildly at her, one hand on the pommel of his sword.

"I need to see the King!" she shouted back with her hands wide apart to indicate she wasn't a threat.

"Courtiers only!" the guard was closer now and Bex's obstinacy had attracted the attention of one of his colleagues. A short sergeant started to march across from one of the small doorways just inside the maw of the gatehouse. It was just then that the first guard made his mistake.

"Courtiers only!" he repeated. "Get your whore ass away from here, at least until I am off duty. Then we...." He had placed his hand firmly on Bex's chest, not just pushing but also groping her breast.

Her hand ripped upwards, the speed of her Qoi charged body exhilarating her, and gripped his hand, her thumb burrowing deep into the web between his forefinger and thumb. Her long fingers stretched over the back of his hand and gripped tight. Bex twisted his wrist and stepped away, pulling him off balance. She accentuated her position by pushing up on his distended elbow with her free hand and left him to fall flat on his face.

"Hold it right there."

She looked up to see the sergeant's blade pointed at her and two more guards with bows trained on to her nearby.

"I want. . . . I need to see the King." She spoke calmly and clearly, her eyes glaring at the sergeant. He was obviously nearing the end of his military career. Slightly overweight and balding, Sergeant Roge had up until that moment liked the humdrum of his life as officer of the Palace Gate. Stop anyone crossing the bridge and move on any wastrels. Easy orders. He looked from the tall, lithe woman in front of him and the guard who she had easily put down and wondered what to do.

A thunder of hooves took the moment from him. A great brown warhorse clattered to a stop, her steel-shod hooves sparking on the cobbles. Sweat lathered across its chest and dripped to the ground. Its rider was a tall man in a chainmail hauberk, his dark hair sweaty and matted and his face bloodied and grimy. His armour was dusty as if he had been riding for days and Bex could make out a faint image of a silver rampant horse on his blue surcoat.

"I need to speak to your King! I am an envoy of Jacarna, and he needs to hear my news."

The sergeant grabbed the bridle of the great horse and one of the guards swept his bow up to aim at the blue coated soldier.

'*I think we may be too late.*' Ishtara spoke inside Bex's head.

'*Tobe's tits. I hope not!*'

"Like we said to the wench here, courtiers only. Get lost or face the consequences." Roge snarled.

"Fools!" the rider spat and wrenching the bridle away from the guard, he made to push his horse past the soldiers onto the bridge. The archer's knuckles whitened as he tensed to let his arrow fly. The horse that had carried Bryn Kar so far and away from certain death in Jacarna again saved his life. Ridden hard but conservatively, the great warhorse now decided to collapse from exhaustion. The arrow flew high and wide as the horse's feet slipped from underneath it, throwing Bryn to the floor. He landed with a dull thud, the thick undershirt beneath his mail helping him to avoid any injury apart from the bruising to his pride.

The horse whinnied pathetically as if it knew that it had let Bryn down, but it lay immobile as if all its energy had drained out, the occasional flick of its tail betraying the fact that it was still alive. The sergeant was quickly upon Bryn before he could rise, and the archer readied another arrow whilst two more guards came running.

"Fools," repeated the downed soldier. "Death is coming to you all and you dare to stop me?" He tried to rise but the sergeant placed his boot on his chest and pushed him back down, drawing his sword.

"You dare to threaten us? At the gateway to the Red Throne

itself?" He sounded incredulous that someone would have the temerity to do such a thing.

'We need to stop him from getting himself killed, Bex.'

'I know.'

Bex took a few steps forward and held her hands up as if to placate the sergeant.

"We should let him speak. I think his message to the King is the same as mine." It could have been her soft voice that calmed the guard sergeant, or the view he had as he glanced sideways at the intrusion, his eyes feasting upon Bex's chest.

"Maybe, woman. But maybe not. Your features do not betray sight of the same horrors that have visited my eyes and mind over the last few days." The soldier continued to stare down the Palace Guard, but also glanced up at Bex as she looked at him.

"Your eyes seem to, though." He seemed to falter as their eyes met.

'My eyes? What does he mean, Ishtara? Others have shunned me because of my eyes since we ......joined.'

'I see through your eyes, Bex. Your eyes are mine and mine are yours.'

'What do you mean?'

'People will see your eyes and mine when they look closely at you.' Bex remembered the burning eyes of the Qoi when she had first seen her in the cage at Yab M'vil's villa and shuddered. No wonder Landa had run when she had looked at him.

"You have come to warn the King about ships that fly through the air as if it was the sea. And you will tell him about death and destruction beyond imaginable scale and the fact that your city is under attack." She spoke in a soft voice, audible only to the soldier and the Palace Guard. She sought his eyes and noticed the pain as she spoke the last sentence and added, "or it has already fallen."

The Palace Guard looked from one to the other, the point of his sword wavering and falling.

"Is this true? Jacarna has fallen?"

The soldier from Jacarna looked crestfallen and both the guard and Bex took it as true.

"You say ships that fly?" The guard was unsure how to take the news and stared at both aghast.

'Bex, the King....'

"We should take this to the King and his council at once." Once again Bex's voice was calm and controlled and this seemed to persuade the sergeant that this was the best course of action.

25

The guard led them through the Palace proper, picking up a further escort of Guardsmen as they went. These wore steel plate with the Barstt insignia of crossed swords mounted central on the breast. A thick woollen cloak was thrown over their left shoulder. As they walked through the corridors, Bex was struck at the grandeur of the interior of the Palace. She wasn't surprised, she knew it would be rich and ostentatious, but it was like nothing she had seen before. Paintings, tapestries, statuettes and furs lined each wall of every corridor. Part of the way the corridor ran past one of the ball rooms in the Palace. Glass doors opened into the ballroom every 10 yards and she gazed in awe at the black and white marble floor laid out in a chequer board pattern.

"You are not normally accustomed to this style, I take it?" the soldier from Jacarna leaned in to speak to Bex.

"No, not really."

"You shouldn't worry, they are exactly the same as you and me, these kings and queens. They all fret and stress, bleed and crap, and just like the scum on the streets, they all die in the end." He said with a light chuckle, just loud enough to be overheard by the Palace Guard. "Though," he added, "they do all that with a lot more gold than you and me."

Bex couldn't help but smile.

"I am Bryn Kar," he held out his hand to Bex, and when she responded with hers, he grasped her wrist and shook it twice. "Bryn Kar, Sergeant at Arms, 5th Regiment of Jacarna." About his wrist was a tattoo of a black snake, and noticing her gaze he added again, "Our regiment's insignia – they call us the Black Serpents."

Bex nodded and replied.

"Bex of Samak. It is under unfortunate circumstances that we meet, Bryn Kar."

"Yes, it is. I apologise for the way I addressed you earlier. Please accept my sincere thanks for intervening when you did."

They had now arrived at the Throne Room. A pair of ornate, dark oaken doors guarded by 4 pike bearing guards barred their way. Seeing the approaching party, they snapped to attention.

"Open the doors! We must speak to the King at once." One of the guards, sensing the urgency of the situation, swung open the door and the party marched in.

The throne room in the Palace of the Red Throne was huge. One side was lit by massive windows that stretched from floor to ceiling some five times the height of a man. They looked out upon the beautiful vista of the Bay of Tann and the Western Seas beyond. Two fires blazed in marble fireplaces that were high enough for a man to stand with arms stretched above him. Banners draped from the wooden beams of the high vaulted ceiling showing King Anjoan's coat of arms, two crossed silver swords on a red background, along with others of the Royal Family.

A large dais was sited at the far end on which sat two thrones, both surmounted by scarlet canopies. The smaller throne was occupied by a middle-aged woman, beautiful despite her advancing years. Her fair complexion was in direct contrast to her striking red hair. Queen Sarsi had served her King well, bringing four children into the world for him and turning a blind eye to his many infidelities. She did, however, concentrate upon her children where she could, yet she kept an auspicious, yet inconspicuous seat to the many twists and turns of political life.

To the right of the Queen, in the larger throne, sat the imposing figure of King Anjoan. A giant of a man, his armour he customarily wore only added to the impressiveness of his stature. He sat with his elbows on his knees, hands grasped in front of him as if in prayer, listening intently to the Privy Council before him who were arranged around a table discussing what the various organizations and representees desired to gain from the future negotiations with Jarl Merick. The Master of the Treasury, Golam Harn, was seated nearest the King. An old man, he had held the post for several years, and was renowned for his frugality. Opposite him, sat Eglebon Dutte, the Master of the Privy Council. He was the youngest of the Council but was held in some esteem about the court, despite the misdemeanours of his great-grandfather. Ser Duncarn, Lord of the Navy was present along with the Lord of the Army, Ser Kilmson. The heads of various Merchant Guilds were seated at the end of the table, opposite the King and Queen. The Hawk took his customary position on the bottom step of the dais. The discussions immediately hushed as the doors crashed open.

Two soldiers wearing the uniform of the City Guard, chain-mail and red livery strode into the centre of the throne room followed closely by two members of the King's Guard in their resplendent plate armour. Accompanying the four guards were Bryn and Bex. The Hawk started at the intrusion, holding his hand up to halt the newcomers.

"Sergeant! What is the meaning of this interference? You

had better have a good reason or you will find yourself patrolling the Hinterlands by the end of the week!" His voice cut through the relative silence of the throne room like a crack of thunder. Bex had heard of Magus Vent and another time, may have felt sorry for the Sergeant. City folklore stated that he had personally executed two of his own cousins for their part in a plot against the King just after he had been granted the role of the King's Marshall.

"My Lord...." stammered the Sergeant of the guard, not knowing how to respond.

Bryn Kar came as an unlikely aid to the faltering Sergeant Roge and brushed past him, hands outstretched to show his was unarmed. Two red clad, visored guards brought him to a halt, their swords already drawn.

"It is not the good Sergeant who is intruding, my Lord. Your King must hear the grave news that I bring from Jacarna."

Anjoan was on his feet, easily he stood taller than any man in the throne room, and that included the two Snow Walker guards and the Jarl.

"Magus, let him speak. I know this lad. This is Bannom Kar's firstborn." He marched down the six steps of the rostrum and motioned to the guardsmen to sheath their weapons. He halted in front of Bryn with his arms outstretched to each side. His teeth shone white in the big grin that split his bushy, black beard and he swept the young soldier up in a ferocious bear hug.

"It is good to see you, my lad. Pray tell, how is your father?" he bellowed, releasing Bryn.

Bryn dropped to his knee, head bowed forward, then raised his head to address the King.

"Right of this moment, your Majesty, my father probably lies dead in the Palace of Jacarna. Jacarna and our sister city Tarim have fallen and my people are being enslaved. Before my captain drew his last breath, he urged me to warn the Western Kingdoms of the horror that will befall us all."

Anjoan turned away from the kneeling soldier and climbed a few of the steps of the dais, struck speechless by the news. The Lords around the table murmured in disbelief. Magus Vent strode forward.

"What do you mean fallen? Who has the power to do that? No army on Maingard could challenge Jacarna and Tarim together – except for our own forces."

"The news is grave indeed, Bryn Kar, son of Bannom Kar. But how has this occurred?" Anjoan faced Bryn once more and asked the question.

"The news I bring is incredible yet true. Jacarna lies in ruins and my liege lord, King Renta is dead at the hands of the enemy warlord. They came from within and above. They call themselves Cassalians. They are an army of several races, barbarians and animals alike and they are not of this world. They have powerful magic that allows their ships to fly and to destroy buildings from the sky."

"Absurd!" shouted a one of the nobles and there was a general humdrum of disbelief and dissent.

"It's true!" Bryn staggered to his feet. "I have another witness!" he waved a hand in Bex's direction. She stepped forward nervously. Even though what she had seen in her dreams from Ishtara collaborated what Bryn had just announced, she knew it sounded completely absurd.

"What Bryn Kar says is right, however absurd it sounds. They do travel the planes, hopping from world to world, stripping each of their resources before they head to their next target."

"This is outrageous!" A noble ranted. Bex couldn't discern whether it was the same one that had interrupted before. "I urge you not to listen to this, Sire".

Magus Vent turned his attention to Bex. She could feel

herself shrink under his purposeful stare and though she had faced down many an intimidating enemy, she imagined herself as a field mouse about to be torn to shreds by the Hawk.

"How do they travel between worlds, girl? And how do they take a city?"

"It is as Bryn says. They have ships that fly, and weapons that can destroy buildings and walls. Their armies have slaves that fight for them and sorcerers that have power of the dark arts." She stared back at the black eyes that pierced her soul.

"I have fulfilled my orders to come here and warn you. You can do with that warning as you will," Bryn took up the speech once more, turning where he stood in order to address all those present. "But heed this, when the palace finally fell, they offered King Renta chance to stand with them and be a client Lord to them, as the Dukes of Karame were client Lords of his. He refused. The Cassalian warlord, an animal called Karchek, tore his head from his shoulders with his bare hands. But not before he made Renta watch his daughters be thrown to the hordes to be their playthings as a reward for their savagery."

Bex looked at the Queen at that point, and noticed her gasp, hand covering her mouth in terror. She beckoned forward one of her advisors and whispered something to him behind her hand. He nodded and turned away, leaving the throne room with one of the guards.

"It is a week's ride from Jacarna, Bryn Kar. How come we have not heard any more reports of this?"

"The assault was over in one night and they now pacify the area around the city. Their patrols range far, plundering farms and villages. I evaded all on my ride here." He allowed a wry smile to cross his tired features.

"It is amazing how fast one can ride when the demons of Hel are at your back."

"Will they come here?" Anjoan asked, already knowing the answer.

"Yes, Bex has told you they will rape this world of the very life she has." Bryn said.

"Can we stop them?" Anjoan echoed the question Bex asked Ishtara earlier.

"Bolam's balls!" Exclaimed one of the Lords. The Master of the Privy Council, Eglebon Dutte, stood and placed his hands upon the table. Imperceptibly, he nodded to someone on the far side of the room, behind the table of Lords. That was where two long tables sat piled with fruit and sweetmeats, with a number of servants in attendance. They wore the scarlet and silver coat of arms of the Barstt family on their tunics and looked resplendent with white hose and gloves.

"If what this young soldier says is true, I think I will require wine in order to take this in." There were murmurs of agreement from the table, and Dutte beckoned to the servants who stood by one of the refreshment tables. They dutifully poured large goblets of red wine and placed two goblets on one silver tray. These were taken to the King and Queen, and a second tray was served around the table.

Dutte took a quick look at the King and inwardly cursed as he realised that Queen Sarsi was wearing her customary gloves as she took her goblet. He cast a quick smile as he noticed Anjoan was bare-handed as he took his. He stared at his own goblet that had been placed on the table before him for a full second before setting his gaze upon a member of the King's guard who had been standing near the servants.

"We need to convene a council of war immediately." Marshall Vent spoke to the King. Anjoan nodded, an odd feeling in his fingers causing him to transfer the goblet to his other hand and stare at his hand. The Hawk carried on.

"And we should ask the guild heads to wait in another chamber. We need to discuss this amongst the Privy Council, but we also need to keep this news inside the palace."

King Anjoan, nodded again. He stared at his hand as blisters started to form on his fingers. He threw down the goblet as his other hand started to itch as well.

"My dear, are you okay?" asked Sarsi, placing a hand concerningly on her husband's arm. He looked at her and tried to speak. He could feel his body struggling to breathe as his throat swelled, constricting his airway. The blisters on his hands made it agonising for him to flex his fingers as he tried to clutch at his throat and mouth. Finally, the convulsions set in, shaking the once mighty man to his knee. By then, mercifully, his body had started to shut down and he felt no more pain.

There was stunned silence as the chamber just froze. Then a piercing scream from Queen Sarsi rent the air and chaos ensued. Dutte along with several of the Council shouted out in unison.

"Poison!" And Dutte pointed at the servants who had just served the goblets to them all.

"Knife!" The two young men looked horrified and one started to raise his hand to point back at Dutte, just as the Guardsman standing closest to them cut them both down with his sword. As the young man fell, a dagger clattered to the stone floor.

Sarsi knelt by Anjoan, stroking his face as he breathed his last breath, a horrid rattling sound as he exhaled one last time, his dying body pushing the air through his tortured windpipe.

"Sergeant! Confine those two for the moment." The Hawk pointed to Bryn and Bex. "And clear the chamber. No one comes in – and no one who is here is let out of your sight. Chain everyone up if you have to!"

The Hawk knelt down at Sarsi's side, placing his hand ever so gently on her shoulder.

"Please, Your Majesty. It is not safe, not until we know what..." He didn't know how to continue, for once lost for words.

"It's a contact toxin, Magus. Taken into the body by touch. It was probably on my goblet as well. We were both targets." She tore the gloves that had protected her from her hand and threw them on the floor. She stifled a sob with the back of her hand, and Bex watched as her body heaved and wracked in torment. Taking a deep breath, Sarsi pushed as much of the grief from her body and rose to her feet, assisted by the Hawk.

The Hawk held her hand as she ascended the steps to the throne. The Queen gripped the arm of the throne as she steadied her legs before sitting. She did not slump but sat proud and elegant.

"Marshall Vent. Find the bastards that organised this. Now!" As the Queen sat back, resting against the throne, Bex saw a single tear form at the corner of her eye.

26

Lord Valon Shuy strode through the palace, looking almost regal in his pale blue jacket. He had been an advisor and chief valet to Queen Sarsi for several years, and now hurried to the classrooms on the lower levels where the Princesses Ingren and Moren spent most of their mornings. When she had learnt the fate of King Renta and his family, Sarsi had felt sick, sick enough to have to physically fight the urge to retch. She had sent Shuy to ensure that her daughters were safe.

Not that he would be defending them himself – Ser Stahl, the guardsman that matched his step pace by pace would do that, his hand ready at the hilt of his sword as it wagged in its scabbard like a dog's tail. Shuy was a cripple, his right arm shattered in a riding accident some years ago. He held it folded grotesquely against his chest as he walked, the elbow bent and wrist crooked.

They turned the last corner, their footsteps echoing along the long corridors and Shuy was relieved to see the guard at the door of the palace school rooms still present. As the two men marched their way towards him, the guardsman took a step from the door as if to present more of an obstacle and barked at the newcomers.

"Apologies, my Lord. My orders are to avoid interruption to the Princesses during class time, direct from Marshall Vent himself."

Valon Shuy waved a hand dismissively and answered without meeting the guards gaze.

"At ease, Guardsman. My orders are from Her Majesty herself. Interfere with me and face the wrath of Queen Sarsi herself. I am here to escort the Princesses back to their chambers once the King's Guard arrives."

The guard seemed to mentally wrestle with his dilemma. It was a choice between death and death, as they said in Tannaheim. Fear of the supernatural seemed to win in the end and he stepped aside. Shuy reached for the door and opened it wide.

Master Tarnal stopped mid flow in his tale of the heroic siege of Tannorn some three centuries ago and looked up at the interruption. The room was large, maps adorning the walls and piles of books and scrolls were stacked haphazardly on tables to the sides and rear of the room. Sat at four desks, dwarfed by the tall backs of the chairs in which they sat were four children.

The two girls were Ingren and Moren, the young princesses. Ingren, older of the two and the tom boy of the pair, wore a simple dark green dress, her long dark hair tied up in a bun. Moren, younger by two years wore a similar style dress but in a more feminine pink decorated with purple brocade. She wound her hair round her finger as she stared at one of the two other occupants of the room, oblivious to the entrance of Shuy and the guard.

Dirian and Klush Dantice were nephews of the King. The same age as Moren they were the spitting image of their father, Lord Edric Dantice. Blond and tall for their age, they were nevertheless haughty and cocksure. Ingren found them intriguing, Moren just found them irritating.

"Lord Shuy, what is the meaning of this..." Master Tarnal stood and placed his hands on the desk in front of him. The long brown robes he wore had seen better days and the chain of large links that hung about his neck were a little tarnished compared to Master Smit's in the throne room.

"It is no concern of yours, Master Tarnal. I have orders from Queen Sarsi to suspend lessons for today and to move the Princesses back to their chambers." Ingren smiled, already planning her afternoon, with class out for the day she might be able to go riding with some of the other young lords. She made to stand up, but Lord Shuy raised his hand to pause her.

"This is most irregular, Lord Shuy," protested the old tutor, who received a glare from the Lord as a reply.

"Please wait, Your Highness, there is no need to move now. A detachment of the King's Guard will be here shortly."

Dirian and Klush looked at each other and then stood to address Lord Shuy. The sons of the King's sister were known for their impetuousness and they raised their voices accordingly and bombarded The Cripple with questions and demands together.

"What is it that you are not telling us, Lord Shuy? Our father will hear of this."

"A detachment of guards to move us within the palace? What is going on?"

"My Lords," Shuy rounded on the young Lords. "My orders are from the Queen herself and they do not include you or your brother in them. Bearing in mind that the Queen enshrined me with these orders herself, whatever threats you dredge up against me from you or your father hold no stead."

EDWOD SCAND, the guard outside the Princesses' class looked right as he heard the boots march towards him. Four King's Guards marched two abreast along the corridor, their red half-plate armour clanking with each step. The front two looked as if they were mirror images of each other, their red cloaks flung over opposite shoulders and one hand gripping the hilt of the short stubby swords issued to the protectors of the King. As they neared, he turned to face them, and raised his hand as if to hold them back. The four soldiers crashed to a halt in unison.

"Are you with Lord Shuy?" he asked, fully aware that he had pulled the short straw this morning when he was assigned guard duty for the Princesses. It didn't take a genius to work out that something wasn't right. First Lord Shuy with a Guardsman and now four more.

"Shuy? The Cripple is here?" the leader of the detachment answered, his eyes flitting sideward to his companions. Scand faltered slightly, sure enough, Shuy was known as the Cripple behind his back, especially by the palace guard and other soldiers but he did expect slightly more respect from a captain of the King's Guard. He gestured over his shoulder at the door and nodded.

"Yes, he went in a few minutes ago." Something clicked in Edwod's mind. There was something wrong, right here and now. These King's Guards weren't here to meet the Cripple, they didn't even know that he was here. He reached out with his hand to bar the captain's way, the palm of his hand pushing against the cold steel of the captain's armour. His other hand reached down to the hilt of his own sword and he opened his mouth to shout out a warning to those inside the room.

Scand felt a hand close over his mouth as his shout was muffled. He struggled against the imposter behind him but only for a second as the pressure increased and his neck was broken.

27

Master Smit bustled to Queen Sarsi's side, dipping to one knee next to her. His hand slipped to the King's neck. When he was confident there was no pulse, he turned to look at the Queen and slowly shook his head. She raised a hand gracefully to her face and wiped a tear away. The elderly Master rose, then helped the Queen to her feet. Her voice was quiet and slightly wavered as she spoke.

"Marshall Vent, please arrange for my husband to be moved to the chapel. Master Smit, can you discover whatever bordello my son is currently in and bring him here. And make sure he is sober." She turned and took her seat on her throne again, adding as she waved her hand towards the dead assassins. "And kindly remove this filth from the chamber."

Queen Sarsi's voice snapped Marshall Vent from his reverie. He snapped at his men as six of the red clad King's Guard bent to lift the dead monarch. After giving orders for the palace to be closed and for his commanders to be fetched, he pointed at Bex and Bryn.

"You two, don't you move. I have more questions for you." He snarled. "Hand over your sword."

'I think you should do it, Bex. We don't want any more trouble.'
Bex felt like arguing, but she took Ishtara's advice and handed her blade to a guard. She looked over at the dead murderers as they lay where they were struck down.

'Their task was to kill the King at any cost. It will certainly weaken your state in the war to come.'

'You still think it will happen?'

'Of course, Bex. I know you don't want to believe it, but it will happen. Bryn Kar's city has fallen, and yours will follow. The Cassalians know nothing else but war and destruction. They will come here, sooner or later.'

Two guards dragged the regicides bodies away, a smear of blood coating the floor. The Queen looked on impassively.

Marshall Vent spat out more orders, sending troops to the servant's quarters to arrest their families for interrogation. The guild masters that were still present in the throne room were all man handled away from the Queen and Vent insisted they were all searched before being let out. Bex stood still as Vent now turned his attention to her and Bryn.

"I want to know everything about these Cassalians. I want to know what preparations we need to make."

At that point the throne room started to refill, this time with more military commanders of the realm. As each lord prepared to take their seats they bowed to the Queen and offered their condolences. Each time she gently smiled and bowed her head in acknowledgement.

"Gentlemen, this is Bryn Kar, a sergeant in the Jacarna Guard, he has come to give you details of a threat to Tannaheim which is almost certainly connected to King Anjoan's murder." Magus Vent started proceedings.

Several of the lords grimaced at the introduction whilst one took it further, banging his fist down on the table.

"Are we now to be addressed by sergeants, Marshall? This is an insult to us all!"

The Hawk glared at him, his hands resting on the table in front of him. But it wasn't the Hawk that answered the general.

"Yes, Lord Kreft, Bryn Kar is a sergeant. He is also son of Earl Bannom Kar of Jacarna. From what information he shared earlier he is now not only Earl Bryn Kar, but possibly one of the highest ranks left in the Jacarna military." Queen Sarsi's voice was more authoritative. Lord Kreft blushed like a schoolboy admonished by his teacher, his bloated face turning a dark shade of scarlet and Bex turned to look at the man who stood next to her.

Queen Sarsi looked over to Marshall Vent.

"Proceed, Marshall."

"Thank you, your majesty." He bowed slightly to the Queen and turned back to the war council.

"Earl Bryn Kar will give you details of what he has faced and what we are likely to face. Please pay attention."

For the next few minutes, the generals listened to the young Earl's account and questioned him strongly. As his statement unfolded, all those present forged a greater respect for the young soldier. War was not unknown in the history of Maingard but for the last century most wars were small actions, border disputes and raids. The horrors of total war had not been experienced in Maingard since the destruction of Keln by one of Anjoan's ancestors a century ago.

Bryn told of the appearance of the dragon ships and the rain of destruction that they had spewed down onto the city below. He told of the make-up of the enemy forces and of the tactics and strategy that they had employed. Finally, he spoke of his escape from Jacarna and his journey through the enemy scouts and forces that had operated in the forests around the Jewel of the East trying to ensure that no one escaped. As Bryn spoke, several minor lords approached Magus Vent, handing him pieces of paper which he studied in detail scanning every word and letter as if he expected his prey to jump out of the ink. He still seemed to never miss a word that Bryn said, often interrupting him with a question as he read.

'The Marshall will question you soon, Bex. You might want to let me answer him' the Qoi warrior spoke.

'How can I do that?'

'Just relax. Don't fight.'

"Thank you, Earl Kar. Please be seated." The Marshall indicated that Bryn Kar's debriefing had finished. Bryn took a seat at the table and turned to look at Bex, she stood there suddenly feeling very alone. A steward walked forward and handed the Earl a goblet of wine. She stared at them all, her eyes settling on each one in turn.

"And now, young lady," The Hawk addressed her. "Who are you and what part do you play in this? How did you manage to escape Jacarna?"

"I am Bex of Samak, a trader." She lied easily; at times she called herself trader, bodyguard, adventurer or even pilgrim, but never what she really did. However, lying about who she was and what she did was easy, she had done it a thousand times. An answer to the other questions would be more difficult.

"Go on, girl." The Queen softly urged her on.

'Go on, Bex. Tell them what has happened and tell them my message.' Ishtara soothed her as well. *'I will speak when I need to.'*

"Your Majesty, Marshall and Gentlemen, I never escaped from Jacarna. I have never been there." At that point, the Hawk leant in more, eying her even more closely than he had done before. "Last night I was outside the City, to the north."

She saw surprise and fear in some of the Lords' eyes and realised that they thought the invaders were much closer than they had thought.

"There I met a creature who told me she had fled her world when the invaders, these Cassalians, had come there. It was she who told me about them and that she had come here to warn this world." The lords seated about the table broke out in muttering ranging from disbelief to utter indignation. She felt Ishtara smart at the term 'creature' and silently enquired whether she would prefer the term 'demon' instead.

"Absurd!"

"Does she take us for fools?"

The muttering rose to a chorus of discontent which was silenced by Queen Sarsi.

"Gentlemen!"

Slowly the chorus quietened until there was only one dissenter, Lord Kreft.

"Total madness! First a sergeant who is an Earl, and now this. I suppose you will tell us all that this girl is actually a general?"

"Anyone can see that she isn't, Lord Kreft." The new voice cut into the proceedings and Bex turned to see who it was. Striding through the throne room with a small entourage at his back was a small wiry man, shorter to Bex by quite a few inches. His blond, wavy locks framed a non-descript face. Bex couldn't tell whether he was older or younger than her. He was dressed in black riding boots and leather trews, and a loose, white silk shirt that was open at the neck. A sword hung at his waist. He strode with an air of arrogance and disdain past the table of assorted military officials. Bex heard the scraping of chairs as the generals at the table rose to attention.

"Mother," he greeted the Queen with a slight bow, and then acknowledged the Lords and generals, and then Marshall Vent, "Gentlemen, Marshall Vent." He moved to the Queen's side and knelt taking her hand in his and touching it to his lips.

"Mother, I am sorry for your loss, the kingdom's loss and mine. I take it my father has been moved to a more private location?"

"Yes, Garlen. He has."

So, this was Prince Garlen, Bex thought. She had obviously heard of him since she had arrived in Tannaheim but had never seen him. His antics were the subject of gossip throughout the city – duels, womanising and partying to excess – and gave rise to a cruel nickname whispered behind his back; The Lord of the Inns. Though much of these were probably exaggerated, what was well known was his estranged relationship with his parents. Since the death of his twin sister, Princess Antht, he had rebelled. The young Prince Garlen seemed to antagonize his father and mother by doing everything that wasn't expected of him. His love of the throne and royalty extended to only those aspects that promoted his lifestyle. Riches, reputation and the knowledge that the Crown would influence or buy the silence of anyone he had offended.

'And now he will be King?' Ishtara had been quiet for some time but now spoke to Bex.

'Yes, Lineage is passed down the male line here on Maingard.'

'Hmmmm' Ishtara harrumphed.

They both looked on as Garlen turned to survey the room, then turned his attention to the vacant throne upon which his father had recently sat. He grimaced with disdain and Bex wasn't sure whether he was imagining the recent events or despised the office into which he was now prematurely thrust.

"Marshall, what have I missed?"

"Earl Kar, Your Majesty," the Hawk gestured towards the still standing soldier from Jarcarna, "has told us of the attack on his city and also the city of Tarim. It appears that the invaders are from another plane. This lady was about to give her brief."

Prince Garlen sat at the head of the table and indicated to one of the companions who had arrived with him. Two of his guards stood behind him, they were in similar armour to the palace guards but whereas the palace guard looked bright and magnificent in their red plate, the plate of Garlen's guards were a dull, dark grey.

"This seems a good time for some wine," he looked about the table. "Or is it too early for you gentlemen?"

His steward stepped forward, placing a goblet of red wine in front of him, and then retired to the side of the throne room.

"You may well need it, Your Majesty," Lord Kreft looked across to the young Prince. "The Samakan woman was telling us of a refugee from another world who came to warn us. A creature that is nowhere to be seen" and laughed heartedly, his face ruddy and bloated. A few of the other lords laughed and it was evident that some were still in denial over the strength of the invasion and believed that other worlds and planes did not exist, despite Earl Kar's statement.

She could sense they were all staring at her now, but the Hawk seemed to take more notice, staring deep into her eyes, intrigued and inquisitive.

"The creature is before you now, Lord Kreft. You really should open your mind and eyes." The words came from Bex's mouth, but the voice was Ishtara's. Bex started to feel the same sensation as she had in Yab M'vil's villa, but not as intense or as painful. The whole room seemed to jump as Ishtara started to take over Bex's form. Several lords leapt back, nearly overturning their chairs, and several shouted in surprise, invoking various oaths and gods. Two guards jumped forward with their swords drawn.

Whilst only Prince Garlen seemed unmoved, Bex had the satisfaction of bringing a look of astonishment to even the Hawk's normally impassive face.

"Guards, wait! Leave her!" Queen Sarsi stood tall and shouted, her voice commanding and loud. The two soldiers stood immobile, their gaze not moving from her. "She did come here to warn us, after all. I would like to hear what she has to say."

Bex looked down to her hands, and noted the change was not as severe as Ishtara's previous manifestation. Her skin was bright red like a cooked lobster and not the appearance of swirling, molten lava that had happened before.

'Relax, there is no need to scare them even more with my full form. This seems to be a cross between both of our looks.'

"Thank you, Your Majesty." Bex/Ishtara bowed slightly to the Queen. "I am Ishtara, you will do well to listen to what I have to say. Earl Kar has spoken and some of you believe him, but I still sense you are under the impression that this force is from your world, a force you have been unaware of. You are wrong.

"My world was taken by them, my people enslaved. This is happening now at Bryn Kar's city. They will come here and do the same to your city, your people."

"Lady Ishtara, I am sorry about your people, your family and I am grateful that you have come here to warn us. What can you tell us about how they work, how they fight?" Queen Sarsi broke in. Marshall Vent moved forward, resting his hands on the guards' shoulders and indicated that they should step back and put up their swords.

"Their sorcerers have the power to cross the planes, their ships can fly; how I do not know. Bryn Kar has told you how they fight and what weapons they have. When they have devastated one city or one nation they will consolidate and enslave the population. The strong from those left become part of their army; the rest go to the misery of the slave pits. Rulers who become vassals to their cause are just puppets to them, a figurehead for the slave army to look up to. Behind them will be a Cassalian Lord poisoning their mind and their soul until they become no more use to them."

She turned and looked at the young Earl from Jarcarna.

"Earl Kar, I know it is little consolation, but if your father died in the initial assault then he would be one of the lucky ones." She froze momentarily when she saw the pain her words caused.

"How do we fight them?" Prince Garlen rose, placing his hands wide on the table in front of him. Despite his opposition to the role of royalty he found himself into, he seemed to realise the seriousness of the situation. His rule as King of the Western Kingdoms could be not only the shortest of his family's line, but also the last. "Can we fight them?" He added.

"I don't know. I spent several weeks hiding near them. I have seen eight or nine races within their 'Chosen Ones', which is how they call their vassal forces. They don't talk of defeats, which may be because they have never been defeated or it may be because they don't talk about failures."

"How much time do we have?" The Hawk spoke.

"Again, I don't know. They have two cities to subdue and the outlying lands. They will then start to offer vassal status to nearby nations, and then they will make another example of a city if they need to."

"Your Majesty, shall I prepare the city forces?" one of the lords stood and addressed Garlen. The young prince stood, forcing the other generals to stand to acknowledge him.

"Mother, Gentlemen, Marshall. I wish to spend a few moments with my father and then I will give my reply. Thank you." He waved his companions away as they went to join him. "I wish to be alone." He bowed slightly to his mother before leaving the room.

'*Well that seemed to go well,*' Ishtara spoke to Bex.

'*It did look a bit hairy to start off with. You could have warned me that you were going to scare them to death!*'

'*I think they needed the shock.*' Bex could feel her smile.

As the heavy doors shut behind the Prince, a low murmur started amongst the nobles around the table. Sarsi sank back in her throne and Bex felt for her. She had seemed to have aged several years in the few hours that Bex had been in her company.

'*She has further to go, Bex. It will be a long journey to rid your world of these murderers.*'

'*I know, Ishtara,*' Bex answered.

28

Narbek cursed everything, long and low under his breath. He sat in his wagon awaiting entrance to the Palace compound. The two guards on gate duty at the southernmost gate were taking their time with the wagon ahead. The merchant on that wagon, a grey-haired man in his early sixties, had had the temerity, no – Narbek thought – the audacity to take his daughter with him today. Now the guards were doing what soldiers all over Maingard would have done. Flirt with the young lady.

Not that she was young, Narbek thought. Or even a lady. She was thirty at a guess, short and plump with a plain face. He smiled to himself, forgetting the urgency of his mission and the wrath of the stranger should he fail. I bet that as soon as she has settled the old fool into bed that night, she would be down here to meet those same guardsmen, maybe here or maybe in one of the inns that were often frequented by the off-duty palace guard.

He frowned again, remembering the time and the task at hand. He must have jerked the reins of the big black shire in his reverie because she snorted and trotted forward a few steps before stopping, noticing that there was nowhere to go due to the wagon ahead. The mare whinnied and snorted again.

One of the guards turned to look at him and shouted.

"Be patient, darkie." Narbek wasn't sure whether the guard was speaking to him or his horse. He presumed the first, as it was true that his mother had had some Theshian in her which had given him his swarthy appearance, but he could be wrong. The horse's impatience had seemed to work though. The guard strode past the old man's wagon down to Narbek's. His partner said something to the old merchant that Narbek couldn't hear but which brought a torrent of giggles from the daughter who received a sly grope on her backside that spilled over the small wagon seat for her troubles. The guard motioned the wagon off and paced the few yards to Narbek's wagon.

A few hours earlier he had waited patiently at the courtyard down the small alley off Coin Street as ordered by the stranger. The buildings were old stone and very worn. A few of the tiles had slipped from the roof and lay smashed to one side. A pair of oaken doors split the monotony of the windowless stone wall. At exactly three bells to midday, the strange old man had appeared with what must have been the biggest man Narbek had ever seen.

The blond giant was over seven feet tall, maybe nearer to eight, Narbek judged. But it was the sheer size of him that caused Narbek to gaze momentarily in awe. A decade ago, he had seen the legendary knight Ser Callom of the House Galon as he left the city for his self-imposed exile. Ser Callom had been a giant of a man himself, able to wield a sword that most men couldn't even lift. But this man who accompanied the stranger was even bigger. The bear skin jerkin he wore left his arms bare, and his biceps bulged obscenely. Around his neck was an iron collar, several inches tall, that Narbek thought could fit him as a belt.

Brant walked to the wagon that Narbek was waiting with.

He slowly circled the four wheeled cart, taking care not to get too close to the black horse that was buckled between the long shafts. After a few seconds of deliberation, he spoke to Narbek.

"This is the wagon that you spoke about?"

"Yes." Narbek replied, jumping down from the seat. Nimbly he skipped to the rear of the wagon and reached into the empty cargo area. Hooking his finger into a small knothole in the wooden base he lifted part of the cargo floor to reveal a shallow compartment hidden away. The area was just big enough for one or two adults to lie flat.

"Is this big enough?" the smuggler asked Brant. The grey cloaked man nodded. He turned and made a gesture to the giant. The huge man strode silently to the doors in the courtyard and pulled them open, a squeak from the rusty hinges breaking the air. He shuffled inside the barns and came out carrying two wooden kegs under his immense arms and loaded them into the wagon. Narbek and Brant watched silently as he returned for more. As the giant loaded another two into the back of the wagon, Brant glared at the smuggler.

"Time is of essence. Help him."

The smuggler looked down at the kegs judging their weight. He knew he wouldn't be able to carry two at a time like the giant.

"You don't keep a dog and bark yourself. Your man looks like he can handle these on his own."

"He can, but time is of essence," he repeated, his eyes seemed to burrow into Narbek's head. "And I have two dogs. . . ."

Groaning, Narbek followed the giant into the barn and saw the stack of kegs that needed loading. He wasn't cut out for this sort of work, but a thousand crowns would make it worthwhile. Narbek wasn't sure whether the mute giant was appreciative of his help but between them they managed to get the wagon loaded. As Narbek clipped the tailgate into place he summoned up the courage to ask the question that had been burning his mind since the stranger had started to formulate his plan.

"Why do you need me? Why don't you smuggle them out of the palace yourself, out the same way that you are going in?"

"It is not as easy as that, Narbek." How could Brant explain to this lowlife the power of the Emperor, more importantly why should he? It was possibly beyond the comprehension of these inferior animals. How could he explain the energy required to move unseen, to cloud everyone's mind and to search for new minds to block as you move? Brant was one of the most senior of the Adept Sinister, the Emperor's mages but even he would not trust his power to try to pass unseen from an enemy's stronghold with an unwilling hostage, yet alone two. He decided against an explanation.

"I must go, time. . ."

"I know. Time is of essence." Narbek sighed and completed his sentence for him.

"Be on time, Narbek. I hope I don't have to provide threats to illustrate my point of how important timing is for this mission."

The grey cloaked man swept away, the cloak billowing as he moved. As he entered the passageway that led out to the alley he seemed to blur and Narbek strained to focus on him as he disappeared from view right in the middle of the alley. Narbek had waited half an hour as they had planned and had then mounted the wagon, pushing the horse on and through the courtyard to the alley beyond.

Now he sat at the eastern most gate of the palace, a gateway gaping like an open mouth that led across the twin draw-bridges to the tower beyond. This was not the same gateway that Bryn Kar and Bex had passed through earlier but the entranceway that was more commonly used, due to its prox-imity to East Street, by merchants delivering stores to the royal household. Now that the old man and his daughter had driven their wagon through the gate, the guards turned their attention to him.

The guard to the left of Narbek poked about in the back of the wagon, using a short stave to poke between the barrels. The other had a wistful look in his eye as he glanced back over his shoulder at the wagon now trundling over the thick and heavy wooden drawbridge.

Narbek started to fret inside and hoped that any worry wouldn't show to either guard. After all, smuggling himself into a heavily fortified palace was not something he would normally do. The second guard had torn himself away from his lusty daydream of the merchant's daughter and he now turned his gaze upon Narbek and his wagon.

"What are you carrying?"

The smuggler fought the urge to answer cockily and instead turned to survey the contents of the cargo area of his wagon.

"Wine, forty kegs for the palace kitchens. From Saret's." He added the name of one of the more celebrated wine merchants of Tannaheim. The guard pretended to check an invisible roster.

"It says here thirtynine only, can you drop the extra one off at the barracks?" he said, grinning.

"I wish I could, friend, I wish I could."

"I know, it was worth a try."

"I tell you something, my friend," Narbek continued, gaining confidence with every second as he was now aware that neither guard had any excuse to disbelieve the cover story that Brant and himself had conjured up. "I started with Saret's last week. It is my first time here. Next time, I will see what I can bring."

The guard that had checked the cargo had circled the entire wagon and now stood at the shoulder of his colleague.

"You said you were from Saret's?" there was a hint of suspicion in his voice.

"That's right, started there last week."

"Saret didn't say anything about another delivery when he delivered earlier."

Narbek cursed inwardly but shrugged his shoulders and spread his hands as he replied.

"I'm only doing what I am told, Sers. I don't know about that. I suppose it is going to be a big feast?"

"Come on Faolder, there is only wine on that wagon, let him go." The first guard patted his comrade on the shoulder and turned back to the gatehouse. Muttering under his breath, Faolder waved Narbek on.

Breathing a sigh of relief, Narbek shook the reins and drove off. The great drawbridge groaned and creaked as the wagon crawled over it. Narbek tried not to look down as his horse led him over the chasm to the palace grounds ahead. He passed through the twin gatehouse and entered into the palace grounds properly. The stone towers soared away to the clouds ahead of him and at the base of the grey fortress and of the concentric walls that circled the promontory, sat ugly squat buildings that formed the service part of the palace. Kitchens, stores and stables all seemed to spawn from the very walls themselves.

Following the directions given by Brant he found one of the furthest most buildings and was grateful to find the area deserted. It was little more than a lean to and had a small low wall near it that would allow some cover for the wagon whilst he waited. Pulling the wagon to next to it he dismounted and pushed open the single door and looked inside. It was evident that it was not often used, and he smiled, maybe the old coot wasn't mad after all.

29

A forceful pounding on the door brought Master Tarnal's room to a fragile silence. Ser Stahl, the guardsman who had accompanied Lord Shuy now looked at him, as if asking for directions. With a slight nod of the head, the Cripple instructed the guardsman to the door. As Stahl stepped towards the door, Lord Shuy looked about the room. The two princesses were aware of the tension emanating from the newcomers to the room and Ingren held her younger sister as if to comfort her. The two young Lords, Dirian and Klush, looked subdued for the moment.

"Identify yourself!" the guardsman ordered the hidden knocker on the other side of the door.

"Captain Murf, under orders to meet with Lord Shuy," came the muffled reply. The guardsman stretched for the door and softly released the handle. Something clicked in Shuy's head. The door guard! Where was the door guard? He should have announced the arrival of Capitan Murf, not the captain himself! He had thought the Queen was chasing shadows with her orders to return her daughters to their rooms but maybe she was right. He called out to the guardsman as he drew his own sword, a thin blade held stubbornly but uselessly in his left hand.

"Guard! Your sword, they are imposters!"

Before the Stahl could react, the door burst inwards and the four counterfeit King's Guards pushed their way in. The solitary guardsman stood no chance, his own sword only half drawn as he fell to a flurry of blows from two of the imposters. The room exploded into a cacophony of noise. The two princesses screamed at once at the shock of the intrusion and the sight of a man viciously hacked down in front of them. The leader of the four assailants pointed his blade at Valon Shuy, snarling as he spat out his ultimatum.

"We've come for the princesses. Give them up or die!"

A thousand thoughts seemed to cascade through Valon Shuy's head but giving up the two young children of his queen was not one of them. He wondered whether he could hold off the attackers until help arrived, if indeed it did arrive. He knew that this was his last day alive; there was no way that the four men would let any of them live even if the princesses were handed over. He wondered whether his wife would grieve for a respectable period and whether Queen Sarsi would honour him for laying down his life, or if he would be remembered as being the one responsible for losing Princess Ingren and Moren.

The Cripple stalled for time, silently hoping that help would arrive.

"You must be mad! This is one of the most fortified palaces in the whole of Maingard and you think that you will get away with this? There is no way that you will get over the bridges and away into the city!" He motioned to the children to keep behind him as he raised his blade to point back at the fake captain. The tips of the two swords wavered closely to each other, a row of desks helping to keep the two antagonists apart.

The two attackers who had killed Ser Stahl stepped over his

inert body to line up with 'Captain Murf' and his compatriot. Blood dripped from their swords and Lord Shuy could see small splatters of Ser Stahl's blood on the face of one of them.

"We got magic on our side, dark magic that would scare even the witch queen herself." The leader of the assailants answered Lord Shuy in a matter of fact tone although Shuy detected a slight trepidation in his words. They were afraid of something or someone. Perhaps he could play on their fears in order to delay the inevitable.

"He will kill you; you do know that. Even shit loving scum like you know when you are dispensable, don't you? Once you are out of here, your employer will put you to the sword. . ."

"I say we kill them all now, take the whores and throw them to the grey cloak." The guard with the blood of Stahl upon his face muttered loudly.

The young Lord Klush Dantice broke, shrieking as he grabbed Moren and moved to push her in front of Lord Shuy, his own voice adding to the discord in the room. As Dirian tried to calm his brother, Master Tarnal struck. No one in the room had been paying attention to the old man. A tutor to the Royal household for nigh on thirty years, Tarnal was old. His grey balding pate, long beard and slightly doddery gait gave lie to the fact that in his past he had once been a competent warrior. Having served in the King's Guard during the reigns of Anjoan's grandfather, Hanjoan II and Anjoan's father, Drajen III, he had left the military life after a difficult mission to rescue an abducted duchess from brigands in the borderlands. Some say it was the horrors that he had seen on that quest that drove him to sheathing his sword forever, whilst others say it was the abhorrent actions he himself had to carry out in order to save the young lady that made him retire.

Now he returned to days of his youth and middle age. How dare these upstarts come into *his* domain, *his* classroom, and make their reprehensible demands. He may not have wielded a sword in anger since before any of the intruders had been born but, in his day, he would have sent all four to their graves before they knew what had hit them. Aware that they thought he wasn't a threat, he had slowly inched his hand across the desk in front of him. Finally, his hand had come to rest on the cane that he sometimes disciplined his students with. It wasn't the best weapon for the circumstances but all he needed to do was gain a few moments so that the real King's Guard could arrive, and maybe offer a diversion for Lord Shuy to act upon. His gaze never left his intended target, the bandit whose face was flecked with the blood of Ser Stahl. Only his fingers moved as he slowly flexed his old, aching fingers around the thin wood.

Tarnal's grey eyes had already sought out the weakness in the would-be abductor in front of him. He had left his cheek pieces to his red helm untied so that they flapped backwards like so many soldiers when they weren't on full duty. The large strap that reached under their chin that normally held the two cheek pieces together also offered protection for the throat when secured properly. Left open, like the attacker's helm, it offered no protection at all and obviously the thug in front of him now clearly did not expect opposition to his impudent demands. Tarnal's martial mind slipped back thirty years and noticed how sloppy the thug had been in trying to pass himself off as a guardsman. The unsecured helm was only part of his failure at disguise, his mailed gloves hung at his belt and his cloak was also secured with the pin badge insignia facing the wrong way.

Like a cobra's strike, Master Tarnal lashed out. The thin cane whipped through the air at breakneck speed. The switch cut deep into the soft skin, ripping into the man's airway. He coughed and spluttered as his vocal cords were cut in two by the vicious penetration of the cane, his expletives cut short. Sinking to his knees, he held his hand up to his ravaged throat, his eyes wide in shock and surprise.

"Impudent scum! Keep your vile hands and your disgusting words to yourself!" the elderly tutor spat the words out.

It was just the diversion that Valon Shuy was waiting for. He lunged forward, the thin blade of his short rapier-like sword thrusting forward to impale his opponent. His opponent though, standing opposite him in the guise of a King's Guardsman was more than equal to Lord Shuy's attack. A veteran of many underground blade fights, Murf was not going to be killed by a onehanded cripple. His own blade came up and across in front of him as he heard one of his compatriots scream at Tarnal. The flat of the blade struck Shuy's forearm, pushing his attack slightly offline. Shuy watched as the point of his sword flashed past Murf's face and he silently eyed the edge of his attacker's sword now started its inevitable path towards him.

Out of the corner of one eye, he caught a glimpse of one of the attackers pounding Master Tarnal repeatedly in the face with a mailed fist, the old man's robe bunched into the grip of the attacker's other hand. The greyness of the elderly knight's beard was nearly covered by his blood that flowed from his broken nose and tortured mouth. Still the old man fought on though, the whip of the cane landing ineffectively on the red armour of his murderer. Tarnal's strikes were getting weaker and weaker as the old tutor was hit again and again. Lord Shuy looked past the blurred edge of Murf's blade as it swept towards him to see the third attacker swing a heavy blow down on the back of Lord Klush as he ran for the door. All around Shuy was noise, screams and shouts of expletives as the attackers carried out their grim task. Finally, he turned towards Moren and Ingren, his eyes fixed upon them as he died knowing that he had let them down.

30

Rothannir, one-time princess of the proud city of Jacarna, lay in a crumpled heap on the floor of the chamber that had once been her mother and father's. A thick chain attached to a cuff around the ankle on her good leg was secured to one of the thick legs of the bed that was the centrepiece of the room. Anyone laying eyes on her now would have struggled to recognize the royal bloodline that coursed through her veins. Her broken leg was wrapped in dirty bandages, blood and pus seeping through the stained linen and whilst the leg had been strapped in splints it was evident that the bone had not been set properly beforehand. Not that it mattered the young princess, she would be dead before the wound healed. That she knew and she prayed to Tomnar every second, that her end be quickened and then she would be free to run with her family in the afterlife.

Her long blonde hair had been hacked short and the haggard remains were matted with blood and grime. Naked apart from the crude bandage that adorned her shattered leg, she was covered in bruises and bites.

Her sisters, Rentanne and Ramene, were both dead. That

she knew also as the giant monster that had killed her father in front of her and had thrown her little sisters to the ravening hordes made sure he told her each time he raped her. It was her sisters, especially young Rentanne, who she wept for. The young, innocent Rentanne, in her eyes, symbolised the people of Jacarna and Tarim – all devastated and destroyed by the invading hordes. Karchek also took great delight in telling her what the crews of the two dragon ships would have done to the beautiful, young and unsullied women before and after they had died.

At first, she had fought like she had in the throne room, striking and scratching as he held her down but as the days and nights had gone by, she struggled less and less as if accepting her fate. Even the comments about her sisters and parents left her seemingly unmoved.

The figure of the old woman hobbled to her side. Narki the Hag, Karchek called her. She had come with the invaders and seemed to hold a position of some power amongst the Cassalians. Rothannir had seen how many of the commanders of the enemy vessels held her in some form of reverence as if she was a matriarch, yet Karchek swore and abused her at every chance. Narki now knelt next to her and raised a small cup of water to her lips. The coldness of the water made her jump, memories of a more peaceful time jumping to the front of her mind before the dark realisation of her plight slapped her in the face.

She tried hard to distinguish Narki's features as the robe of the old woman was pulled up over her head obscuring most of her face. What skin she could see was dark and gnarled, gnarled like an old oak tree that had stood for centuries. She nodded in thanks to the old woman, the briefest of nods as any movement made her pain wracked body ache. When she spoke, her lips hardly moved and the sound of her voice was hard and rasping, surprising herself at how different she sounded.

"Let me die, hag. Let me die."

Narki the Hag lowered her hands slowly and gave a small chuckle that Rothannir had come to hate as much over the last week as the sound of Karchek's voice.

"He has need of you, girl. Your death is not yet, but I am sure it won't be long before he sends you on your way." Narki still crouched down next to the crippled princess. Rothannir wasn't sure who smelt worse. The pus oozing from her wound on her leg reeked enough without the addition of the waste of her own body as she was unable to clean herself. But the old hag stank of death and decay, a stench that possibly overpowered even the repugnant state of her own body. Narki chuckled again and carried on.

"It won't be the end of your suffering, girl. Oh no. He will replace you, one from the slave pen, no doubt. But he will keep you as well. He will give your broken and used body no respite. He will fuck you in death as much as now. And when you finally rot away, he will keep parts of you." She chuckled again, longer this time as she saw the look of horror on Rothannir's face. The horrible cackle rattled to a stop as the hag noticed the steely resistance return to the young woman's eyes.

"Go away, Hag! Keep your filthy hands to yourself and crawl away and die." Though the Princess never raised her voice above a whisper, there was no way that Narki failed to note the determination in her voice. "And when you do die, I hope your bones are trodden down into the earth like the body of a beetle and whatever soul you have flits from sanctuary to sanctuary, never to rest. May even Jarm shun you like the filthy bitch you are!" She gathered up the phlegm in her mouth and hawked a glob of spittle at the hag only to feel even more disappointed when the bubbly sputum land only on Narki's robe.

Rothannir's outburst sparked the hag into life and she

danced backwards out of the way of Rothannir's grasp. She cackled once again and hitched her robe up to reveal her nakedness underneath. She arched her back as she urinated, a stream of acrid, yellow piss splashed down on the outstretched arm of the princess, who recoiled in disgust.

"Piss on the whore, piss on the whore," the old hag sang out, her voice hoarse and grating. Rothannir tried to push herself back but Narki followed, arcing the stream on to the poor girl. When she had done, she spat back at the princess, the aim of the old woman much better than Rothannir, as the glob of spittle landed on the stricken girl's cheek.

Rothannir lay still, only the movement of her chest as she sobbed gave any indication of whether the princess lived or not. Face down on the floor, she listened as the cackle of the old woman disappeared. She lay still for what seemed like minutes but when she next looked up she could see that the sun had started to rise, its feeble rays had invaded the chamber yet barely had enough energy to warm her aching skin as it rose in the sky. Rothannir let out a low groan, knowing that Karchek would be returning soon. He had made it his routine to see her after his morning briefings with his commanders. He would then inspect certain parts of the city himself, speaking to the troops in the field, before retiring late at night to use her again.

She turned to face the sun and noticed something gleam on the floor under a side table. The young princess focused her weary eyes on it and crawled towards it, her fingers reaching for the joints in the flagstones to give her weak body leverage. She made slow progress across the floor as if she was climbing the vertical wall of the outside of the palace.

As her eyes focused on it, the gleam took shape revealing a shattered crystal stem of a wine goblet. She remembered a few nights earlier when Karchek had received a message that had driven him furious. He had been drinking, like most nights, and was about to use her when then the knock on the chamber door interrupted him. The young page entered nervously and stammered whilst passing the note over to the huge general. Rothannir had recognized the young page as Farnan, a former member of the royal household. No doubt, she thought, that Karchek had kept many of the servants on after all due to their familiarity of the palace.

She had looked up to the baby-faced page imploringly, all too aware that he was completely powerless to help her. Their eyes had locked for a moment and he had reddened as he recognized her. She had been oblivious to the fact that she was broken and naked, now all too used to it.

Karchek had exploded madly after reading the message. He had sworn in many languages and had then thrown the goblet at Farnan, missing him by the closest of margins. He had turned and kicked out wildly at Rothannir catching her in the hip with his bare foot. Farnan had wisely backed away and turned and fled from the room, leaving his former princess to the mercy of the enraged giant. Karchek's appetite for Rothannir had been quelled and he had spent several more minutes pacing the room, screaming at the top of his voice and lashing out at her before dressing and leaving. The fact that she had avoided the humiliation of his lust seemed scant reward for the aches and pain that was left from the blows, and she had then fallen into an uneasy sleep.

She now crawled towards the shard, a plan for revenge forming quickly in her mind. The fetter about her ankle tautened, holding her fast and she stretched her arm out. Her fingers wavered agonisingly close and she extended her arm again, feeling the shackle cut into her skin as she reached out. Rothannir cried out as she pushed her body past its already broken limits. Still her fingertips were a sword's breadth away from the crystal.

The captive princess curled herself up and reached down to the chain that held her fast, all the time focusing past the pain from her broken leg. She tried vainly to pull with both hands on her shackle, knowing that even if she were fit and healthy, that she wouldn't be able to move the heavy bed or break the chain that held her. Sobbing uncontrollably, she collapsed, her head on the stone floor.

It was as her hand strayed down to her broken leg and touched the rude linen dressing that swathed her wound, that she realised that her body had failed her temporarily but not her mind. She pulled at some of the dressing until a length as long as her arm had come away. The pain intensified in her leg as she tugged on the linen and then tore it off crossways. Rothannir looped it in her hand so that it looked like a crude sling and once again reached out to the shard, but this time used the linen to drag it towards her. Finally, the crystal shard was in her grasp. It looked a little shorter in her hand than when she had first spied it but felt that it would do as a makeshift dagger. Rothannir, daughter of King Renta and of the line of Frentarn the Holy would have her revenge.

31

The battle had lasted mere seconds and what had once been a peaceful room of learning now resembled a charnel house. The two princesses knelt, their hands bound, and mouths gagged, their eyes wide with terror. The leader of the four attackers was crouched over the body of Master Tarnal, cleaning his blade on the teacher's robes whilst another stood over the two captive girls. The third stood by the door as he held it ajar, peering into the corridor. The final attacker sat slumped in a chair, blood still seeping from the wound on his neck that the elderly master had dealt him. His breaths were laboured, his chest rising and falling in a haphazard rhythm and his throat rattled.

"I don't like this. We need to get going now." The man who stood over the girls said aloud.

"Shut up!" Murf replied, standing up and making a move as if to sheath his sword. He thought better of it, not necessarily should any more guards stumble upon them but he felt the edginess in his colleague's voice. He had to control the situation.

"Someone is coming," hissed the man at the door only to

add before the others could react, "It's the grey cloak!" He stood back from the doorway, pulling the door open as Brant entered. The elderly but imposing figure of the old man surveyed the scene then nodded briefly before speaking.

"You have done well, Murf."

"You walked into the palace like that? You have more steel than others, Brant."

The old man sighed before replying.

"An Adept has ways of passing unseen or unnoticed. The minds of inferior species are easy to cloud." He walked over the slaughter, lifting the hem of his robe where necessary to avoid it getting soiled.

"We must leave, now! The Cripple said that he was to move the princesses back to their chambers when a guard detachment arrives." Murf shifted the grip on his sword and indicated the dead figure of Shuy as if to accentuate his point. Brant ignored him and stooped to inspect the princesses.

As he lowered his face to draw level with Moren, the young princess found that she was unable to avert her terrified eyes away from the piercing black gaze of the old man. Brant raised his hands to her gag, loosened it and lifted it over her head. Strands of her dark hair matted to her tearful, wet face.

"Tobes Tits! She'll bring the palace down upon us!" The guard who stood over them hissed loudly.

"Gags are so crude." Brant replied without turning and lifted his hand with fingers spread in front of Moren's face. He slowly closed his fingers until the tips of all met and whispered a word.

"*Slud*"

Moren felt an intense feeling of exhaustion overcome her and the room seemed to close in as her eyelids grew heavy and weak. She found it impossible to resist and slipped into a heavy slumber, her head bowing forward to rest on her chest. Brant turned to Ingren and noted the fire in her eyes.

"This one is different." His eyes pierced deep into Ingren's as his mind probed hers. Leaving the gag fixed in place, he placed his hand on her forehead and muttered another incantation.

"*Tinest intor duk.*"

There was a dull thud and Ingren collapsed backwards with a start, unconscious with her knees still folded under her. Brant stood and turned to the others handing them two large black sacks.

"They won't struggle or make a sound now. Now it is time to go." He seemed to notice the stricken figure of the fourth attacker for the first time. He motioned to the Murf that the princesses should be picked up and walked over to stand in front of the coughing thug.

"Yoris, Tanner. Take the girls." Murf stood next to Brant and kicked the dead body of Master Tarnal. "This old man had a bit more fight in him than we thought. Dannad took a blow to the throat. He'll be okay."

"He will hold us up. We have enough encumbrance with the princesses." Dannad looked first at Brant and then up to Murf. With a stricken look he understood what Brant was saying but tried to implore Murf to intervene. Had they not worked together for years? Murf stared at his friend, unmoved and silent.

Brant's blade appeared magically from his forearm sheath and speared deep into Dannad's chest. It penetrated his armour as if it was mere cloth and the invisible blade reached his heart. His eyes lowered and a look of shock appeared stiltedly as they took in the blood that seeped from the new wound in his chest. He coughed again, a cough that ended in a splutter as he passed into the next world.

Brant withdrew his hand and there was an almost inaudible shlurp as he pulled the mystic blade from Dannad. He stood and adjusted his robe.

"Now it is time to go." He repeated and made for the door.

32

Garlen returned to the throne room a quarter of an hour later. In that time Queen Sarsi had requested refreshment for Bex and Bryn Kar and the palace staff had brought in platters of freshly baked bread and hams. The generals had retired to talk between themselves so Bex and Bryn sat at the table in the centre of the throne room. Queen Sarsi perched herself on the chair next to Bex and waved her handmaidens away.

Bex studied her closely. By all accounts Queen Sarsi was nearly fifty years old and the years had not been too unkind to the monarch. She had a few crow's feet around her eyes and the odd blemish but other than that her skin belied a younger age than her physical age. Her vibrant red hair was offset by piercing green eyes, and her voice when she spoke conveyed the exact tone that every word deserved in a precise manner. Not once did she sound condescending or patronising.

"Earl Kar, I am dreadfully sorry what has befallen your people and city and I can only apologize that our walls here may not offer any greater protection to you. I thank you for your warning to us, as I am sure my husband would have been just as grateful." She turned to Bex who was suddenly all too aware that she was just a commoner in a room full of nobles.

"And many thanks to you and your... unique friend." She struggled to find the right word. "For what it is worth, I offer you my friendship and the eternal gratitude of the Crown."

'*Thank you, your Majesty.*' Ishtara replied in Bex's head who passed on the comments to the Queen.

At that point Prince Garlen entered the throne room. The guards at the door snapped to attention whilst Marshall Vent announced the new arrival.

"Your Majesty, Ladies and Gentlemen, I announce His Royal Highness, King Garlen!"

The Queen looked on, a slight smile of pride showing on her face despite the circumstances of her son's promotion. The young Lord however, looked solemn and pensive.

"Thank you as ever, My Lord Marshall, however there is no need for that title. I have decided against accepting the normal line of succession. The Western Kingdoms, if not the whole of Maingard, face a terrible and uncertain future. What the Western Kingdoms need now is stability and experience. Because of that, I will bow down to my mother and acknowledge her, Queen Sarsi, to become absolute ruler of the Danaria. I doubt that she will need it as I know for sure that behind the Crown of my father, she made many important decisions on his behalf, but she will always have the guidance and support of Marshall Vent.

"My place will be with the forces of the Western Kingdoms, in order to prepare defences against the invaders." A hum of excitement and wonder circulated the throne room at Prince Garlen's announcement. He took himself to one side and sought the company of his mother who hugged him. Bex wasn't sure but she thought she could see both shed a tear. Marshall Vent gave them a moment or two and then walked towards them, bowing as he approached. The three whispered amongst themselves with Bex and Bryn only catching snippets of the conversation. After a moment Marshall Vent stepped forward and addressed the court.

"Ser Duncarn!" A bald, older man stepped forward that Bex recognised from those who had sat around the table listening to her and Bryn Kar's debriefing. He wore the black leather armour of the marines except that gold braids were woven across the hardened leather breast of his cuirass.

"Marshall, Your Majesties." He bowed lowering the bald pate of his head towards Vent and then slowly stood ramrod straight. Bex likened the way he stood waiting for Vent to reply to a loyal dog waiting for his master's approval.

"Duncarn, we currently have the Third and Fourth Squadrons stationed at or on their way to the Isle of Winds. We need to get them back here ready to meet any threat from the invaders."

"Certainly, Marshall. I can have a light ship from the Fifth Squadron ready to leave tomorrow. It should make the Isles in three days and may even catch Visney's Squadron before he docks."

"Three days to reach them. And then three or four to return. How will that leave our defences here, Marshall?" asked Queen Sarsi.

"It seems unlikely that the cassalians will attack by sea due to their own flying ships. But Visney's marines will add another three hundred swords and the Third will add another three hundred."

"Can we afford to wait that long?"

A fair-haired nobleman stepped forward to stand next to the Admiral. Count Eglebon Dutte lowered his head slightly then spoke without waiting for Vent to acknowledge him.

"Marshall, Your Majesties, one of my own personal ships is about to sail for Marneheim right now. I could divert the ship to the Isle of Winds with orders for Visney and Neechy to return. It's a faster ship than the navy's light ships."

Queen Sarsi returned Dutte's bow with a slight nod of her head.

"Count Dutte, that is most kind. I shall see that a herald is ready for when your ship leaves. Can you please liaise with Marshall Vent?"

"Of course, Your Majesty." Dutte moved to Vent's left and spoke for several minutes before leaving the throne room.

"So, people aren't always what they seem?" Bex snapped out of her reverie to look up and see Bryn Kar.

"Indeed, Earl Kar." She countered back. "I met a lowly sergeant a few hours ago who gave me the advice that Kings and Queens and nobles are just the same as us. Now, it seems, that sergeant is in fact, one of them."

"I apologize for that, Bex of Samak. To be honest, I do not see myself as an Earl, even now. I disliked the backstabbing and gossip of the court and prefer the mostly straight forward barrack room life. Soldiers aren't afraid to say what they like or feel."

Bex reached out a hand and touched his forearm gently.

"I know, Earl Kar. I feel out of my depth here. I hate this probably as much as you do."

"Thank you, Bex. And please, no Earl. Call me Bryn or sergeant. That I can relate to. Earl is very redundant here as my father's lands are taken. As well as the fact that the old goat practically disinherited me when I joined the Black Serpents," he chuckled.

'You are quiet at the moment.' She asked Ishtara.

'I am remembering my people. All this talk is bringing the pain back.'

'You did come here to warn us. You must have known it would be painful.'

'Maybe. I didn't think about it.'

She became aware that Bryn was talking to her again. She looked inquisitively at him and he smiled and repeated himself.

"What happened to you? When you spoke to us all?"

"That was Ishtara, she lives inside of me, I suppose. We can let each other out, I think when we need to. I am not sure, though," she smiled.

"Ishtara lives inside of you?"

"Yes. It is a strange feeling and I am still getting used to it. I don't think either of us know what we can do together yet."

'That is true.' Giggled Ishtara.

"What is she like?" Bryn continued.

"Very nosey," laughed Bex.

"Nosey?"

'Nosey?' they both questioned at the same time.

"Yes, it appears we cannot have a separate conversation and she can root through my memories as well. That and our imaginations being linked. She is finding certain aspects of this world quite interesting."

A picture formed in Bex's imagination. Herself and Bryn were alone in the throne room. Sunlight cascading through the tall windows shone on their clothes strewn like footprints on the marble floor. The soldier's body was rough and muscular, and scarred in places. She flung her arms around his neck and he lifted her up, carrying her effortlessly to the table. As he let her down, her naked cheeks touching the polished oak, their lips met, pressing together urgently and passionately.

"Ishtara!" the thought came out loud, as well as screamed inside her head.

'Yes?'

'Stop that!'

'Oh,' replied the Qoi, *'that wasn't me.'*

Bex blushed profusely.

33

K archek opened the door to the chamber and strode in. His captive, the Princess Rothannir, was sobbing on the floor curled up in the foetal position, the chain on her ankle keeping her secured to the heavy bed. This morning he had met with the men who were tasked with patrolling the outskirts of the city and the subjugation of the outlying villages and farmsteads. He was quite pleased with the way the *knartevilder* was going; however, there was something that would annoy him later. This evening, he would receive the visit of Margran.

Margran was, in his eyes, a thug and an incompetent fool. But Margran was his equal in rank – a General and Lord Commander of the Emperor's Host. Margran commanded the forces that had dealt with Jacarna's sister city, Tarim. His forces were as numerous as Karchek's and that infuriated him. How the Emperor, in all his wisdom, could trust Margran with similar responsibility as Karchek was beyond him. Still, despite his incompetence, Margran garnered results. *Knartevilders* were completed and planets conquered and raped. They had commanded forces together on the last dozen world plunders and had come to an uneasy truce. This time Karchek was responsible for the lands west of Jacarna, whilst the small blue-skinned dwarf used his forces to subdue the lands east of the Twins.

He stripped of his armour leaving his chest bare whilst keeping his under trousers and boots on. He drank heavily from the flask of wine that sat on his bedside table and looked across at the crumpled form of Rothannir. Her leg was bleeding again, he noted from the fresh crimson patch that showed through the dirty linen. She was not long for this world, he thought but secretly admired her for the strength that she had shown. Many others would have given up long before now, letting their body slip into death rather than take the seemingly endless punishment.

He wanted her now. Karchek drained the flask and strode over to her, loosening the tie at the front of his under trousers. As he neared her, he pulled himself free of his garments, his member already reacting to his wants. He wanted her and was more than ready for her. Reaching down, he grabbed her hair and lifted her effortlessly. She made no attempt to grab his wrist or hand to alleviate the strain on her long hair and he thrust his left hand in between her legs.

Karchek was caught unawares by the speed of her attack and only just managed to turn his head in time. Her hand came up quickly and struck him in the face just over the eye. The shard of crystal carved through the flesh, striking bone, and the vision in his left eye went dark. A second later he felt his groin explode in agony as she drove the shard deep into his genital area.

"That's for my father and Jacarna, you pig!" she screamed as she attacked him, before her screams extended to naming her sisters in her revenge.

Karchek brought his left hand up to block her intended third blow and caught her slender wrist in his meaty fist. With a bellow of rage, he snapped her forearm in two, cutting her rant off in midstream. She screamed shrilly. With a flick of his right arm, he flung her away from him. Her trajectory was abruptly cut short as the chain around her ankle tautened with her still in mid-air and with a bone jarring crunch, Rothannir fell to the hard floor.

The Lord Commander of the Emperor's Host reached up to his torn eyebrow, wiping blood from his sight as he discovered the torn flap of skin that hung over his eye. He looked down at his groin and saw the puncture wound that sat near to the root of his penis. Blood coated his hand and dripped from his face wound, however, there didn't seem to be the same amount of flow from his lower wound. He turned his attention to Rothannir who lay shattered on the floor. The crystal had fallen from her grasp and she held her fractured arm in her good hand.

With a snarl he pounced on her, kicking her viciously in the stomach so hard that she was propelled off the floor. There was only a modicum of satisfaction as he heard one of her ribs' crack under the ferocity of his kick. Grabbing her hair again, he pulled her over onto all fours, her bad leg akimbo and her shattered wrist wavering tentatively over the floor as she tried to keep herself upright without using it. Her bottom protruded into the air because of her ungainly stance. Karchek knew that despite his wounds he was more than a match for the unarmed and heavily injured girl. He would show her one last time that he still owned her and held her fate in his hands despite her pitiful attempt to fight back.

He drove her face downwards towards the hard flagstones of the floor and cruelly manhandled her around to face away from him. Kneeling behind her, he thrust deep into her, bringing a yelp from her as she fought for breath. He reached forward and clasped his bloody hand onto her forehead, bringing it upwards and backwards, extending her throat. He thrust hard and mercilessly, ignoring the pitiful sounds that emanated from her tortured and raped body. At the point of his climax he reached round her face with his right hand and his mighty paw clenched the left side of her agonised features, obliterating her vision. As he came, he whipped his hand back, snapping her neck with one clean jerk that left her blood-stained face staring obscenely back over her shoulder.

Karchek stood and reached for a sheet to clean himself. He pressed the cold linen against his wound to staunch the seepage of blood. After a couple of presses, he tore part of the sheet off and wound it tight around his abdomen. He pulled his under trousers up and secured them over the crude bandage and then strode to the door of the chambers, shouting for his aide. As he stepped over the dead princess, he missed what could only be described as the beginnings of a wry smile on Rothannir's face.

34

Brant led the way down the dimly lit corridor, his flowing robe merging with the shadows cast by the torch carried by Murf. Yoris and Tanner followed with the sacks containing the inert princesses held over their shoulders. Murf brought up the rear, his hand gripping the pommel of his sheathed sword. He looked nervously about him as they marched deeper into the palace. The minute that had passed since they had left the scene of devastation in the school room seemed to have lasted an eternity and all three were relieved when Brant led them into a small room.

The room was empty except for a few crates lined along the back wall. Set into the centre of the floor was an iron grating which Brant crouched down at and lifted.

"Quickly, down!" and he indicated that his accomplices should climb down through the grating. Yoris lifted the sack off his shoulder and lowered it to the floor before peering down into the darkness. He looked enquiringly at Murf.

"You want to stay here in the palace? After kidnapping the princesses and murdering the King's nephews?" He lowered his torch over the hole and saw that the grating covered a small sewer like tunnel.

Yoris grunted and lowered himself through the hole before dropping from sight. From the flame of the torch the others could see Yoris's hands reaching up to take the princesses. Tanner handed the sacks down before following. As Brant made to descend, Murf grabbed his sleeve and hissed.

"Where does this lead to?"

"Under the courtyard to the outbuildings."

"How are we getting out of the palace?" Murf hissed again, his voice full of malice and apprehension.

"It is all in hand, now, do not touch me again if you value your life." Brant tore his arm away from Murf and dropped neatly through the hole.

Murf shook his head. There was something the old man was not telling him. He wasn't sure that the thousand crowns he was paying for their complicity in this crime was worth it. He had never believed in the old man's crusade or story of an impending invasion and a war to end all wars. Murf was, and always had been, a mercenary. Once he was out of the palace and had collected his fee, he would journey to the lands beyond the Eastern Ports and find employment there. No more crazy old men. He laid the torch on the floor near the edge of the hole and climbed through. Reaching up, he retrieved the torch and pulled the grating shut.

The tunnel below was a sewer, old and out of commission. A narrow path edged a narrower conduit that had barely a trickle of water in it. The other three waited along the wall of the tunnel that seemed to have been hewn out of the solid rock. Tanner held out a new torch towards Murf.

"We need another light."

Grunting an acknowledgement Murf held the tip of his lit torch against the tip of the new brand. It flared as it caught light and added its illumination to the gloom of the tunnel. Brant's face gave no indication of the altercation that had passed between them.

"Which way?"

"East." Brant smiled and indicated along the tunnel.

They took the same order as before with Brant leading and approximately five minutes later came to another open grating in the ceiling. Brant stood under it and softly whistled. He paused; ear cocked towards the opening. He whistled again, a little louder this time and sure enough a reply came.

"We go up here. Our way out of the palace waits above."

Yoris lowered his princess to the floor and reached up to the sides of the hole. As he pulled himself up, he met Narbek face to face. The swarthy face grinned at him and held out his hand to help him up. Grunting, Yoris reached out with his hand as his knee found the edge of the hole. As he propelled himself up with Narbek's help he found himself impaled on Narbek's dagger. The thin blade buried itself deep in Yoris's neck and the murderer of Lord Klush died silently with a surprised look on his face.

Oblivious to the killing of their compatriot, Murf and Tanner hefted one of the sacks up so that the top protruded through the aperture above. Narbek wiped the dagger on Yoris's cloak and then pulled the sacks up one by one as they appeared. Murf looked up at the hole and formed a stirrup with his hands, and nodded for Tanner to climb up. As Tanner lifted himself up to the opening above, Narbek and Brant struck together. The smuggler stabbed downwards into the face of the unsuspecting Tanner whilst Brant despatched Murf with his sword into his chest. Murf slumped to the floor with a knowing look on his face that seemed to tell Brant that he had always suspected the old man of treachery. Tanner struggled for a few seconds as he tried to ward off Narbek's repeated blows, but his grasp gave way and he crashed to the floor below.

Brant climbed up through the ceiling into the room above with surprising agility for an old man. Without a second glance to Narbek he walked to the door and looked out into the courtyard. He liked what he saw. The courtyard was empty except for a few of the palace staff and there was little evidence of any extra guards. It was this part of the plan that had always unsettled him, getting out of the palace without detection was always going to be risky. However, he had hoped that a suitable length of time would occur between the kidnapping and its discovery. He turned back to Narbek.

"Hurry! Grab the sacks and get them in your wagon. We must leave immediately."

Narbek paused from his task of tipping Yoris's body down the hole to the sewer below, with the upper half of the dead thug disappearing into the void below.

"As soon as we are at your contact, I get the remainder of my fee?" the thief enquired.

"Of course! And not before. We must be far from the gates of the city before the disappearance of the princesses is discovered." Narbek let go of Yoris's legs and the corpse thudded to the floor of the sewer below. Brant continued, "You will get your reward, Narbek. Don't you fret about that. Murf and his gang were expendable. They would never have the honour of true rogues."

'Rogues,' thought Narbek as he hefted one of the sacks onto his shoulder. Is that how he thinks of us? We have just carried out one of the most heinous crimes ever committed in Tannaheim and we are just 'rogues'? Bolam's Balls!

A minute or two later, with the sacks concealed in the secret compartment under the cargo bay of the wagon, Narbek and Brant made their way to the palace gate. Brant appeared asleep as they neared the gate, his hands in his lap and his eyes shut as the black horse pulled the wagon onwards.

"Shit!" Narbek hissed sideways.

Brant did not respond or even open his eyes.

"The gate guard has doubled! We've been discovered!"

"The gate guard has indeed been doubled, Narbek." Brant's voice was soft, as if he was speaking from far away. "They haven't discovered what we have done....yet. The guard is doubled because of something else." His mind, stretched almost to its limits in reaching out to those nearby and affecting what they saw so he literally disappeared from view, allowed him a glance of the school room from which they carried off the princesses. Seeing it untouched, his sub consciousness flittered about the palace.

"What shall we do?" Narbek spat the words through gritted teeth, a bead of sweat appearing on his brow as he thought of all the ways that Anjoan and the crown would take their revenge upon his body and mind.

"Just carry on. And shut up!" There! He had it, his mind saw a glimpse of the mighty frame of Anjoan lying on a bed. His arms folded across his chest and the look of agony etched upon his face.

'Dutte!' He had initially doubted the man as not having the nerve to carry out his plan, but the traitor had done well. He hoped that the Master of the Privy Council could now keep it. By now the wagon was upon the gate and two guards in chainmail and red surcoats stepped out in front of it. Narbek briefly wondered about urging the black horse on and crashing straight through but he knew it would be folly. He would rely on his mind and the gift of the gab which had always seen him through trouble in the past.

"Hold!" The guard was commanding and held his hand out, his other hand coming up and taking hold of the bridle of Narbek's horse. Narbek could see the guards were jumpy. Their hands held their weapons tight and their eyes jumped furtively from Narbek and the wagon to each other.

"What have you just delivered?" the guard demanded, his red hair sticking out from under his round helmet.

"Wine, from Saret's" Narbek replied, hoping that his voice didn't betray any lie or guilt.

"The wagon is empty." A third soldier shouted from the back and Narbek prayed to Tobe that they wouldn't look harder at the wagon.

"He's sweating. That's a sign of nervousness. He has something to hide." The guard was itching for confrontation and he took a step closer to the wagon.

"Of course I'm fucking sweating! I've just unloaded forty barrels by myself whilst that lazy toe rag in the stores just stood and watched. You'd sweat as well!" Narbek swallowed nervously despite the brash exterior. Something else had happened that had left all the guards on edge.

"The wagon is empty, Jordu." The third soldier shouted again. "Let him go! They have, after all, killed the assassins." Narbek's eyes widened ever so slightly. Assassins? Was that why the guards were on edge? Who had been killed? The redhaired guard snorted derisively.

"Were they working alone? We don't know." He didn't sound as sure as he had when he had first spoke.

The guard at the rear of the wagon now moved to where the other two soldiers stood. He had sheathed his sword and spoke softly to Red Hair. Narbek was only able to hear a few words but swore afterwards that he heard the words 'king' and 'dead'. Reluctantly Red Hair turned and stomped off to the guardhouse waving his hand impetuously.

"On you go." The remaining two guards stood back, allowing Narbek to drive his horse on over the drawbridge and out of the palace. With every fibre of his being, Narbek managed to control the urge to lash the reins and bring the long crop down hard on the rump of the black horse. Instead Narbek's wagon trundled to safety instead of careening over the drawbridge. The wily smuggler still expected a shout from the guards and nearly risked a look over his shoulder.

"Keep calm!" His heart jumped into his mouth as a disjointed voice hissed in his ear. In his terror he had forgotten about Brant. The blurry figure of the old man materialised next to him as he sprung back to mind.

"Keep facing forward and don't go any faster." Brant spoke again and looked over his shoulder at the gate. He turned and faced forward again and sighed. Narbek didn't say a word until they had turned out of sight of the palace and were heading towards the East Gate.

"Did you hear them?" he hissed sideways at the old man who sat still with his face screwed up in concentration as he tried to keep himself hidden in plain sight from others. He needn't had worried, life went on as usual in the busy city, the populace unaware of the assassination of their King and the threat of invasion and slavery that hung over them and took no notice of one of many wagons driving through the crowded streets. Merchants called out from stalls and shops at the side of the street, announcing their wares and prices and the sounds of children darting amongst the throng of people added to the cacophony. Smells of spices and cooking food mingled with the aroma of animals being driven to market.

"Did you hear them?" Narbek repeated.

"Yes." Brant replied matter of factly, hoping that the conversation would end there. It didn't.

"The king..... murdered!" Narbek spat out. The words being said aloud shocked him more than when they were just thoughts in his head.

"Fool! Keep quiet."

"Quiet!? Is this your doing?"

"No, no it is not!" Brant lied, just a little too crossly. Narbek's questioning was starting to annoy him and was also starting to draw attention from passers-by. It did seem to many that the wagon driver was speaking to himself. As Narbek opened his mouth to speak again, Brant grabbed his wrist. The coldness struck him numb. It was like the coldness when Brant had first met him in the Scalloper's Inn and this time the cold spread quickly outwards from the old man's grip. Narbek could feel his fingers stiffen as they turned blue and he saw his veins grow icy up his arm.

"Keep your mouth closed. Do not speak again until we are out of the city." There was no need for Brant to add a threat. The tone of his voice carried all the threat that was needed. Narbek closed his mouth and kept driving. As Brant released his grip, Narbek could feel a little warmth and feeling seep back into his arm.

35

The door to the throne room opened. Not the main doors to the exterior parts of the palace but one of the inner ones. Two newcomers stood at the open door whilst a palace guard, resplendent in his red armour, marched into the throne room towards Marshall Vent. All heads turned to see who had intervened on the solemn occasion. The Hawk, sensing urgency in the faces of the two and the pace of the guard walked across the throne room flagstones to meet him.

One of the pair was an elderly master, Master Smit, his creamy white robes hanging awkwardly. Bex noticed that the hem of the master's robe, although always slightly dirty from dragging across the dusty corridors, was flecked with scarlet. The old man was close to collapse, his face red from exertion and his hand was on the shoulder of the young maid who accompanied him. She wrung her hands and sobbed uncontrollably, tears running down her pale face and onto her plain grey dress.

As the Hawk spoke quietly with the guard, the maid ran forward to the base of the steps leading to the throne. There she stood looking more wretched. Bex started to make her way to her and was stopped in her tracks as the girl let out the most awful wail. The old master had trotted forward and now stood with the Hawk.

"Polian! Whatever is the matter?" Queen Sarsi swept down from the throne area from where she had been speaking with Garlen.

"Oh Mistress, they are gone! They are gone!" sobbed the unfortunate Polian.

"Please, Polian. Control yourself and calm down!" The Queen placed her hand on the maid's hand who wrenched it away, only to let out another dreadful wail. Marshall Vent, fresh from hearing the news from the elderly master, paced to the Queen's side and spoke softly.

"Your Majesty, it is grave news. There has been another attack," he paused, the look on his face evident that he wished that the day could not get any worse. He stammered on, struggling to get the horrific words out. "There has been another attack, at the school quarters. Lord Shuy and the two young Lords have been killed." The Queen went white. Garlen started down the steps towards his mother, shouting.

"What of my sisters, Marshall? What of my sisters?" one hand was already on the pommel of his sword as the other swept his blond hair out of his face. Bex felt for the hardened Marshall as he fought to speak.

"They are gone, Prince Garlen. They have been taken!"

'*It carries on, Bex*' Ishtara whispered in Bex's head.

Garlen shot off like a hound, indicating to his guards to follow. Bex and Bryn ran out with him, Bex pausing for a second to snatch her scabbarded sword from a guard. They ran at breakneck speed along corridors and down staircases keeping up with Garlen and the two guards who were with him. Neither Bryn nor Bex took any notice of what they passed but Bex could feel Ishtara making notes as they ran.

Finally, Garlen flung open a door in a wide corridor and

stood in the doorway surveying the scene that met his eyes. The others came to a halt behind him and Bex and Bryn looked past the Prince into the room. Bex had killed people and had seen people killed but the carnage inside the room shocked her. Even Bryn was aghast.

'By the All Giving Fire!' exclaimed Ishtara, her voice trembling inside Bex's head.

The furniture was overturned, the half dozen desks and chairs smashed and splintered to pieces. A palace guard lay dead on the floor with his neck snapped at a grotesque angle. The corpse of a King's guardsman was just inside the doorway in a pool of blood whilst another sat slumped in a chair, his throat a mess of bruising and welts and a puncture wound central in his red plate.

Garlen cautiously entered the room with one of his guards and Bex and Bryn behind him. Bex covered her mouth with her hand, trying not to look. They found Lord Valon Shuy dead with sword in hand, his right hand bent uselessly across his chest. Next to him were the bodies of the two young lords, their lives cut down before they had turned into men. Laid out on the master's desk was the worst sight of all. Master Tarnal's old body lay still on the large oaken desk, his grey robes nearly indistinguishable from the vast quantity of blood that had been spilt. His face was battered beyond recognition and his throat had been cut.

"Ingren! Moren!" Garlen shouted for his sisters, though he knew that they had gone.

'A Cassalian has been here.' Ishtara warned Bex who pictured the tall Qoi standing, sniffing the air about her.

'They stink, Bex. They reek of absolute evil.'

"Garlen, Ishtara says that a Cassalian has been here." Bex inched her way further into the room, her sword drawn.

'A proper Cassalian, not a Chosen One.'

"Not a turncoat or a traitor, but one of the true Cassalians."

"Whoever they were, they were well armed." Garlen's black garbed guard said. He pointed to the bodies of the dead soldiers and continued, "Strong enough to take out two of the King's Guard and another soldier."

Bex crouched down inspecting the body in the chair.

"Only one Guardsman. This is an imposter."

"Are you sure?" Garlen turned to her. She held Dannad's bare hand up indicating a blue sun tattoo on the webbing between his thumb and forefinger.

"Unless the King's Guard are now accepting applications from members of the Thieves' Guild? This tattoo shows he is a member of the Day Watch."

"So, they took them by surprise, poor sods." Bryn mourned sorrowfully.

The Prince knelt by the body of Valon Shuy and straightened the dead man's tunic. He looked up and saw Bryn watching him. He reached for Shuy's sword that had fallen from the lord's grasp when he had died, and placed it back in his hand.

"He was always impeccably dressed, Earl Kar. He was my mother's assistant for many years, before Ingren and Moren were even born." Even as he mentioned his sisters' names his demeanour changed. The wistful look was chased from his face by a determined, steely look and he stood up.

"Mayko," Garlen turned to the guard that had accompanied him into the room. "Get back to Marshall Vent – tell him to close the city and the palace. Shut the docks down as well. No-one leaves Tannaheim unless I say so. And then raise Col and get him to call the men to roster." Mayko turned and hurried from the room.

"Garlen, come here!" The second guard called from the corridor. Bex looked at Bryn, both astonished at the way the two ordinary soldiers addressed their Prince. As Garlen passed them he seemed to notice their inquisitive look.

"Mayko and Gordin are part of my special retinue. I made it clear to all that I want to be addressed as Garlen; not 'Prince' or 'Your Majesty'. I would appreciate the same from you both." He swept the hair from his face and marched past to see what Gordin had found.

The second black armoured guard stood still in the centre of the corridor about five metres away from the door. With his dark garb and short closely cropped hair, the armoured figure looked sinister. Bryn wondered exactly what Garlen's retinue did for him. Gordin indicated the floor ahead with the tip of his sword.

"Blood. There are more drops ahead as well. One of the attackers was injured."

"Could it be from the maid who found them?" Bryn asked.

"No, she would have gone back the way we came. They went that way." Garlen cut in and strode defiantly down the corridor.

36

F ar to the north, beyond the Hinterlands, a figure
scurried through the undergrowth. The tall oaks of the
forest cast shadows in the midday sun and Jerone
Witchboy took advantage of them as he darted from tree to
tree, scanning the forest floor for the plants he was tasked to
collect. He was unique among his tribe, having failed the Test
of Manhood twice yet having received an agnomen to his first
name. Witchboy, however, was more of an insult than a name
given purely for descriptive reasons. Shunned by most his tribe
due to his failings, he found his only ally to be Janda, the witch
of the forest.

And ally she was, rather than friend. She had made it clear
when she had first offered him shelter that it was purely a business arrangement. The old woman would keep him safe and
offer some protection from the other young men of the tribe as
his status amongst his people would allow him little rights. In
return he would fetch and carry for the witch and clean and
cook. He had carried out his duties with great diligence and
had been rewarded over the last few moons with a basic introduction to the art of witchcraft.

As he picked the last berries, he checked the contents of the small belt purse he wore. He thought he had covered the list of required ingredients that he had been given at dawn by Janda. There was the mandrake root and the firewort, and several others – dreadweed, faery cap and dawn grass among them. He nodded thoughtfully, adding the dark red earthberries to the purse. Janda had been agitated recently, her temper fluctuating more than ever, and it had coincided with the appearance of the green lights in the sky.

"It is trouble, trouble it is," Janda had cackled as she hobbled around her tower. "Trouble for us all, trouble and death will come."

It hadn't been just Janda that had seen the lights. The elders of the village had come to her tower and asked for reading of the lights, whether they meant ill or good. Without a thought, she had answered.

"Death."

The elders had implored her to look again at the signs and read what nature and the spirits had said. 'Death' was not what they wanted. 'Death' would not placate the tribe and keep the people focused. They had brought her an ox to sacrifice in the hope that it would provide a better divination. Bathed in the blood of the animal the naked Janda had once again pronounced the future.

"Death."

The elders retreated, not wanting to waste further time and effort on her and the tribe carried on nervously with its day to day life. Until the dragon arrived. Janda had sensed it and had run to the top of her tower to watch as it soared above. It had also been seen by many of the tribe, including Jerone. He stood petrified as the great beast flew above him and it took Janda several minutes to shake him from his near catatonic trance.

"The beast, Hern protect us, the beast has come for us," was all he could say as the old woman had grabbed his shoulders and violently shook him. If it hadn't been a serious moment between them, it would have looked comical. The small crone, her spine bent leaving her no taller than a child, standing on her tiptoes so that she could reach the young man's shoulders. Jerone wasn't bulky, his build was that of a young teen, but even his arms made the frail, old woman's arms look like twigs. Somehow, she had managed to get him into the tower and sat him down.

She had calmed him down by pushing eldersage leaves into his mouth and getting him to slowly chew them.

"But the dragon will kill us all..."

"It wasn't a dragon, idiot!"

"But I saw the teeth, the horns . . . ." Jerone was confused. If it wasn't a dragon then what could it be?

"How does a dragon fly?" the old woman asked, wrapping her black cloak around her tighter. Her face was creased and lined, just like the bark of the old, dead oak that formed part of her tower. Her toothless grin expanded into a black hole of a guffaw as she laughed at his confusion.

"With wings, mother Janda."

"Aye, idiot. Jerone Idiotboy, they should have named you, not Witchboy. Aye, on wings, and can you tell me how many wings were on that foul creature just now?"

Jerone scrunched his face up as he tried to concentrate and answer. He could only visualise the great beast flying overhead, its vast wings flapping and its head turning to look down – right at him!

"Two." He answered but then it came to him, he could see the teeth and the tail of the dragon, but the body in between stayed rigid and firm and there was definitely not a wing in sight. "None." He corrected himself.

"Correct, boy!" Janda patted his cheek, quite hard. He smarted under her touch. "There were no wings. It was a ship. A ship that flies, but no dragon."

"So, we aren't going to die?" The relief in his voice was evident and he sank back on the stool that he was sitting on to lean back against the wall of the tower. It took a second or so before he sat bolt upright. "A ship? How does it fly?"

"By magic, boy. I told you that magic can do anything, do you not remember? And we may still all die," she added as an afterthought.

The elders returned that evening, this time with other men from the tribe. They numbered around thirty and called out to Janda to help protect them from the dragon. They beat their shields with their clubs and swords, calling out to her. Jerone had recognized several of the young warriors as those that he had carried out his Test of Manhood with, including Anders Whitehair, the white-haired son of the tribal elder, Veng Stonefist.

Janda had stayed out of sight and the delegation from the tribe withered away in the cold night leaving the tower alone. Jerone had crept uneasily to his bed of furs and pulled the old black bear fur up around him. Sleep eventually came and he drifted off to a slumber that neither refreshed him nor comforted him.

Janda had shaken him awake just before dawn and urged him to gather the ingredients that she needed to refresh her stores. Rubbing his eyes, he had left the tower and ventured out into the morning, carrying nothing apart from the small belt purse and a small knife. The cold had cut into his bare torso like a knife and the fur trousers he wore only just kept his long legs warm. Like most of the tribe he had long dark hair, almost black.

As he was not a man in the eyes of the tribal elders, his chest and face were not adorned with tattoos, unlike that of Anders and the other warriors. For passing the Test of Manhood, a young man in the tribe was welcomed into manhood with a long cut running from shoulder to shoulder along his clavicle. Whilst the blood from this cut still ran, soot was rubbed into the open wound giving the scar a darker colour once healed. For each act of bravery another cut would be added underneath whilst a scar would be added on the cheek for each warrior killed in battle.

Jerone made his way back to the tower. He listened to the forest around him, trying to take in the noises and movement to understand his surroundings and then stopped dead in his tracks. Something wasn't right. Something had scared most of the wildlife in the area close by and there was a smell of smoke in the air. Dreading the worst, he ran home, the undergrowth whipping against his skin as he leapt over fallen branches and rocks.

He skidded to a halt a short way from the tower, shocked at what he saw. Janda's tower was a ramshackle affair, built on and in the remains of an old oak tree. Ivy and other plants covered the wooden walls and crept upwards into the remaining branches. The old oak was surrounded by young warriors from the tribe and Anders Whitehair stood tall over the others, barking out commands. The tattooed warriors rushed forward and threw more faggots onto the piles of branches and twigs that smouldered around the base of the tower. He crept forward to see closer when a twig snapped behind him.

He spun round; knife held out in front of him. A young warrior stood facing him, club in hand. The newcomer was slightly shorter that Jerone but bigger built. In fact, his stomach was large making him look fat and obese despite the broad shoulders. A single black scar ran across his chest and his long black hair framed his youthful unmarked face.

"Shit, Taukem! I nearly stabbed you then!" Jerone hissed upon recognizing the only youngster in the tribe who had never bullied him. Taukem Twoguts crouched down as if to comically hide his great bulk behind the skinnier man.

"Jerone! What are you doing here? You must get away. He will kill you as well as Janda!"

There was no need for Jerone to ask who 'He' was. The tall white-haired figure of Anders stood nearly head and shoulders above any other warrior at the base of the tower. Despite passing the Test of Manhood just twelve months ago, the tall youth's chest was already adorned with five dark ridges of scars. His long white hair framed the pale skin of his face, pale except for the four black scars under each eye. He waved his long spear as he gesticulated to his cohorts to build the fires up.

The tower wouldn't last long when the fires got going. There was a loud crack and a roar as the flames took hold on the side nearest Jerone. Yellow flames the height of a man greedily licked up the walls consuming the thin branches and vines of the parasitic plants that covered the tower.

"Taukem! Why is he doing this?"

"He has always hated you, Jerone. He laughs because you failed the Test." He blushed, realising he had offended the young man.

"I know that, Taukem. But Janda? He wants to fight her magic?"

"He hates the power that she has in the tribe. He sees this as a chance to turn the whole tribe against her. He has already spoken out to the elders about it."

"About what? You aren't making sense!" Jerone grabbed Taukem by his meaty shoulders and hissed urgently. Taukem crouched down, pulling the Witchboy with him, suddenly conscious that the conversation was getting a little loud.

"Don't you see? It's the dragon, Anders has convinced the tribe that Janda summoned it to destroy us all."

"The dragon? You dolt! It's a flying ship, not a dragon!" Jerone looked up at the tower knowing that he had to get in there and save Janda. There was a tall tree at the edge of the clearing that had branches that overlapped with the old oak.

Maybe he could use that to get to Janda. He looked at Taukem eye to eye, his dark brown eyes meeting the gaze of his tribal compatriot.

"Janda is our only hope. I have to save her!" and he stood and ran in a loping gait through the undergrowth to the base of the tree he had noted and began to climb.

37

Garlen led them down corridors deep into parts of the palace seldom used. The black garbed Gordin helped spot the occasional drop of blood which helped convince them they were on the right track. Bryn and Bex followed, the tall solder from Jacarna having taken the sword of the deceased Dannad. They were all in a grim silence, a silence that felt all to necessary following the day's malefic events. Bex and Ishtara, however, were able to keep up a dialogue as they walked.

'*Who could do such a thing, Ishtara. You saw the Queen's nephews.....*'

'*I told you they were despicable creatures, Bex.*'

'*I know, but still – those poor boys.*' The tattooed woman reached to her eye to wipe away the early bud of a tear as it formed.

'*You might have to control me when we catch up with this...*' Bex could feel Ishtara reach for the right word in her mind. She helped by forming a few for the Qoi to use. '*With this bastard,*' she continued.

'*I think Garlen will be in your way for that, Ishtara.*' She focused on the steely faced Prince as he strode forward. The determination and anger had seemed to make him grow in stature, so he now looked even more imposing than the tall, chainmail clad Bryn.

'*Good. I hope he doesn't kill them too quick. I can help him torture these foul bastards.*' Having found the word, she seemed fond of it.

'*They won't hurt the princesses, will they?*' Bex was starting to get used to portraying emotion in her thought voice to Ishtara. The Qoi paused before answering.

'*I am not sure, Bex. I know it is not what you want to hear but we must hurry. Hold on!*' Bex stopped in her tracks as she caught an image of Ishtara once again checking for scent. They had just passed a door to a storeroom, one of many in the seemingly endless corridors.

'I can't smell them anymore.'

Bryn had paused now, turning back to face Bex.

"What is it?"

"Ishtara can't smell the Cassalian anymore. They must have gone into one of these rooms." Garlen noted the broken silence and turned back.

"Are you sure?" Bex gave an enquiring nudge to her symbiotic partner.

'*Yes, definite.*' Bex nodded to Garlen. The Prince reached for the door with his free hand pushing it open and stepping into the room nimbly. It was empty apart from a few storage boxes. Garlen turned back to Bex, his face red with anger.

"Really sure?"

Gordin had entered just behind Garlen and now crouched by a grating that was in the centre of the room. He looked up to the others and Bex caught a good look at his face for the first time. Bex put his age at forty, though he could have been a few years younger. A bristly stubble coated most of his lower face apart from a scar along his jaw line. As he spoke, she noted several gaps between his yellowing teeth.

"Blood, Garlen. She was right."

The Prince gave a look that could only just be interpreted as an apologetic one and then turned on Gordin.

"What are you waiting for? Open it up!"

"You are welcome." Bex muttered under her breath. Garlen heard it though. He drew himself up to his full height and turned slowly. His hand made the now too customary sweep through his hair and he stared at Bex.

"Bex, my father has just been murdered and my sisters have been taken, under threat of death or torture now doubt. Once I have rescued them, which I will do, I have the small problem of my kingdom, the kingdom that I was born and raised to rule, facing imminent destruction from a force that seems unstoppable. So, forgive me if I seem terse. My sisters' lives are at stake here and also the fate of the kingdom, which is also your home, the kingdom that you serve."

There was nothing in his delivery that seemed apologetic rather an irritation that his command was not automatically being followed. Bryn groaned as he saw Bex pull her shoulders back and stand tall. She was already taller than the small blond nobleman. She swept her own hand through her black shock of hair in a parody of Garlen.

"You may have been raised to rule but I only had the misfortune to be born into a kingdom where the majority of your subjects have to beg, steal, kill or whore themselves out just to face another day. I understand your anger at the perpetrators of these crimes today but whilst Ishtara and I wish to help – and help we will – bear in mind we are not in your service or pay." Garlen looked like he was about to explode but Bex continued. "Ishtara and I are your best chance to rescue Moren and Ingren."

At the mention of his sisters' names Garlen softened

slightly. Bryn stepped closer and put his hand on Bex's shoulder.

"Perhaps we should get after the princesses?"

"Yes, Mori and Ingren." Garlen nodded humbly and distantly. He once again settled his gaze on Bex and reasserted himself.

"Bex, Lady Ishtara. I forget myself and apologise. I spent too long on at war where a split second is the difference between breathing again in this world and feasting in Kani's Hall. Be reassured your assistance is appreciated."

Gordin had the grating open and held it for Garlen to lower himself down. They all followed and found themselves in a sewer tunnel only just big enough to stand in without stooping. The void was only lit from above, a solitary torch struggling to cast light from the corridor above through into the room and down through the grating.

'*Hold out your hand*' Ishtara told Bex. The tall thief held out her left hand. She could feel Ishtara concentrate and watched as her hand started to glow, the skin starting to redden first before seeming to split at the knuckles. Flames licked from the open wounds and leapt forth to illuminate the darkness. Garlen turned around and grunted in acknowledgement whilst Bryn grimaced then spat to one side.

"It's going to take me a while to get used to this," the seasoned warrior said.

"You and me both, Bryn." Bex stared at the flames flickering across her hand.

"Which way, Bex?" Garlen asked, trusting Ishtara to pick up the scent.

'*I can't tell to be sure. This stench is confusing the scent.*' Bex caught an image of the fiery Qoi wrinkling her nose in disgust. Finally, she added, '*That way,*' and pointed down the tunnel.

They soon came across the bodies of Murf and his accomplices. A quick check of the dead showed that two had a tattoo on the hand like the body of the unfortunate Dannad in the school room.

"He is tying up loose ends. They had served their purpose." Garlen pointed to the grating above them. "They must have got out here."

Climbing through, they found themselves in an old room that was a dilapidated animal shelter, little more than a lean to against the wall of the palace complex. Heavy blood splatter was evident around the edge of the grating. The door was slightly open, letting a shaft of light illuminate the interior. Standing in the doorway, Garlen took note of his surroundings and gauged his position.

"We are still in the palace. Are they still inside as well or have they managed to get out? And if so, how?"

Bryn pointed to a pile of horse dung in the small enclosure. It was still fresh.

"My guess is they had a wagon here. Drove straight out through the gate."

"Brazen." Gordin noted.

"Brazen they maybe, but these bastards have my sisters. Let us hope the Hawk has closed the city gates in time."

"Even if they have, that leaves them in the city. And it is a very big city, Garlen." Bex added, not wanting to add to his worries but feeling the need to lower his expectations. "Two girls can be hidden away, and it could take years to find them."

"I have my means, Bex. Let us check with the gate and see whether Earl Kar is right about wagons."

38

Narbek looked back at the city. They had passed the final gate with no problems and now had the open countryside ahead of them. With every step that the black horse took, the city shrank and Narbek felt safer and safer. He looked ahead and grunted as he saw the crest of the hill that the paved road took them to. Another few moments and even the tall spires of Tannaheim might disappear. Then he would feel even safer. The smuggler looked sideways at the old man who sat next to him. Now out of the city Brant no longer concentrated on clouding the minds of those around him. Indeed, there were few people on the road for this time of day and even less in the immediate vicinity. He looked a little less on edge himself.

"So, can we now talk?"

Brant sighed. He supposed it didn't matter what the smuggler knew now. He nodded and drew his cloak about him a little more. Damn this cold!

"Anjoan is dead?" It was more of a statement than a question. Brant nodded again.

"How?"

Brant harrumphed but it didn't put Narbek off.

"How? And who or what is Dutte? Do you mean Eglebon Dutte?" Brant sighed again, this time inwardly. They had another hour to drive before he could hand the princesses over. He decided that, whilst they drove, he would have fun with Narbek and let him know exactly what he had done.

"The kidnapping of the princesses is nothing to do with a political statement or revenge. The story I told Murf and his associates about a forthcoming war is the truth. He didn't believe it." The old man laughed. "Your land, nay – your world is about to be invaded in the name of the Emperor. I am an Adept Sinister in the Emperor's Host, a force incomprehensible to your pitiful minds. The inhabitants of your world will bow before us or be crushed underfoot." He paused to give his words affect.

Narbek was a mercenary thief anyway. He held no allegiance to the crown or to Tannaheim. If the power shifted in Tannaheim, or in Maingard overall, then he would seek out opportunities to prosper from it. It didn't matter to him who was wearing the crown. Brant sensed this and despised him. He was just like Dutte, no loyalty and not to be trusted.

"The cities of Jacarna and Tarim have already fallen. General Karchek is already preparing his forces to subdue the West. The taking of Anjoan's daughters is to provide the General with a bargaining tool. Hopefully Anjoan would bow to the Emperor and save the need for unnecessary bloodshed."

"But Anjoan is now dead?"

"Yes,"

"Look, I don't want to know the full details. If I get paid then I work for you and your Emperor. I just want to get my money and stay out of the way of Anjoan's – well I mean Garlen's retaliation. I take it, he is king now if his father is dead." Narbek was unsure now, doubt creeping back into his mind. Maybe he should have disappeared after meeting the strange old man in the Scalloper's Inn. He wasn't sure if he could trust what the old man was saying.

"Don't worry, Narbek. You have served the Emperor well. I won't let Garlen harm you."

They settled into an uneasy silence as they drove onwards, passing the occasional rider or wagon. Once they passed a troop of Tannaheim cavalry which caused Narbek to sweat and panic. The old man had put him to ease.

"Don't worry. They are returning to Tannaheim. They have no way of knowing about their King, let alone their Princesses. Now, if they were coming from behind us, then we have a problem." With that Narbek relaxed a little but still threw a quick, nervous glance over his shoulder after they had passed the last soldier.

A little while later Brant indicated that Narbek should turn off the main highway. A track ran from the paved road that led to a small copse of trees. Whilst not a well-worn track, its destination indicated that it was used occasionally as a campsite. The copse was a few hundred yards from the road and overgrown. As they neared it, two men stepped out from the undergrowth. Brant motioned to Narbek to pull up the wagon near the two men and jumped down with a spritely step.

The men were tall, taller than Narbek and garbed in armour. It was worn and dark with gouges and scratches covering it. A relief of a skull adorned the steel breastplate of one whilst the other wore bulky leather armour but had gloves fashioned as claws. They didn't wear helmets, but their lower faces were obscured by leathers masks held in place by straps that were tight to their greying skin. Their eyes were black and buried deep in darkened pits, so much so that Narbek at first thought they had been blinded.

"Well met, Adept Brant. Lord Carmig awaits you on board. He wishes to leave immediately." The man in the skull armour spoke loudly and assuredly.

"Very well, help us carry the girls on board. Then you can leave." Narbek climbed down from the driver's seat and lifted the base of the cargo hold to reveal the Princesses still encased in their sacks. The soldier with the clawed gloves grabbed both and threw them over his shoulder effortlessly. He walked off towards a small single-track path through the undergrowth. As Narbek and Brant went to follow, Skull Armour stopped them.

"Lord Carmig's orders, only you and the Princesses allowed on board." He gestured towards Narbek. "No witnesses." As if to make his point, he drew his sword.

"He is with me, Silda. I will take it up with Carmig." Reluctantly the soldier sheathed his sword and stepped aside.

As they walked into the copse Narbek was astonished to see a sailing ship sitting in a clearing in the middle of the small wood. It was about thirty yards long and slightly higher and bulkier than one of the drakkars that the northmen sailed. The bulwarks stood twice the size of a man and there were three cabins situated on the deck with two short stubby masts in between. The masts had no yardarms and looked as if they served only as flag posts for pennants and signals. A hideous dragon head was carved into the bow, its jaws open as if to consume whatever the beast wanted.

The ship lay beached at a slight angle. On the lower side a gangplank reached down to the ground allowing a steep but easy access. All four climbed on board and Narbek saw the deck was deserted.

"Lord Carmig awaits you in his quarters."

"Take the girls to the spare quarters, and take Narbek down to the Tandorian for his reward"

Silda, the soldier with the skull armour nodded, opening a hatch set at an angle into the deck. Narbek watched apprehensively as Brant walked to the door of the middle cabin. Even though he didn't trust the old man, he felt that his only ally on this strange ship was leaving him. Silda motioned for Narbek to enter and he did so reluctantly.

A set of wooden stairs, wide enough for three men, led down into the murky gloom below. Narbek mouthed a silent prayer to Tomnar, the first prayer he had muttered to the Father God for a long time. The deck they had descended to was low and even the short Narbek stooped slightly. The only light was coming from the cracks in a door ahead and it took a few seconds for his eyes to become accustomed to the darkness. As they approached the door an overpowering sense of fear and oppression hit him. He was aware of Silda standing behind him, as if his personal space was invaded. The door swung open slowly and Silda took a step forward, forcing Narbek into the room beyond.

He raised his hand to his mouth as he tried hard not to retch as the foulest stench seemed to seep into his very pores. Now he understood the masks that the soldiers wore, they were to aid breathing. His eyes focused on the sight ahead and the horror that met him was etched forever on his mind for the rest of his life, which was mercifully, not very long.

39

G arlen led them across the courtyards to the palace gate. The imposing tower was set into the palace wall and its base was surrounded by a milieu of added buildings, some made of stone and some of wood. The great portcullis was down, its thick iron bars helping to partly obscure the interior of the gate tower which was only lit by the flickering of a single torch. They all noted grimly that the drawbridge to the city was pulled up. Several guards lounged about the gate, clearly thinking that their duties were easier due to the closure of the palace.

The Prince was equally imposing though, the strides of the smaller man out pacing those of the others. A light breeze billowed his silken shirt and the coldness brought a chill to Bex's skin.

"Guard! How long has the gate been shut?" Garlen called out as he approached the gate. One of the red, surcoated guards, sitting with his back to the portcullis and with his head bowed down made the mistake of replying without looking who had called him.

"Who wants to know?"

Another guard, seeing who approached them, struggled awkwardly to his feet. As he straightened himself to an 'at attention' pose, he muttered something under his breath to the others. There was a hurried reaction as they all realised who was addressing them.

Garlen stopped several paces away from them and stood with his hands on his hips. Gordin however, marched straight past and grabbed the guard who had answered his commander insubordinately. With his hands grasping the chainmail clad soldier's surcoat, he pushed the unfortunate soul up against the portcullis. There was a large clang as armour met iron and the guard's helm fell off, displaying a blast of red, lank hair.

"Your Prince wants to know, you ignorant oaf! Just be glad that we are going to need all the swords that we have over the next few months else I would be feeding your guts to the crows right now for your insubordination!" Gordin screamed at him, his face inches away from the guard. The black garbed soldier dropped the guard and took a step backwards.

The red-haired guard, Jordu, regained his composure and stood to attention. His skin flushed red, almost enough to match his flaming hair. Bex could sense their confusion. Their Prince was with a soldier from another city and a strange woman who looked unlike any of Garlen's normal consorts. Finally, Jordu managed to stammer out an answer to Garlen's enquiry.

"About an hour, your Highness."

"How many wagons went through just before it was closed?" The guards looked between themselves questionably before one spoke up.

"Three, your Highness."

"How many of the three were drawn by one horse?" Bryn joined in. Sensing a look from Garlen he turned and shrugged his shoulders. "One pile of dung, one horse? I am just guessing." The Prince nodded and looked back at the guards.

"Well?"

"Just the one, a black horse and the drover was dark as well."

"Maybe a Theshian. Said he was from Saret's"

Between them the guards managed to give a description of Narbek and his wagon, however from this side of the gate tower they were unable to see which way the wagon had gone once it had left. Garlen ordered the guards to lower the bridge. They waited impatiently as the chains clinked and clattered as the two great bridges lowered into place. crossed to the far side.

The tower on the city side of the gorge was a replica of the palace side but with the deep chasm dropping away there was no need for a wall. Whilst Garlen and Bryn questioned the guards at the gate, Bex looked up and down the street. She could picture Ishtara with her nose up in the air sniffing. The streets right outside the palace were all part of the merchant's quarter. She looked each way but at this time of day the way was busy. Merchants shouted from small stalls and customers milled about. There wouldn't have been much space to move a wagon here either and if that was the case then that would have made it all the more memorable.

'Well?' she asked Ishtara.

'I can't tell, the scent seems diluted, too many others walking the route.'

Bex glanced anxiously one way then the other. She didn't need Garlen to spell out the importance of getting a lead on where the girls had been taken. Suddenly she saw what she was after, a beggar, sitting in between a couple of the stalls. His one leg was stretched out in front of him, the other was cut off at the knee and a crutch laid alongside. A small bowl was in his hand, a few copper coins rattling in the bottom of it as he shook it forlornly as people walked by. Bex crossed the street, walking towards him.

"Hey, friend!" she shouted, "have you been here all day?"

"What's it to you?" he started to reply, fearful that he was going to get moved on or set upon. He glanced momentarily to one side as if looking for someone. Bex could see out of the corner of her eye another man leaning against the wall suddenly take a step towards them both and smiled.

'Oh!' Ishtara exclaimed, *'he only has one leg!'*

'Don't worry about it, it's a sham.'

Bex dropped a few coppers into his bowl and knelt down near him. The other man stopped and returned to his post.

'What do you mean, a sham?'

'He hasn't really lost a leg, it is just tied up to make people think he has so they feel sorry for him.' Bex replied, *'though we humans can live with disabilities like the loss of a leg. Can't the Qoi?'*

'No! But why would he do this?'

'I'll explain in a minute.'

"I just wondered if you could help me, you been here all day?" Bex spoke aloud to the beggar.

"Tomnar bless you, my darling. Thank you for the coins, it is cold and lonely here on the streets," the beggar invoked the name of one of the Western Kingdom's principal deities, Tomnar, God of Life and Joy. "I have been here for a while, I don't get chance to move much," he patted his thigh just above where the limb was 'severed'.

"I have business with someone who left the palace a short while ago."

The beggar stared at here, not sure what to say. He glanced once again over Bex's shoulder to the man who was clearly overseeing him. She moved her left hand from under her cloak and absentmindedly rubbed her chin. His eyes betrayed two things, firstly the recognition of her tattoo on her hand, a small moon between the thumb and first finger, and secondly a glance and a shake of the head to the man behind Bex. The thief turned her head slightly and saw that the overseer had moved off. On the same place on his left hand the man had a similar tattoo; however, his was a small faint sun.

"Did you see my friend? He was in a wagon, by himself, drawn by a black horse."

"I saw him, my lady. Just before they shut the gate. He must have been the last one before the bridge was pulled up. But he wasn't alone. There was someone sitting next to him, I think. There was something odd about that one. He wore a grey cloak and he didn't want to be seen."

"What do you mean?"

"At first I didn't see him but then he was there..."

Bex added a couple more coins to his bowl.

"Did you see which way he went?"

"That way." He nodded to his left.

"Thank you, my friend. May Lady Tobes smile on you and your prize be bountiful, today and all days." She smiled and stood, speaking to him the Beggar's Orison.

"And may she smile upon you, today and all days," the beggar gave the standard reply to the guild prayer.

She turned and strode back to the passageway, calling Garlen to her and giving him the news. Both Garlen and Bryn were amazed at the beggar's news about the mysterious second driver.

"If they went out of the City they will be heading for the North Gate. I will ride there with a detachment of guardsmen. Gordin, fetch my horse and tell Col to meet me at the North Gate. I pray that the Hawk was in time and the gates are closed. You two, please return to the Palace and tell my mother."

40

J erone inched his way along the branch and nervously clambered across to the oak tree. So far no-one on the ground had spotted them and he looked back to see Taukem standing stock still staring at him. The idiot! He thought. If Whitehair looks about and sees the fat boy standing like that, he will follow his gaze. With his mind on his rival below and the need for speed to save Janda, he didn't notice the branch he stepped on was weak. With a large crack it snapped and with it his balance went. He managed to fling himself forward and grab a branch of the oak tree which he prayed to Hern, the Forest God, would be substantial enough to hold his weight. He hung precariously above the ground, a drop of four times his height to the ground below.

Jerone looked down at the fires that were getting stronger and found himself staring straight into the eyes of Anders Whitehair. Even from that distance he could see the hate in the eyes of the young warrior and as the white-haired wolf saw the boy's predicament, an evil smile came to his lips.

Anders called to some of his warriors who started towards Jerone. Jerone struggled to gain a foothold and pull himself up to stand on the branch. Just as he managed to do so, a rock flew past his face causing him to nearly lose his balance again.

"Witchboy! Come down here and let me put you down like the whelp you are!" Anders called out, shaking his spear at Jerone. "I'll put you out of your misery just like your old hag. I won't cut my face in your name though, Witchboy! True warriors don't get a scar for killing sheep." He burst into a fit of laughter and several of his men followed suit.

One of the warriors started to climb the same tree that Jerone had done, with obvious intent to follow him and bring him down. Jerone turned and concentrated on the task at hand – getting into the tower. The branch he was on led straight to the huge trunk of the oak and to the left of that was a window in the man-made portion of wall. He scrambled along the branch and jumped instinctively for the window. As he landed heavily on the window frame, his chest catching the base and his arms snatching wildy at anything just inside the room to pull himself up, a rock struck his forehead gouging a deep cut above his eye.

Looking down he spied a couple of the warriors running forward with short hunting bows and he knew he had to move quickly. With an almost inhuman effort he pulled himself into the room and to safety. Relative safety - as he could feel the heat as the lower rooms of the tower ignited and sensed the smoke start to rise from below through gaps in the floor. He could hear Janda moving in the far room and called out to her.

She hobbled through the doorway clutching the small bag she always carried. As usual she was wearing her thin cotton robe and her white hair, long and straggly reminded Jerone of his enemy below. Jerone gasped as he saw how thin she appeared. The old witch looked even older than when he had left that morning. As he rushed forward to help the frail, old crone he felt a blow to his back, and he hurtled forward. How could he have forgotten the warrior who climbed up to follow him!

He landed face down and watched helplessly as the bare-chested brave ran forward and brought his club smashing downwards onto Janda's arm that she had thrown up to protect herself. Jerone heard the crack and knew she was now defence-less against the next attack.

As the warrior raised his club in a two-handed grip, whooping in the infernal way of the tribe, a cloud came across his vision. Only Janda and her assailant were clear in his mind and he could see everything as clear as if it was crystal. He saw the flecks of Janda's blood spray from the club as it reached the apex of its curved journey. He could see the muscles of the brave flex and tense as he readied the blow that would kill the witch. Jerone momentarily caught her eyes in his gaze and was astonished to see no fear in them. The old woman looked impassively up at the warrior as he was about to dispense her death and she cradled her shattered arm with her good one.

Jerone suddenly acted. He sprang forward, his right hand drawing the small knife from his belt and smashed into his opponent with his left shoulder. The charge took the warrior by surprise and caught him across the ribs on the left side of his torso. The impetus propelled him into the wall and, as he felt the crunch of body against wood, Jerone started stabbing. He repeatedly drove the small blade into the assailant's lower back as his left hand moved upwards to reach the man's face.

Caught by surprise, the warrior did little to fight back. His right arm and club were stuck between his body and the wall and he struck out with his left hand striking Jerone's back. Jerone's hand reached the man's chin and with a sharp push, smashed the man's head into the wall. The warrior's blows became weaker as Jerone continued to stab and smash, and then they stopped altogether.

Jerone stopped and took a step back pulling the warrior

with him so that he fell to the ground away from Janda. He looked down at the carnage that he had wrought, and his bloodied hands shook.

"Jerone. I knew you would come." He was shocked at the weakness in Janda's voice. She spoke slowly and laboured over every word. Snapping out of his shock he crouched down at her side.

Her wounds were more serious than he had first seen. The blow had shattered her arm completely and a shard of bone protruded from her thin flesh above the elbow. The club had also caught the side of her head and a sea of blood now flowed from the nasty gash above her ear.

"I had to. I had to come and save you. I am glad I got here in time." He leant forward to lift her to her feet. "Come, let me see to your wounds."

"There is no time," she raised her good hand in an effort to wave him away, "and there is no need, it is my time." As she spoke, she coughed and spat a splatter of thin blood onto her robe.

"But we have to get away. They will kill us!" Jerone was confused. Why was she saying this? Surely, she knew what position they were in? He looked about, the interior walls were starting to blacken and there was more smoke now. He knew they didn't have long.

"No Jerone, this body has lasted past its time. You must go alone."

"No! You can't die, Janda!"

The old woman raised her head again and looked at Jerone. Although her body was frail and weak, her eyes still showed a lot of fire. Had she been wrong about this young man? She reached out, at first with her hand as the old, gnarled fingers gripped the bare arm of the man who had risked his life to save her, and then with her mind. She nodded, the potential was still there, growing a little each day.

"Die? Who said anything about dying?" She coughed again and wiped the sputum that frothed at her lips from her mouth. "Bring me my bag." Jerone stood and sought the witch's small bag. It was the one that she carried whenever they left the tower and contained many tools and ingredients.

"Remember what I told you when I first took you in? What your people call 'Magic' comes from another plane. That plane exists in line with this, overlapping with ours. It is power emanating from beings that reside in that world and that power leaks into this world. With the help of familiar spirits, certain people can channel that energy to affect this world. We call ourselves 'Channelers', you call us witches, shaman or seers. There are other ways in the world but ours is the True Way, the Way of Maingard, the Mother's Path."

Jerone handed her the small bag and nodded. She carried on.

"I have seen many winters, many many winters. My birth name has not been used for most of them. Indeed, I doubt if anyone alive in the tribe now had been born the last time I was called by my birth name. Janda, the name you call me, is the name of one of those familiar spirits.

"When this body dies, Janda will find another channeler. You must find her and help her." Jerone stared at her, amazed at the revelation and confused even more.

"Where will she be?" he stammered.

"If I knew that, dolt, I would tell you where to go!" The stern exclamation brought another coughing fit, this time stronger than the last. It took her a minute to recover.

"When Janda finds another channeler, you will know. She will guide you to her." She rummaged through the small satchel before taking out several items. She bound some small animal bones and twigs together in the crude form of a man and then mounted a mouse skull and on the neck using some gum.

"Who leads the warriors outside?" She asked, knowing the answer before it came.

"Anders Whitehair"

She fished out two small, white feathers and bound them around the skull with a thin twine giving the small charm the appearance of having long, white hair.

"Take this when you go. When you confront Whitehair, this will protect you if you still believe in me. There is one other gift I must bestow on you. Pass me your knife."

Jerone took the charm and reverently placed it in his own pouch with the ingredients that he had collected that morning. He handed his knife over, the dull steel still coated in the thick, sticky blood of the man he had just killed. Janda rooted through her bag one last time, bringing out a small drawstring pouch. She opened it to reveal a black powder. She placed the tip of the knife against Jerone's chest, at the end of the collar bone.

"As an elder of our tribe, I confirm to all that Jerone has reached Manhood. He is entitled to wear the scars of honour in recognition of his courage." As she spoke, she drove the point into his skin and dragged it along his chest, following the line of his collar bone. At first the incision did not hurt but then his chest erupted in an agonising fire as the tip of the knife was dragged through his skin. The thin cut parted slowly, almost as an afterthought as the steel moved on and blood began to flow. As she cut him, he gritted his teeth and tensed his muscles to push against the knife rather than draw away. He had seen some men in the tribe who only had a part scar as they had pulled back in shock. Grimacing, he clenched his eyes shut as the knife finally edged towards the end of its journey.

If the pain of the cut had been just about bearable, the next part was not. The small particles of grit and soot that Janda rubbed into the wound burnt like nothing that Jerone had felt before. He let out a short scream. The old woman dropped her hand and shut her eyes, exhausted.

"Now it is your time. Witchboy no more. Go, Jerone Witchguardian. Take your new name and duty and find me again." Her chest rose ever so slowly and Jerone stood staring down at her. He stepped over her into the room that she had appeared from just a few minutes before. All the time he could hear the cracking of beams as the flames took hold. He made for the window and looked out. Most of the warriors below were standing round near the entrance to the tower, waiting for his final exit. The faggots piled against the tower wall below still smouldered, perhaps they were too wet this side. This side also offered the less distance between the forest and the base of the tower, perhaps twenty feet. He made to climb through but then turned and went back to Janda.

Crouching down he raised her chin. The old woman was nearly gone. Slowly she sensed someone there and opened her eyes.

"What was it? I mean, what is it?" He asked.

She looked blankly at him.

"Your birth name, Janda. What is your true name?"

He could barely hear the answer as her lips slowly mouthed the words.

"Shoola, Shoola Brighteyes." A look of wistfulness came over her as she breathed one last time before passing.

Jerone closed her eyes with his hand and then made for the window again. Before climbing out, he turned and spoke softly.

"Goodbye Shoola Brighteyes."

41

Brant had met with the captain of the ship and had then disembarked. Pulling the hood of his cloak up he started back to the city. The evening was drawing in and the temperature was already dropping. As he reached the highway, he turned and watched as the ship lifted off and soared slowly into the air. Several minutes later it had disappeared into the fading light.

Thirty minutes later he was approached by a party of horsemen. The six riders wore chainmail and a surcoat displaying a blue star on a white background, with red cloak thrown over their shoulders as they rode. As they got nearer, Brant could discern the silver crossed swords of the Barst family crest mounted on the cloak. The surcoat denoted that they were kinsmen of Count Dutte, whilst the red cloak bearing Anjoan's crest displayed their allegiance. All the same, he steadied himself if needs required it.

The riders pulled their horses up close to him and the leader raised his hand in salute. The young man, in his twentieth year, bore an uncanny resemblance to Count Dutte and Brant realised he must be one of his four sons. His hair was slightly longer than the Count's, but his eyes were the same piercing blue of his father.

"Lord Brant, I am Earl Monteth, son of Count Eglebon Dutte. He ordered me to meet you along this highway and escort you back to the city." He beckoned one of his men forward who held the reins of a spare horse. Brant sighed. He had hoped to make it back to the city without others knowing but he had to agree; his legs were old, and it was a cold night. He allowed himself to be helped up onto the horse. In the name of the Emperor, the faith they put in these animals, he thought warily.

The mounted men turned and trotted back to the city, Brant and Earl Monteth leading, with the five men at arms following at a respectful distance. Brant found himself under scrutiny from the young man. He looked across as he gripped the reins tightly.

"Forgive me, Lord Brant. I am merely curious. My father has told me a lot about you." Brant seethed inside. He had instructed Eglebon Dutte not to divulge their allegiance to anyone.

"For what it is worth, Lord Brant, I would happily give my life if my father or one of my brothers could ascend the Red Throne. I pledge to you my sword, as do my siblings." Brant relaxed slightly but was still mad at the Count. Now he had five tools to use but also five to control.

"My father had hoped to meet you himself, however he is dealing with a problem that has arisen in Tannaheim. He asks that you let me speak for you should we need to explain your appearance."

"What is the problem?"

"The bearded bastard, Anjoan, is dead. That you may know already. Garlen has renounced the Throne, handing it back to his mother. Queen Sarsi has sent a messenger to recall the Third and Fourth Squadrons from the Isle of Winds. That will mean another six hundred men arriving here to bolster any defences should you attack."

"Six hundred well trained men could make a difference. When are they due to return?"

"A ship has been despatched that should make the Isles in three days, then another four or five to return. But they will never get the orders, Lord Brant. My father thought it best if the Third and Fourth stayed where they are."

Brant smiled, perhaps Count Dutte was the best man for the job after all. He did like independent thinking, something that was lacking in the military hierarchy of the Cassalian Host.

"Very well, Earl Monteth. I am sure your father will elaborate when we speak."

They rode on in silence for a while until the tall towers of Tannaheim were easily in sight with the sun starting to fall behind them. Along the highway they could see a small force of men riding at speed toward them. His own men behind closed the gap between them and they rode on.

As the newcomers approached, Brant and Monteth could see that they were all dressed in black except for their leader who wore a white shirt underneath a black cloak. The blackness was the only thing uniform about them. Their armour was a mix of chain, plate, brigandine and hardened leather, some carried bows, some lances. The leader's blond hair identified him long before he came close enough to recognise him.

"It's Garlen!" Monteth exclaimed, his hand straying to his blade.

"Fool!" hissed Brant. "Twenty swords to six. Even with surprise on our side, he will win. Besides, your father wishes to deal with him his self."

Brant could feel the young Lord seethe at the insult, but his hand moved back to hold the reins of his large white horse. It wasn't long before the two parties met, and they reined their horses in. The black and grey horses that Garlen and his men rode were lathered in sweat and snorted heavily in the chilly air.

"Your Highness," The young Earl acknowledged the Prince. "I have not had the chance to pass on my condolences regarding your father. May he rest in peace and I hope you are able to avenge his death." Monteth blushed ever so slightly as he spoke.

"Earl Monteth, I thank you for your words. It is good that my mother can rely on the allegiance of all the noble families of Tannaheim and in particular, the House Dutte. This darkness that is rising threatens to extinguish the light of our world. We must stay united else Tannaheim and Danaria will fall."

The Earl nodded in agreement and flinched slightly as the Prince caught his eye.

"We are tracking a wagon that left Tannaheim from the North Gate about two hours ago."

"We haven't seen or passed one, Your Highness. Though we have not yet ridden an hour ourselves. My father asked that I ride out and meet Frar Stenos, the brother of the Seneschal of Tar Dutte. He comes with a report on the holdings of my father's lands." Earl Monteth introduced Brant who bowed slightly as he had seen the Earl do in salute to the Prince.

"Your Majesty. I have hardly seen anyone since leaving the last village and certainly not a wagon." Garlen turned his attention away from Brant back to the Earl. Count Dutte was certainly right about this young upstart, thought Brant, his face impassive despite being dismissed from the conversation so quickly.

"We must keep up with our pursuit, Earl Monteth."

"Very well, Your Highness. Good luck with the hunt." The Prince kicked his tall grey on past the mounted men of Monteth's retinue. As he did so, he turned and spoke to Brant.

"Frar Stenos! Please pass on my regards to your brother and

mention that when this crisis has been averted, I would be pleased to visit Marneheim and Tar Dutte."

"Of course, it will be our pleasure, Your Highness. You must visit again."

The two sets of soldiers parted company. Monteth and his men headed for Tannaheim whilst the sinister black-clad troops and Garlen carried on the main highway. The blond Prince gave a pensive backwards glance at the departing messenger and his escort. Something puzzled him about them, but he wasn't quite sure what. The light started to fade, and he brought his attention back to the task at hand, finding his sisters. It was some fifteen minutes later that Tobes, Lady Luck, shone down on him.

"Garlen!" It was Col, his sergeant who spoke. Col was a thick set man of about forty with thick curly shoulder length hair. A jagged scar ran down the right-side of his face crossing his eye, an eye which was milky white and unseeing – a result of a goblin sword four years back. His black chainmail had hand sized discs of blackened steel riveted to it to add extra protection and a great sword was strapped over his back. As he called out, Garlen raised his hand bringing the twenty men to a halt.

"There's something in the trees there. Sounds like a horse."

"Gordin, come with Col and me. The rest of you, give your mounts a break." The three men walked their horses tentatively over the beaten track that led to the small copse of trees. Garlen's grey whinnied as they neared the treeline and sure enough a loud neigh came in response. They dismounted leaving their horses untethered and slowly drew their swords. Only the faintest of scrapes of metal on leather gave any indication of their action and they gradually moved into the copse.

As the undergrowth thinned out, they could see the wagon, empty with the black horse still harnessed to it. Garlen fought the urge to run to it until they had made sure the area was secure. A quick circle of the small clearing confirmed that they were alone, and they moved in towards the wagon.

Though Garlen was expecting it, he was disappointed to find it empty. No trace of drover or his sisters could be seen. He dispatched Gordin to instruct the men to search the immediate surroundings whilst he and Col investigated further. It was Garlen himself who found the secret compartment under the storage area of the wagon that had hidden his sisters and it was Col who noticed the weird depression in the soil of the clearing.

"If I didn't know better, then I would say it's from a boat, Garlen. Back in Samak we used to draw the fishing boats up out of the waters over winter and they would leave a mark like this." Garlen walked over to where his sergeant stood and crouched down to inspect the ground. When his comment and inquisitive look didn't get a reply, Col carried on.

"So, if it isn't a boat, what is it?" The scarred warrior looked at his commander, who stood and pensively stared in the direction of the Eastern Cities. After a moment Garlen spoke.

"You're right, Col. It's a ship. Bryn Kar was telling the truth. And my sisters are being taken to Jacarna as we speak. Get the men together. We return to Tannaheim tonight, but I want forty Ghosts ready to leave at dawn. Full gear. We are going to war!" With a grim look of determination, he continued to stare at the far horizon and clenched and unclenched his fist several times.

42

"Did you find my daughters?" Queen Sarsi stood up from the throne and asked Bex and Earl Bryn. As she stood, she placed one hand on the arm of the great seat and Bex could see her tremble. Bex felt for the Queen. This must have been the worst day of her life – her husband murdered in front of her, her two younger children taken and the kingdom under threat.

"Where is Garlen?"

"We traced the route the princesses were taken through the old sewer system and then out through the main gate, hidden in a wagon. From there we think they were taken to the North Gate. Your son has taken a detachment of troops there." Bex answered.

"So, we know nothing!" the Queen sat down, slumped in the throne. She looked close to collapse. Bex climbed the dais steps and knelt in front of the Queen. As she did so, the guards took a step forward, but were waved back by the Hawk. Bex reached out and took Sarsi's hand in hers. The one-time beggar and prostitute, killer and thief held the most powerful woman in the West's hand and consoled her.

'Tell her we will get her children back, Bex.' Ishtara's voice sounded in her mind.

'And how will we do that?' she answered back.

'We know who took them. The same ones who destroyed my world and the same ones who threaten your world.'

'We think we know who took them.'

'We know!'

'Am I getting any choice in this matter?'

'No, the Cassalians are here, your world will die anyway.'

Bex knew it was pointless to argue. She had made up her mind anyway to stand up to the Cassalians.

"We will do whatever we can to get them back to you, my Queen," she lifted her eyes to the Queen and could see the tears form in Sarsi's eyes.

"Do so, Bex, and I will give you anything."

Earl Kar stepped forward but only as far as the lower step of the dais. He clasped his hands together in front of his face in the salute of Jarcarna.

"Your Majesty. I will also get your daughters back to you or die trying. I have no land, no country. My only cause to live is to take the fight to the invaders and to avenge my fallen people."

"Thank you, but my manners have deserted me. You must be tired and hungry. Please rest and as soon as my son returns with news, I will send word to you." She waved one of her valets forward.

"Come this way, please," he indicated that the audience was over, and they should leave. Marshall Vent stepped forward and walked with them as they left the throne room.

"My thanks to you for what you have done today."

"It's my duty," the Earl answered.

"If you have no objections, Marshall, I wish to return to my lodgings to wash and collect my belongings. I am at the Black Dragon Inn on Water Street." Bex asked.

"Ahh, Ol' One Eye. I know it well. I can send an escort with you if you wish. The streets in that area can be dangerous when darkness falls."

"I don't think that will be necessary, do you, Marshall?" Bex smiled. Then the Hawk surprised Bex. He laughed, only a small, short laugh but it was a laugh, nonetheless.

"No, young lady, I don't think it will."

She bade Bryn and the Hawk goodnight and left the palace. The walk back to Water Street and her lodgings at the Inn of the Black Dragon wasn't too long and she enjoyed the chill of the night air. As she progressed from the more affluent areas of Tannaheim from around the palace towards the Poor Quarter she passed less and less people. From the bridge at the top end of Water Street to the Inn she would have been surprised if she saw a member of the City Guard. All the way from the palace she spoke to Ishtara.

'*That man you spoke to in the street, why was he faking his injury?*' the demoness asked.

'*To prey on the goodwill and charity of others.*'

'*Charity?*' it was obviously not a concept that was well known to the Qoi.

'*Some people here on Maingard find it part of their nature to help others less fortunate.*' Bex explained.

'*Some people? Why not everyone?*' Ishtara asked.

'*Some people here are good, some are not. That is the easy answer. It is a lot more complicated than that though,*' the tall thief replied knowing that Ishtara could soon tie her up in knots with her thinking and questioning.

'*How did you know he was faking it?*' Bex knew it was going to be a long walk home and maybe a long night so decided to answer her resident demoness.

'*He hadn't completed his disguise properly, a two-year-old could have seen through it. And he also had an Eye, someone to watch over him in case he got into trouble. Did you see the man he kept glancing at? That was his Eye. Another one of the Beggar's Guild.*'

'Guild?'

'*Originally tradesmen carrying out similar trades would band together to help protect each other in business. You would have guilds for moneylenders, goldsmiths and the like. However, the idea soon lent itself to the criminal elements of society, so you have a guild for thieves, beggars and assassins for example. Someone cannot operate as a thief in an area unless he belongs to that guild.*'

'*These notions of trade and crime intrigue me, Bex. We had neither on my world.*'

'*Neither?!*' Bex exclaimed both out loud and in her mind. Her outburst resulted in her getting a weird look from a couple of passer-byes.

'*No, neither. That surprises you?*'

'*Yes, I can't see how it would work. It would be nice though – all my life has been a constant struggle for coin and wealth. And with wealth and riches, there is always someone who wants to take it.*' Bex pondered.

'*Our world was peaceful and harmonious. No war or killing, everyone lived for each other. Maybe it is a good thing I found your world, Bex. Your people may be more suited to fighting the Cassalians, maybe in your world I can have my revenge.*'

'*Maybe, Ishtara, maybe.*' They both fell silent for a while, then Bex spoke again, sensing that Ishtara needed something to talk about and take her mind away from the painful memories of her world.

'*Here in Maingard we primarily use coins to use as wealth, though gemstones and other valuables are also used.*' Bex went on to explain the monetary system in Danaria, how gold crowns are the standard and each one is divided into silver and copper pieces. She explained how other countries and other states minted their own coins and that the values varied from time to time depending upon markets states. What was a more alien concept than currency to Ishtara, was the notion of trading currency to others for work. The Qoi had no need for food, clothing or items. Their only need was shelter, and they all worked collectively to accomplish that through their knowledge of fire and heat. They took sustenance from the fiery sun that circled their world and did not wear clothes.

'You don't eat?' It was Bex's turn to be shocked.

'Not at all, the power of the All Giving Fire is all that we need.'

They arrived at the Black Dragon, its windows alight with the glow of the fires and lanterns inside. A steady stream of singing and laughter echoed from the doorway as they approached. As Bex pushed open the door Ishtara exclaimed as she was met with the first scene of the human world being joyous. The lounge was packed, with every table taken. Patrons from all walks of life swilled flagons of ale or wine, whilst others ate hearty meals. A minstrel stood on a table nearest the stairs, strumming away on his lyre and singing a raucous ditty. A table of off duty guardsmen cheered and tried to out sing him with verses that were more barrack room than coach house.

Bex peered through the crowd and spied Mon and her staff tending tables and the bar. She made her way through to Mon and caught the smaller woman's arm.

"Hey, Bex. How are you tonight?" Mon was local, born and bred in Tannaheim, though she was coy about her adult years. Rumour had it that she had been a sword for hire herself before buying the Black Dragon a decade ago. She was a good head shorter than the tall thief and nearly twice her age. However, she wore her years well, looking striking and still turning as many patron's heads as her younger staff. This attention may have been down to her easy nature and ability to chat and talk to anyone; sharing problems, giving advice and offering support where needed. Mon Baxt had dark hair, worn long and pulled back into a ponytail and her dark eyes scrutinized the younger woman as she spoke.

"I am well, Mon, but I need to speak with you, urgently."

The Innkeeper turned back to the table she had just served, a platter of warm meat and vegetables.

"Enjoy your meal, Sonde. Just shout for Kilde if you need anything else." She placed her hand on Bex's arm. "We can talk in the back room. Wine?" she never waited for an answer and waved at one of her staff at the long bar, a younger, full-bodied dark-skinned girl from Thesh. "Tomhew! Bring me a bottle of red wine to the back office please. One of the spiced wines from Jacarna." Bex smirked at her apt choice and marvelled at the woman she considered to be her best friend in the city.

She led Bex round the back of the bar and into the office behind. It was small and cramped with a small desk submerged under a stack of papers. Bex perched on the edge of the desk and Mon stood with her back to the door.

A short rap indicated that Tomhew had brought the wine and she passed a tray holding a dark red glass bottle and two leather flagons to her employer. As Mon shut the door behind her, she spoke to Bex.

"Well, dear, what is it?"

The thief wasn't sure where to start. She took a gulp of the wine. It was full bodied and she could taste the fruit and spices that the vineyards of Jacarna were famous for. She stopped mid gulp and realised that she had meant 'had been'.

"You have to get out of the city."

Mon paused, her flagon halfway to her lips and a questioning look on her face.

"Why?"

'*You can't say why, Bex.*' Ishtara cut in.

'*Why not?*'

'*She could cause a panic and you need to be united in fighting the Cassalians.*'

'*I would be surprised if half the city doesn't know already, or by morning at the latest.*' Bex knew knowledge of the murder of Anjoan wouldn't stay within the palace for long. '*I am sure the*

Hawk will have it under control. Anyway, you came here to warn us – and I will warn my friends, no matter what.'

"Spit it out, Bex. I have never known you to be stuck for words." The innkeeper joked with Bex, but she could obviously tell the tall thief was worried.

"There's a war coming, Maingard is being invaded."

"Who would be mad enough to invade the Western Kingdoms?" Mon was incredulous.

"Not just the Western Kingdoms, the whole of Maingard. Jacarna and Tarim have fallen already and King Anjoan is dead, murdered by a spy." Mon stared at Bex, then hurriedly downed her wine and poured herself another. Bex went on to recount the day's events explaining about Cassalians and Ishtara.

"Bex, I have seen some pretty wild things in my life, including a dragon and giants. But creatures from another plane are something else. What is going to happen?"

"I am not sure, Garlen, I mean Prince Garlen, is chasing down the abductors now. The Queen and the Hawk are preparing for war. Can you leave Tannaheim?"

"Leave the city? No way – I risked everything to gain the gold I needed to buy Ol' One Eye here, I won't leave until there is no other choice."

"But it's going to be war, Mon. War like we haven't seen before. This could be the end for Maingard."

"I will leave when there is no more hope, Bex."

When she lowered her flagon, it was the old Mon again, bright and optimistic about everything. "Now tell me about this 'demon' of yours." As they both sipped their wine, with the world about them ready to fall apart, Mon, Bex and Ishtara laughed and chatted until the small hours.

EPILOGUE

Bex, Mon and Ishtara while the night away, getting to know each other better. Bottle after bottle disappears as they drink and make small talk, trying to keep any mention of the forthcoming war from marring the conversation. Ishtara laughs along with the two old friends, finally glad to be part of something.

Far from the frivolity of the friends and their impromptu get together, a more sedate Queen Sarsi sits on the edge of the canopied bed. Next to her lies the still corpse of her husband, his body covered with a white sheet, his face still showing the anguish he felt in his last moments. The heady scent of the incense that burns in the small braziers either side of the bed hangs in the air. Unlike the three friends gathered away in the back room of the tavern across the city, her thoughts are all on the forthcoming struggle, the fate of her two daughters kidnapped by the Cassalians.

She simmers as she sips her wine, her motherly instinct competing with her love for the man who lays in rest next to her; her lover, her soulmate – Anjoan. Her delicate fingers reach out to stroke his face and she leans down to whisper in his ear.

'Until we stand and fight together again, my love.' Standing, she throws her goblet to one side and as it clatters across the flagstones, she storms from the chamber.

Garlen, prince but foremost a soldier, moves between his men as they check and recheck weapons and equipment. He raises questions and offers encouragement, his voice subdued and quiet. Here and there, he clasps shoulders, pats backs, and grips hands. Outside the barracks, his stable hands check over the horses for the third time, before offering them hay and letting them rest. Despite the troubles coursing through is mind like a raging river, he has learnt the art of snatching sleep where normal men could not, and his mind drifts off into a tormented slumber, wondering what lays ahead in their journey into the unknown.

Far away, in a city destroyed and in ruins, another warrior lies prone, this one not yet in the Hall of the Dead, yet his hand reaches out to open the door. Poison seeps through the veins of Radnak the half-orc. Tended by his forbidden love, the healer Iga, the Goblin Lady. Her two sons, the young Goblin lords Igant and Janis look on anxious and slightly scared. Their secret past is safe for now, unknown even to themselves. The four hide, quiet and still deep in the cellars of the palace of Jacarna, unaware that the rooms above are now quarters of the Cassallian Host and it's terrifying commander, the giant warlod Karchek.

Jerone Witchguardian sprints through the forest, branches and leaves whipping across his face. Smarting as they brush across the open wound on his chest. He runs for his life, pursued by his nemesis, the hateful Anders Whitehair. Tasked with an impossible mission, to find a woman he doesn't know, who could be anywhere in the world.

And finally, in a world away in a dimension across the voids, a gnarled hand grips the arms of his throne, skulls of strange beings forming the basis of the very throne itself. The figure slumps rather than sits in the massive seat, the obsidian back arching upwards over him. From the depths below, a bell chimes and its toll rings out, echoing from wall to wall until the resonance reaches the figure. He looks up, all his features obscured with the folds of his cloak. All his features are hidden, except his thin bloodless lips that, upon hearing the bell, start to smile.

PRONUNCIATION GUIDE

Pronunciation Guide – The Darkness Rising

When I first read Fritz Leiber's Lankhmar series it was in the pre-internet era, so I had to take a wild stab at the pronunciation of Fafhrd. I didn't think at the time that Mr Leiber would be to upset if he heard my possible mangling one of the heroes moniker's, but by the time I reached 'Ill Met in Lankhmar' I found out that I was roughly right.

I am not so precious with my names, after all, the reader is asked to add a lot of other visual description to the narrative as well. But I thought it would be nice to add a few explanations of how I hear the names when I write. Most of the names are simple; Bex, Radnak, Bryn etc, so I haven't included them.

Iga Ee-ga (a hard G as in gantry)
    Igant Ee-gant (a hard G as in gantry)
    Janis Ya-nis
    Sarsi Sar-see
    Magus Vent May-gus Vent (a hard G again)
    Ishtara Ish-tar-ra

Danaria Da-nar-ia (Da as in Dan, nar as in narwhal)
    Tannaheim Tan-na-hime
    Jacarna Ja-car-na (Ja as in Jack)

Cassalian Cas-sail-le-an

Anyone or anywhere else that I haven't added, feel free to go with it. I promise I won't get mad.

BOOK 2: THE DEMONS WITHIN

The Maingard Chronicles Book2: The Demons Within is coming soon! Here's a taster to whet your appetite as the saga continues.

PROLOGUE

The small ship had cast its moorings and had slipped from the Royal Harbour. Flying the Royal Pennant to indicate that it was on the business of the Crown, it had been let through the blockade that had been in force since the discovery of the kidnapping. The ship was *The Dagger*, a small brig owned by Count Eglebon Dutte. It was aptly named as its sleek, low hull made it one of the fastest ships in Tannaheim and it cut easily through the early evening waters.

The captain, Raust, looked out and nervously spied the black clouds ahead. He didn't like the look of the weather and spat to his side for good luck. He rubbed his shaved head as he looked over his crew. Four good men were on deck right now with another four resting in bunks below. The ship's cook would be cleaning the galley as the main meal had been taken early as was usual when passengers were on board.

Raust looked back at the cabin door and gave a slight chuckle. The passenger had annoyed him since he had come aboard but had retired after the evening meal looking worse than wear from the ship's movement. If the landlubber had thought that bit of the journey had been rough, then he would get a rude shock when that weather ahead hit.

He felt the rain on his weathered face and knew it was going to be a rough journey and not just from the weather ahead. For ten years he had been in the employ of Count Dutte and never had he seen him like he had been that afternoon. The Count had been agitated beyond words, wringing his hands as he passed his orders on. The previous orders to sail to Marneheim had been succeeded by new ones to sail to the Isle of Winds. A passenger, a herald from the court, was to be transported to either Lord Visney or Count Neechy commanding the Fourth and Third Squadrons respectively.

The Count had returned later with the herald, a middle-aged man wearing the red livery of the palace and carrying a small bag containing his orders for Visney and Neechy.

For a man who had just conveyed orders of utmost urgency, Eglebon Dutte had acted strangely after ushering the herald on board. He had held Raust in conversation for nigh on quarter of an hour, ignoring the herald's frantic attempts to interrupt. As he spoke had looked anxiously up and down the quay and had then finally acknowledged the herald's protestations and left Raust speaking midsentence.

Raust pulled himself back into the present and sighed. Nobles seemed to have nothing and everything to worry about. He looked across to the mainmast and saw that Grose had not reefed the sail yet.

"Grose! Hurry it up, you lazy bastard!" He couldn't see the young sailor and wondered whether he had gone overboard as the waves rose around the now struggling ship. He switched his gaze to the other side of the ship and called out to the crew.

"Ganner, Yorik! Where's Grose?" He shifted from his vantage point and made his way over to where the young boy had been working. The deck was wet from the rain but no worse than the area he had just left. No ropes were unbelayed so it seemed that the youngster hadn't started to reef the sail. Still there was no sign of him. Raust gripped the rail, his big fists clenched hard, as he leant out and peered into the darkness. He called out again, louder than before. It was then that he realised that there hadn't been a response from Ganner or Yorik.

"Tobe's Tits!" he exclaimed to no-one but himself. If they had all gone below, he would skin the lot of them. He stepped lithely of the deck of the rocking ship only to find the port side empty of life as well. He turned and looked back to the stern of 'The Dagger'.

His heart leapt into his mouth as a shadow rose seemingly out of the deck. The dark shape shifted into the figure of a man, taller but more slender than the captain. The ghostly figure lunged forward and Raust sank to his knees, finding it hard to focus as his eyes clouded over. He died without making a sound as the short sword penetrated his throat. The sword slowly withdrew, and he sagged forward to fall onto the deck. The last thing he saw were the black felt boots of his murderer turn and walk softly and silently to the cabin in the stern.

ABOUT THE AUTHOR

Inspired by a misspent youth playing Dungeons & Dragons, and reading the deeds of heroes such as Fafhrd & the Grey Mouser, Conan and others, Carl F Northwood creates his own heroes and heroines, all eager to wield swords and mutter incantations at sinister and fantastical villains.

Having grown upon a leafy and green village in Bedfordshire, he now resides in a leafy and green village in East Yorkshire with his partner and two of his five children, surrounded by horses and dogs.